SWEET OBEDIENCE

THE ISLAND SERIES - BOOK THREE

EROTICWRITERGIRL

KINKY INK PRESS

First paperback edition May 2025

Cover design by eroticwritergirl

ISBN 978-1-968079-03-1 (paperback)

Published by Kinky Ink Press

www.kinkyinkpress.com

ALSO BY EROTICWRITERGIRL

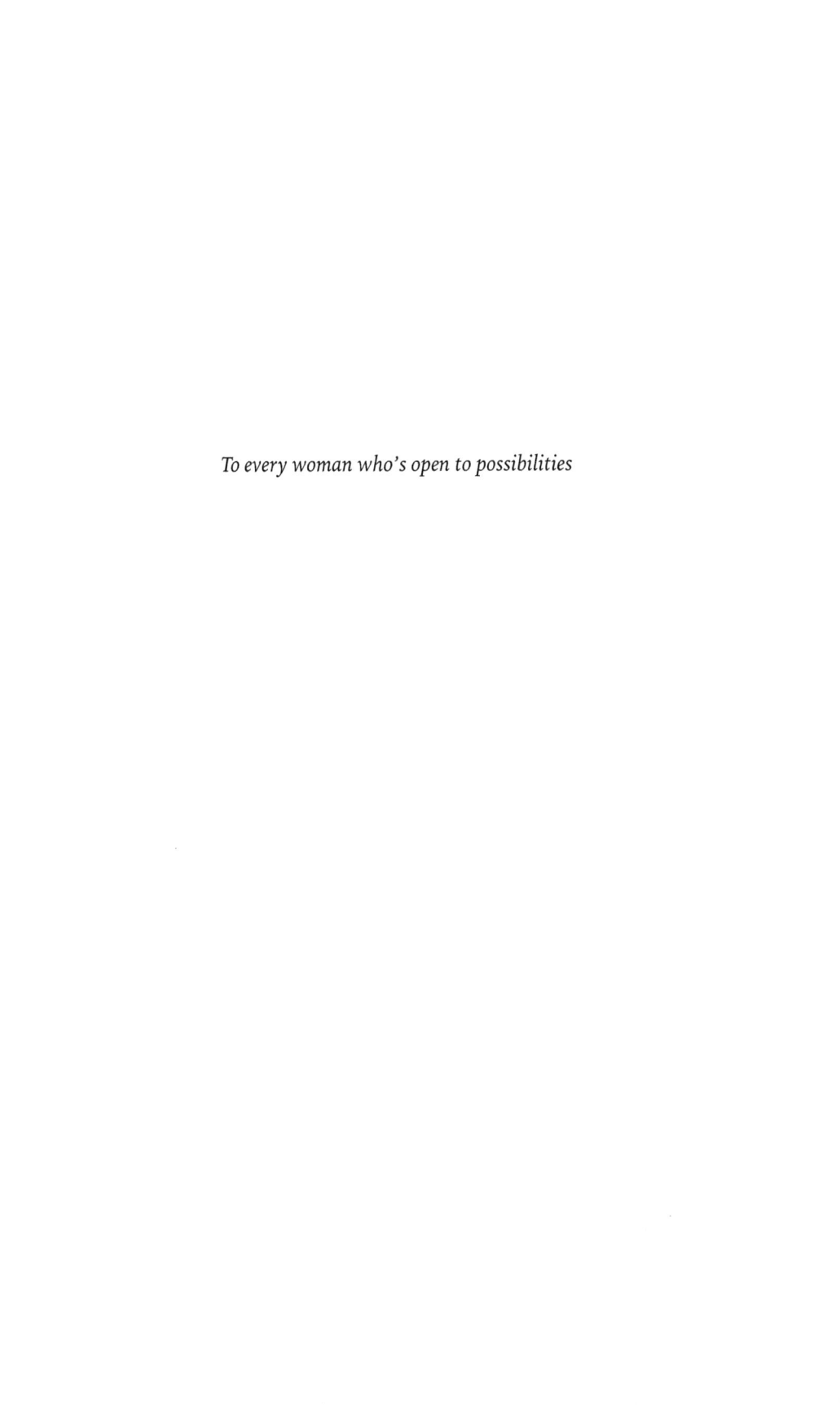

To every woman who's open to possibilities

ONE

I smiled when I saw Annabelle walk into the kitchen wearing nothing but a green collar and a smile. She glowed, happiness beaming off her from being re-collared by Luke. Luke stood behind her in loose grey sweats, leaving his muscular chest bare, a wide smile on his face.

Jealousy snaked through me. Even though Luke owned me, I wondered for how long. He had recently reclaimed Annabelle after she had struggled with their growing relationship. Even though it was common for men on the island to own several women, the relationship between Luke and Annabelle had always been different, stronger and more connected. They had fallen madly in love with each other which left me feeling left out. I was truly happy for them—they both found what they didn't even know they were looking for—but I longed for the same type of connection.

I had wanted to squeal with delight when Master Grant had shown up with Annabelle last night. He had returned her after she left thinking Luke no longer wanted her. Her contract was up and she had decided it was better if she returned home. Thankfully, someone helped change her mind, encouraging her to give it one more chance.

My heart had hammered at the sight of Master Grant, one of the new trainers at the new training facility on the island. Mr. Wood had created it to help women new to the island transition to this lifestyle easier. He also wanted a place where women could obtain additional training. Annabelle and I had been sent there for a week to help them test out their new trainers and the whole set up. I haven't been able to stop thinking about Master Grant since.

I had been working on breakfast before they came down—an egg scramble with bacon and hash browns. I heard them when they woke from my bedroom next door and thought it'd be a fun surprise to cook breakfast for all of us. I had set the table in the dining room with Luke's fanciest plates and had brought in flowers from the garden as a centerpiece. Luke's place was rather simple, lacking in decoration, so I tried whenever I could to liven it up. He never commented but I liked how it looked.

"Good morning," I said to them, my smile wide and genuine. "How'd you sleep?"

Annabelle blushed as Luke said, "Very well. Something smells delicious."

"I made us breakfast," I said, happy to please him. Even though my place in his household felt precarious with Annabelle back, I still wanted to please him. "Why don't you two head into the dining room and I'll bring everything out."

"Do you want help?" Annabelle asked.

"No thanks," I said. "I'll be right in."

I watched them as they rounded the corner to the dining room. I liked that you couldn't see the kitchen from there. It made sense. Who wanted to see the mess in the kitchen while they ate?

I plated two servings and carried them into the dining room. Annabelle and Luke sat next to each other, making eyes at each other. They stopped talking when I walked in. I served them like I was a waitress at a restaurant but I didn't mind. I put the plates in front of them before returning to the kitchen for Luke's coffee and Annabelle's herbal tea. The women weren't allowed caffeine on the island for some reason.

I returned with their drinks, setting them down in front of them. I smiled then came back into the kitchen for my helping. I debated staying in the kitchen, letting them have their space, but I decided against it since I had told them I made breakfast for all of us. I didn't want them to think anything was wrong.

I returned to the dining room with my plate and a herbal tea for myself. I sat on the other side of Luke. Luke allowed us to sit on the furniture in his house so I didn't hesitate to use the chair. Everywhere else on the island, women needed permission to sit on the furniture otherwise they had to stand or kneel. It was another way to remind the women of their place here.

"This is delicious," Luke said once I settled into my chair. "Thank you for making it for us."

"My pleasure," I said, meaning it. "I figured you'd be hungry this morning."

I caught the twinkle in Luke's eye when I said that and smiled to myself. They hadn't exactly been quiet last night or this morning as they reconciled again and again. Annabelle had always been Luke's favorite since the day she arrived. Her stay was supposed to be temporary. Luke's brother owned her but had sent her to Luke when he needed more time and space to accommodate his new acquisitions. Luke didn't mind and when Annabelle was supposed to return to his brother, Luke fought for her to stay with him. It was a true love story and I knew they were meant to be together. Now I needed to figure out how I fit into all of this. I couldn't come out and ask—women weren't allowed to initiate conversation here—so I needed to wait and see.

"You outdid yourself," Annabelle said. "Maybe you can teach me how to cook."

"Of course," I said. "It'd be my pleasure."

I didn't know how to cook when I arrived on the island but I had spent the past few months studying cookbooks and experimenting in the kitchen. Luke had been busy with Annabelle, leaving me a lot of time to play around with different recipes. He didn't seem to mind the increase in the grocery bill and had always given me a lot of freedom to do what I wanted. His only quirk was not allowing me the freedom to leave the house but lately, he'd been allowing me to do more of that, too. I would have gone mad with boredom if I hadn't found some productive outlet for my time. We didn't have access to TV or the internet, leaving only cooking, cleaning, reading and writing letters to family and friends.

We ate in silence for a few minutes. I felt the tension build in the room, squeezing my chest with its uncertainty. I savored each bite, not knowing my future, not knowing where I might be tomorrow. I came to the island to explore this lifestyle and mindset. I had always considered myself submissive but had never had the chance to explore it. The few boyfriends I had over the years never did it for me. They played at dominating me but never in the way I needed. It always felt more like a game to them than a lifestyle. It wasn't until I stumbled on an ad for the island that I felt I might have found my place in the world.

A group of men had created the island based on the belief that women would be happier submitting to men and being treated like property. The women lined up to come here and were compensated handsomely for their time as long as they stuck it out for their entire contract. Most contracts ran six months, including mine. It was long enough for women to shift their mindset and truly experience this lifestyle without it feeling like forever.

I had felt lost before I came here. I had just dropped out of college and was working at a bookstore, barely getting by, not knowing what I wanted to do with my life. Not only had the ad promised me enough money to buy me a year or two to figure out my life, but it also spoke to a deeper part of me that knew I needed to experience complete submission.

I told my parents I was volunteering for six months building schools for orphans in Haiti and wouldn't be able to be in touch with anyone. Only a few friends knew the truth. My friends thought I was crazy but supported me in their way. Most thought I was going through some crazy phase and would work it out of my system by coming here. It reassured me knowing that my friends knew where I was in case things went sideways. But I had never felt anything but safe since arriving.

Since the men on the island wanted the women to stay, they treated them well, almost like loving pets that sometimes needed to be disciplined. We signed our rights away as soon as we arrived, agreeing to become property and to relinquish the ability to own anything, including any salaries if we worked. We could leave at any time but we wouldn't be compensated if we left early unless there was a legitimate reason. I liked having an exit option. It made staying easier and kept me from feeling trapped.

The women were auctioned off upon arrival, having no say in who acquired them. Now with the new training facility, the new women would spend a couple of weeks being trained before being auctioned. I felt lucky to have been purchased by Luke right away. He had been new to the island, too, and his brother had encouraged him to acquire me. I didn't know where the money went from the auctions but I assumed it went into maintaining the island. There was no official government here but there were strict rules and felt governed by the men who owned it. Every man seemed to contribute to the island in some way, similar to a co-op.

Once purchased, the men gave their women collars that represented that they were owned along with what level other men could use them. I wore a black collar, allowing other men to use me without restriction, including fucking and punishing me. Annabelle wore a green collar, allowing other men to fuck her but without pain.

Whenever we were with Luke, men asked his permission before using us. It was a sign of respect. The men needed to follow the collars' restrictions or else risk being kicked off the island. The men took the rules seriously, not putting up with rule-breakers, which made me feel safer. I assumed they screened the men before they came to the island but it was reassuring that they kept a strict tab on the men, too.

I was lost in thought and almost didn't hear Luke ask me if I wanted to join them in town today.

"Yes, I'd love to," I said, hoping I hadn't paused too much.

Luke gave me one of his charming smiles. "That'd be great. Wear one of your short dresses and join us in the family room in about 20 minutes."

"Yes, Luke," I said, my heart warming at being included. Luke didn't want to be called master or sir or anything other than Luke like some of the men on the island but he still wanted acknowledgment when he spoke. "I'll wash up here and be down ASAP."

I cleared plates while Luke escorted Annabelle upstairs. It wasn't unusual for Luke to mess around with Annabelle in front of me but since she came back yesterday, they had done everything behind closed doors, reinforcing the sense that my days in Luke's household were numbered.

I put the dishes in the dishwasher and turned it on before slipping upstairs to my room. Annabelle and I had our own rooms upstairs, next to Luke's. I enjoyed having my own space to retreat to. Luke had encouraged me to decorate it how I wanted. I mostly had postcards from my friends stuck to the walls with a few group shots of friends from the summer. I missed them but I was happy I came here. I needed this. I needed to experience this level of submission. I would have regretted it if I hadn't come.

TWO

I slipped into a sheer royal blue dress with no undergarments and my silver platform heels. I ran my hands through my short blond hair, giving it a bit of a messed up look, knowing that's how Luke liked it best. I had quickly learned that my appearance was meant for my owner and the men on the island, not me. Women were kept either nude or in sheer dresses unless they worked in an office. Then they wore crisp white blouses that could be gaped open with short black pencil skirts. The men figured they needed to be able to focus on their work somewhat but that didn't keep them from fucking their secretaries over their desks whenever they wanted. Undergarments were never worn.

I checked my reflection in the mirror, happy with what I saw, before going downstairs to the family room. I had beat Luke and Annabelle down and wasn't surprised. I knew he wasn't even close to being done with her. He had practically gone out of his mind once he realized she had left this last time. I still didn't know what happened and resigned myself to the fact that I may never know. I couldn't ask Luke, of course, and I wasn't sure I wanted to get into it with Annabelle. She seemed so much happier now that I didn't want to drag her back to more unhappy times.

I waited on my knees with my palms face-up on my thighs like a proper submissive and like we were taught at the training facility. Luke wasn't a strict owner but I knew he'd appreciate the gesture. Even though I felt my role in the house was precarious, I still wanted to please him and show him I was more than willing to be submissive to him.

I heard them upstairs, the door opening, their voices floating down the stairs, before they appeared in the entrance to the family room.

Luke walked up to me, leaving Annabelle at the entrance.

"Very nice, Riley," he said, his words warming me. "Please stand."

I uncurled myself as gracefully as I could, my eyes lowered, until I was standing in front of him. He smelled nice, like a fresh shower, and I couldn't help imagining him in the shower with Annabelle. Jealousy coiled through me for a moment before I shook it away.

Luke attached a black leather leash to my collar which surprised me. He didn't typically do that when we went out. Some men on the island made it a regular occurrence so I knew people wouldn't find it odd but it felt odd for Luke to do it.

"I thought we'd have a little fun today," Luke said.

He gave my leash a little tug and I followed him to where Annabelle stood. He attached a black leather leash to her collar, too, and led us out the door.

The sun kissed us as we stepped outside. I loved living on a tropical island where we rarely needed to worry about being cold. The rains came through every few days, usually late in the afternoon, cooling things down for a moment and washing things clean.

Only a few people passed us as we walked. Women weren't allowed to talk on the island when men were present, unless asked a direct question or inside their household with its own rules, so things were mostly quiet. I was grateful that Luke allowed us to talk inside his house but outside we had to follow the island's rules.

I'm not sure what would happen if a woman talked out of turn but I didn't want to find out. Annabelle had been sent to the pillories a couple of times for some of her indiscretions although she never described it to me in detail. All I knew was that I didn't want that to happen to me. I was a natural rule-follower so this was just another rule to adhere to. I didn't mind. It allowed my mind to wander and to take in the beauty of my surroundings.

Luke led us through the women's side of town before reaching the men's side. The island was somewhat segregated by sex to allow women the opportunity to socialize while they were out. The women's side consisted of clothing boutiques, book shops, a few cafés and the island's only grocery store—all the places you'd most likely find women. The men's side contained more restaurants, including the fancier ones, along with several bars. The women weren't allowed to drink alcohol unless given some by a man so the women's side was an alcohol-free zone.

I followed behind Luke, enjoying the day, sharing a smile here and there with Annabelle as we walked. She couldn't stop smiling, her face like a glow stick, and I couldn't stop myself from feeling jealous. Even though I knew that most of the men on the island weren't looking for the kind of relationship Luke and Annabelle had managed to find, I still hoped that somehow I would stumble upon something serious. Even though Luke had fucked me more times than I could remember, we were lacking that deeper connection that he seemed to share with Annabelle. I hadn't minded at the time but now that they seemed to be more of a couple than anything else, I wanted to be in a position where I could find that kind of connection, too.

Hands reached out and groped my ass and grabbed my tits as we walked. I was used to this, especially now that Luke let me out of the house more often solo. It still aroused me and I held my head up a little higher as I walked. I knew I had a body that most men appreciated with curves in all the right places and breasts that pointed up. I was only 5'2" but with the heels, I was about 5'6". I had never been much into heels before coming to the island and now I couldn't imagine my life without them.

Luke led us to one of the more popular restaurants. The interior opened to an expansive beach with a marina in the distance. A platform was situated in the middle of the restaurant where women were sometimes displayed, used or both. I'd never been up there and wasn't sure how I'd feel if Luke wanted that. Of course, I'd do it—there was no question of that—but even though I appreciated the male attention, I wasn't sure I wanted to be the center of attention.

Luke stopped to talk with a few men he seemed to know. Annabelle and I stood slightly behind him as he chatted. Men walked by, running their hands along our bodies, grabbing our ass, pinching a nipple.

I craved this kind of attention. My body reacted. My nipples hardened. I keep my eyes lowered as I was taught, the perfect submissive, allowing them to touch me. Since Luke was present, I knew they wouldn't do more than touch without permission. It had been a while since I was properly fucked. Luke had been caught up with Annabelle and I hadn't left the house on my own in a while. I ached to be used, to fulfill my purpose.

I had never considered myself a slutty girl but I knew deep in my heart that I was always submissive. I hadn't slept around back home— only with a few guys I dated more seriously—but here I was free to explore that part of myself. I was surprised how much I craved being used and how I often didn't care who did it. Sometimes not knowing the guy made it more exciting. Some of the men didn't care who they fucked—they would take whatever woman was available. We all had thorough health screenings before being allowed on the island and all the women were given powerful birth control shots. I never thought about being a mother but the thought of being knocked up by some random guy thrilled me.

Luke pulled us forward by our leashes and introduced us to his friends. They gave us the once over. One reached out and pulled on my nipple. I wanted to lean into it and moan—pleasure rolled through me—but I remained still and like I was unaffected. He pulled on the other nipple before releasing it.

"She's gorgeous," the man said. "Mind if I take her for a spin?"

Luke knew me well enough to know I'd be up for it so he smiled at his friend and said sure.

The man wasted no time pulling me forward, the leash still being held by Luke dangling between us. He pinched and pulled my nipples until I squirmed. Pain and pleasure shot straight to my pussy. He pulled my hair back, forcing me to look into his dark eyes. He wore a smirk and looked like his nose had been broken more than once. He wasn't the most handsome man but that didn't matter. Sometimes the uglier guys fucked the best, like they had something to prove.

He growled something at me that I didn't understand. I blushed anyway because I knew it wasn't a compliment. Luke handing him the end of the leash as if to say she's all yours which made my stomach flip. I knew it was only temporary but fear rushed through me. The man leered at me as he took the leash, his fingers finding a nipple and pulling as he guided me away.

At first, I thought he might take me up on the platform and my heart hammered at the thought. But he led me to the lounge area where a couple of men were already playing with women. I kept my eyes lowered, not wanting to catch anyone's eyes, as the man pulled me along by a nipple.

"You're a nice looking cunt," he said in my ear when we finally stopped near an easy chair in the corner. "Maybe I can persuade Luke to let me have you for good."

God, I hoped not but kept that thought to myself.

The man continued to pull on my nipples, making me squirm. I was wet despite myself, reminding me once again that I was made for this lifestyle. My body didn't care who fucked it as long as it was used in some way.

"I should have you suck my cock first," the man said, "but I'm meeting some friends soon and would rather get right to it."

He let go of my nipples before slapping my breasts, seeming to be pleased by the way they bounced back into place. He slapped them a few more times, the sting radiating through me. I wasn't much for pain but the idea of letting this man do whatever he wanted to me turned me on to no end. My pussy ached with desire as he slapped my breasts a few more times. A smile played on his lips before he leaned in and sucked one of my nipples into his hot mouth.

I sucked in my breath as he bit down on it. It wasn't hard enough to break the skin but hard enough to hurt. He nibbled on my nipple, sucking it in then biting it again and again until my head spun from the assault.

He reached a hand up my skirt and through my wetness before twirling me around and pushed me face forward over the arm of the easy chair. He flipped up my skirt, revealing my bare ass, and gave it a hard slap. I jumped from the sting and surprise of it. He chuckled.

"Good girl," he said. "I love how your ass reddens so easily. Maybe I will have to acquire you from Luke."

Before I could get my mind around that, he smacked my ass again before plunging his cock into my dripping pussy. He was big and thick and my pussy stretched to accommodate him. He didn't let this deter him as he pushed himself in until the tip of his cock tickled my cervix. He gripped my hips for leverage as he plowed into me again and again. My face rested on the chair's cushion, pushed deeper and deeper into its softness as the man relentlessly fucked me.

Pressure built low in my abdomen as my head spun. I gave myself over to the experience, knowing I was nothing more than a cunt to be filled. I reveled in my role.

He picked up the pace, showing me no mercy, focusing on his pleasure alone as I took everything he had to give. He slapped my ass a few more times, the sting radiating through my body and making me wetter and more turned on than ever. I rarely came from penetration alone despite how turned on I became and even when I did feel like I was about to come, I purposely held back like I was taught to do at the training facility. They taught us that we never knew how often we'd be fucked in a day and that it would be to our benefit to keep ourselves aroused by not allowing ourselves to come.

The man pushed into me and stilled, filling me completely, as he spilled himself deep inside me. He smacked my ass one more time, leaving it red and wanting, before he slowly pulled out and walked away. I waited a couple of minutes to be sure he was done with me before I slowly straightened myself up. As I stood, I felt his semen leak down my leg but I did nothing to stop it. I knew the men liked the women to keep reminders of them for as long as possible.

I looked around, trying to find Luke in the crowded restaurant.

Thankfully most of the people were seated while a mass of people hung out at the bar. Luke was taller than most but that didn't matter if he was sitting.

I craned my neck as I slowly walked through the restaurant. A few hands found their way to my ass but I ignored them. I was on a mission to return to Luke before another man could take his turn fucking me. The random man's come leaked down my legs, making me feel like a major slut, and I needed a moment to collect myself before I moved onto someone else.

I heard Luke's deep voice before I saw him. Relief washed over me. He sat at a table with Annabelle and a few men and women. I felt so relieved to see Luke that I didn't bother to notice anyone else as I moved closer.

A smile broke out over Luke's face as he saw me.

"Riley," he said, his voice warm and genuine. "I'm so happy you made it back to us. I was afraid Bryan was going to keep you to himself for the night."

I gave Luke a weak smile.

"I saved you a seat in case you returned," Luke said but there wasn't a seat open next to him. Annabelle sat on one side and a woman I never saw before was on the other. When Luke saw my confusion, he indicated an open seat at the other side of the large round table. My eyes followed where he pointed only to land on intense blue eyes that were staring directly at me.

My heart skipped as I froze in place. Master Grant's lips curled into a slow deviant smile as I forced my legs to work to sit next to him. I felt his eyes on me as I moved around the table. Heat inched up my neck, making me suddenly flush. There was something about this man that pushed me over the edge. He had been one of my main trainers during my week at the training facility and my heart did crazy things when I was near him.

I felt him watch me as I sank into the seat next to him. Heat radiated off him, the air crackling between us. I kept my eyes lowered as my body tingled from being near to him. I knew I was nothing more than another submissive woman on the island to him but to me, he was the only man that elicited this type of reaction in me. I wondered if this was how Annabelle felt with Luke. I knew I could never have what Annabelle and Luke had with Master Grant, especially since he was a trainer and had his hands full every week with the new arrivals, but a girl could dream.

The men continued to talk, not acknowledging me, as a waitress set plates of steaks in front of them. The women were served fish with a mixture of fresh vegetables. I had gotten used to not having a say in what was ordered for me while we were out and actually preferred it.

I was taking a bite of the flaky fish, marveling at how the chef could make it taste so incredible, when I felt a firm hand on my upper thigh. Pleasure shot through me as the hand inched higher. I kept my eyes lowered but my heart hammered as I realized the hand belonged to Master Grant. The man on my other side was busy chatting with the other men, a buxom blonde on his other side, and had no interest in me.

The hand traveled further up until it slid through my wetness. I'd been turned on since the moment I saw him and knew Master Grant would be pleased by my arousal. I knew he liked to keep the women wet and wanting. He had said that was the most appropriate way for a woman to be, especially while on the island, since she never knew when a man might decide to fuck her. It was better for everyone if she was in a constant state of arousal.

I took small bites of fish, letting the flavors dance on my tongue, as his fingers dipped my wetness, pushing into me. I opened my legs for him, allowing better access, as he talked with the men like nothing was happening under the table. I felt thankful for the privacy of the tablecloth even though it was common for women to be fucked wherever. I liked that this was an intimate moment just between the two of us. It felt like our little secret.

He pushed his fingers all the way in, impaling me most delightfully. I wanted to throw my head back, to moan, to push into his fingers even more, but I managed to control myself and act as if nothing was happening as my head began to spin. Master Grant knew me enough to know the effect he was having on me which made it all that more delicious.

I managed to finish my plate with Master Grant's fingers deep inside me. He slowly pumped in and out, teasing my clit, working me up. My nipples strained against the sheer fabric of my dress, making it obvious that I was fully aroused. I made a point not to look up and catch anyone's eye. The men continued to talk about business and things way over my head. I only knew Annabelle out of the women and knew if I looked at her, I'd lose it. She knew how I felt about Master Grant.

I clamped my pussy around Master Grant's fingers, not to push him out but as a way of acknowledging him. He chuckled as he pushed in deeper then pulled his fingers out. I felt vacant and disappointed as he wiped my wetness off with his napkin and finished eating his meal. I guess it was difficult to cut steak with one hand.

I sat with my eyes lowered, feeling sad, as everyone finished their meals. The waitress cleared plates as soon as people finished before placing little cheesecakes topped with fresh strawberries in front of everyone, including the women, along with glasses of sparkling champagne.

"I want to toast to a successful first month of the training facility," Mr. Wood, Luke's brother, said from across the table, holding up his glass of champagne. I hadn't noticed him when I sat down. "I know we're on the right track with this and I want to thank everyone for their hard work and effort in making this month a success."

Everyone raised their glasses before taking sips of champagne, including the women. I loved how the bubbles tickled my tongue and instantly made me lightheaded. Since coming to the island, my alcohol tolerance had plummeted. The women were only allowed alcohol when the men provided it which wasn't often. I thought it was to get us drunk quicker when they wanted because it seriously didn't take much. I took another sip and reveled in its dry sweetness.

Mr. Wood talked about the success of the training facility, thanking Annabelle and me for being the first trainees. Luke had sent us there for a week of advanced training before the new shipment of women arrived. It was their way of doing a soft launch and working out the kinks. While Annabelle had spent most of her time with Master Owen, Master Grant had taken charge of me.

My body involuntarily shivered as I remembered Master Grant dominating me during my training. Annabelle and I were taught various submissive poses as well as retaught the laws of the island. Those times felt like kindergarten compared to my solo sessions with Master Grant which were positively explosive.

I blushed at the thought as I finished my dessert. Mr. Wood continued to talk about the training facility and his plans to improve it.

"I'll be adding a few more trainers in the coming months," Mr. Wood said. "Not that Owen and Grant can't handle things but I'm anticipating a boom of women to the island as word continues to get out about it on the mainland. We've implemented tighter screening processes for the interested women to help ensure that the ones who come intend to stay. Plus we'd like our trainers to have a life outside of the training facility as well."

My ears perked up as Mr. Wood's words sank in. Right now I knew Master Grant and Master Owen lived at the training facility since someone needed to be there 24 hours a day. The thought of Master Grant being able to have a life outside of the training facility thrilled me.

The waitress brought out cordials for the men and more water for the women. I was happy she didn't pour more champagne for the women because I felt buzzed and didn't think I could handle any more.

I was very conscious of Master Grant next to me. My body radiated with the warmth coming off of him. I wanted to touch him, to put my hand on his thigh and inch it up to his thick cock. I wanted to squeeze him then drop to my knees under the table, taking his thick, hard cock in my mouth. But I couldn't do that. Women weren't allowed to initiate contact with a man, especially one that wasn't her owner. Plus Luke, who was my owner, sat directly across from me and I didn't want to do anything to disrespect him. But I wished Master Grant's hand would snake out and touch me again.

I kept my eyes lowered as the men talked about business and their plans for the island. I was happy that the island was thriving. That meant I'd be able to stay as long as I wanted. I intended to renew my contract once it expired in a couple of months but I knew that would depend on where I was at the time. I doubted Luke would keep me in his household or, if he did, I would continue to play backseat to his relationship with Annabelle. I had never been in an open relationship —it wasn't done back home—but after being here, I could see where it could work. I was open to it but I wanted to be more than just a cook and housekeeper in the house. I wanted to have a connection with the man, something more than sex and housework.

My mind debated this while the waitress cleared plates and empty glasses. She wore a black collar so it was no surprise when one of the men stopped her to have her suck his cock. She squeezed in under the table and I couldn't help but wish that had been me. But with Luke here, the men would be less inclined to touch me without his permission. The only reason I thought Master Grant did was that he had been given permission previously when I had been sent to the training facility. Maybe once permission was granted, the man didn't need it again.

The table ignored the waitress sucking off the man as another waitress swooped in and finished clearing plates. This time no one stopped her from doing her job and as soon as she finished, she was off to help another table.

Mr. Wood was the first to stand and declare that he was heading back to the office. This caused the other men to jump up and excuse themselves as well. I guessed that most if not all of them worked for Mr. Wood so would be going back to the office with him. Luke also worked for his brother but in a different office. Annabelle thought it was because Mr. Wood liked to have a little separation from him and it also allowed Luke to do more of his own thing.

My eyes watched Master Grant as he stood, shaking hands with a few of the men, before leaving. My heart plummeted when he didn't give me another look.

Luke stood once everyone else cleared. He helped Annabelle to her feet before coming around the table to help me. His hand felt warm, sending a little jolt of electricity through me. I had always been attracted to Luke—he was a handsome man with dark green eyes and a killer body—but lately I had been feeling more like an unwelcome visitor than a woman he owned. I wondered if the spark was still there for him or if it had all gone to Annabelle.

Jealousy rolled through me, surprising me, as Luke escorted us out onto the street. More people milled about, the women mostly trailing behind their men. I assumed most of the men on the island worked but a lot of them were independently wealthy, either via business ventures or their families. The men needed to be financially independent to come to the island—most of them with successful businesses that were off the island. They needed to be able to support themselves as well as whatever women they owned. There wasn't a lot of commerce on the island besides the restaurants and boutiques which I had a feeling were mostly owned by Mr. Wood.

Luke whispered something to Annabelle. She nodded. Then he looked to me, a smile on his face.

"I need to head into the office for a bit, too, unfortunately," he said. "I trust you two can make it home safely. I thought maybe you'd want to spend some time in the shops. Buy whatever you want and put it on my account."

"Thank you, Luke," I said, meaning it. A shopping spree sounded wonderful. Luke had always been a generous owner. "Sounds fun."

Luke's face lit up. He leaned in and kissed me on the cheek.

"Don't get into too much trouble," he said. "I'll be back after dinner so don't worry about me. Have fun."

Annabelle and I smiled after him as he walked into the crowd and was gone. I wasn't sure how much trouble we could get into on the island but I was happy to find out.

THREE

Once Annabelle and I made our way to the women's side of the island, I let out the breath I'd been holding. I felt relieved and surprised no one bothered us during our walk through the men's side of town. A few men swiped at my nipples and grabbed my ass but that was it. My pussy still ached from Master Grant playing with it and I wanted to release more than anything. I doubted Luke would use me later since Annabelle was back in the house.

"Don't think I didn't see," Annabelle said as soon as there weren't any men around. We walked by the shops bustling with women. I never considered myself a shopping girl but since it was one of the few things for women to do together, I embraced it. I looked at the shops longingly as I dodged Annabelle's insinuation. "Want to grab a coffee?"

We stopped at a cute coffee shop with a wide patio out front with views of the shops. It reminded me of something I'd see in Paris and usually I'd be all over it but I didn't feel like being interrogated about Master Grant.

Annabelle sensed my hesitation. She smiled and grabbed my arm.

"Come on," she said as she dragged me to one of the tables facing the street. Only women sat inside so we were able to talk. Men rarely came to this side of town and, of course, no men worked here. I allowed myself to settle into the chair, one of the luxuries afforded us on this side of town. It was the men's way to give us a little normality.

A cute petite waitress showed up almost immediately and took our drink orders. We weren't allowed caffeine on the island so everything was decaf but I liked the taste just the same. I ordered a cappuccino while Annabelle ordered a coffee with cream.

Once the waitress left, Annabelle turned her attention to me.

I tried not to blush but I felt myself redden. I'd be a horrible poker player.

"Was it that obvious?" I asked, hoping to God it wasn't. I didn't want to disrespect Luke, especially with his brother present.

"Only to me because I was paying attention," Annabelle said. "The men were too wrapped up in their discussion to notice. Don't worry about it."

I let out my breath.

"Are you sure Luke didn't see?" I asked, worry snaking through me. Luke wasn't one for punishment but I didn't want to push him to find out.

"No, not at all. When I saw what was going on, I looked over at Luke and he was in deep conversation with the other men. He didn't notice a thing."

Whew. I allowed myself to relax a little.

"You know I would never purposely do anything to disrespect Luke, especially in front of Mr. Wood."

Annabelle smiled and put her hand over mine.

"You didn't do anything wrong. And even if Luke noticed, you wear a black collar which means men can do anything to you at any time. Sure, Master Grant should have gotten Luke's permission before touching you, but who knows, maybe Luke gave him an all-encompassing pass somewhere along the line. You don't know. It was out of your hands. It would have been worse for you and everyone if you had tried to deny Master Grant."

I took this in.

"That's true," I said, feeling slightly better. "It wasn't up to me."

"I'm sure you didn't initiate things," Annabelle said with a little wink.

"God, no. I would never."

Annabelle smiled. "I know you wouldn't. Relax."

The waitress returned with our drinks. I took a moment to savor the smooth creaminess of the cappuccino. I felt relieved to be reminded that I wasn't responsible for Master Grant touching me but was I responsible for how I responded to him and how I wanted more? My mind felt jumbled as I considered this.

I felt Annabelle watching me. I looked up and met her eyes. She had a slight smile on her lips.

"You like him, don't you?"

"Who?" I blushed.

Annabelle laughed. "Master Grant. It seemed like you didn't mind him touching you. You looked like you were enjoying it."

I let out a sigh.

"Master Grant is hot," I said, stating the obvious, "and we had a bit of connection during training. That's all it was."

"Yea, right," Annabelle said, taking a sip of her coffee.

She let it go while we enjoyed our coffee, shifting the conversation to other things. She told me how Luke was going to get more involved with the training facility, something to do with legal stuff, and how he was overseeing the new trainers that were coming.

"Luke mentioned he might take us over to the training facility with him since he'll be spending a lot of time there," Annabelle said. "They may even use us for demos. Of course, you more than me since I have a green collar."

My heart sped up at the thought. I wasn't sure how I could keep my feelings under control while being forced to be near Master Grant in such an intimate way again. My sessions with him before had been nothing short of electric. He knew exactly how to toy with me, how to work me up, until I was out of my mind and exploding all over the place. I didn't want Luke to witness any of that but, then again, I doubted Luke would be sitting in on any training sessions.

"Relax," Annabelle said. "It's Luke's idea to take us there. He knows how much we enjoyed our time there and he'd rather us be there than sitting home doing nothing."

"What about your job?" I asked. Annabelle had worked as Mr. Wood's secretary since coming to the island over six months ago. She liked working there because it made her feel useful. I couldn't see Luke denying her that.

"I'll still be working," Annabelle said, "but I hardly work full time. I'll go there about three days a week and to the training facility with Luke the other days. Of course, I'm sure there will be time off, too. Luke doesn't work seven days a week."

Sometimes he does, I thought but didn't say.

"Well, that's good," I said. "I know how important your job is to you."

Annabelle smiled. "It does give me more of a sense of purpose than being a fucktoy."

BACK AT HOME, I cleaned and organized things in the kitchen while Annabelle disappeared upstairs. I didn't ask her what she was planning to do and she didn't offer it. She spent most nights in Luke's room these days, leaving her room empty. My room was across the hall from hers where I spent most nights reading salacious books I got from the bookstore in town. The themes all dealt with men dominating women. It was supposed to help keep us in the right mindset and for me, it worked.

I scrubbed the kitchen counters after putting everything back in its place. Luke and Annabelle weren't messy but since Annabelle arrived, I had taken over the kitchen as part of my sanctuary. I had bought a stack of cookbooks and taught myself how to cook. I wasn't great or anything but I was learning and always getting better. I figured it was a skill that any man would love for me to possess.

Annabelle didn't cook much so she was more than happy to let me take over this job. I now considered the kitchen my domain and I made sure that everything was always exactly how I wanted it. Luke let me buy whatever I needed at the stores in town and even offered to order things to be shipped in if needed. I hadn't taken him up on that yet but who knew, maybe one day I might as my cooking started to get more adventurous.

I was scrubbing the kitchen floor on my hands and knees—the last bit of my cleaning—when I heard Luke come in the back door. I had stripped off my sheer dress, not wanting to get it dirty, so I was scrubbing the floor in nothing but my collar and heels. Luke saw me naked all the time—I preferred it to the sheer dresses—but I wasn't usually on my hands and knees cleaning.

I stopped when I heard him come into the kitchen and sat back on my heels. My back was to him but I wanted to present myself properly like I was taught at the training facility.

"Why did I know you'd be in here?" Luke asked with a little laugh. "My dear Riley, always in the kitchen."

I didn't say anything even though he had asked a question. I figured it was rhetorical.

Luke came around until he was standing in front of me. I kept my eyes lowered.

I could feel him smiling at me. Luke and I always had an easy relationship. We never argued. Even though he saw me naked all the time, I felt he viewed me more like a friend than a woman he owned, especially lately.

"What can I do for you, Luke?" I asked in my most submissive voice. Even though I had calmed down from earlier, my pussy still ached to be filled.

Luke tilted my chin up until my eyes met his. A little spark of something ran through me. Luke was a handsome man with intense green eyes and a muscular body. He once told me he rarely worked out, that he was just built that way, but I didn't believe him. A man didn't get arms like that from sitting in an office.

"I know I've been neglecting you since Annabelle came back," Luke said, surprising me. He smiled at the surprise in my eyes, holding my chin up so I couldn't lower my eyes. "You've been patient with me and I appreciate that. I have a special relationship with Annabelle, as I'm sure you know, but I don't want that to diminish the relationship I have with you. If there has been any doubt on your part, I want you to know that I want you here and I want you to be part of my household. Do you want to stay in my household? I don't want you to be here if you don't want to be."

Knowing there was nowhere else for me to go except back on the auction block, I shook my head. "I want to stay."

Luke smiled. "Good. We'll figure this out, I promise. This is all new to me, too. I never had to juggle two women before. My brother is pushing me to take on a third but I can't do that until I'm comfortable managing two. And I have to say, I haven't been that great at it."

I gave him a smile. "You've always been great," I said, meaning it.

"I want to be better. Please stand."

I straightened myself up until I was standing in front of him, my eyes never leaving his. He had a warmth in his eyes that I always found comforting, like I could trust him. And I did trust him. He had never given me a reason to doubt him.

"You're an amazing and beautiful woman," Luke said as he trailed his fingers along the top of my shoulder and my collar bone. "I knew the moment I saw you that I wanted you to be in my household."

I let his words sink in as his fingers trailed lower across the top of my breasts. I inhaled as his fingers lightly grazed my pert nipples. They hardened under his touch, sending a wave of arousal through me.

He pinched one nipple and pulled until I was leaning into it, heat spreading through me.

Luke smiled, pleased with the effect he was having on me. He knew how to get me going—that was never an issue.

He released that nipple before moving on to the other one. He pinched and pulled, a wicked smile on his lips. I gave myself over to it. This man was my owner and I liked him. Maybe I could be happy in this household. I liked Annabelle, too, so maybe we could make this work. I was open to it.

Thoughts scattered from my mind as he took hold of both nipples and gave them a forceful pull. The pain went straight to my pussy, stirring up the arousal that was already there.

"Gorgeous," Luke said before releasing me. "You've always made me happy, Riley, I hope you know that."

I smiled. "I do."

"I will do better at showing that to you. Now scoot up to my room. I'll be up in a few minutes."

I bolted up the stairs, delighted to be invited to his room. It had been a while. I didn't even pause to see where Annabelle was. I half expected to find her in Luke's room but she wasn't there. I positioned myself next to his bed in a kneeling position, my eyes lowered, my hands resting on my knees, my heart pounding. It was one thing to be fucked by some random guy while in town and it was another to be taken by my owner, especially after having felt a bit neglected lately.

I didn't wait long before Luke appeared in the doorway. I felt his approval even though I didn't look up to meet his eyes. He closed the door before approaching me which signaled to me that we'd be going solo. He had fucked me in front of Annabelle before but I think he was trying to prove something to her at the time. I hadn't minded. I felt like that was why I was here—to be used in whatever way he desired. But now, I don't know, something changed. I wanted more, too. I saw what he had with Annabelle and I wanted that.

He stood in front of me a moment as if waiting for me to do something but I knew better than to look up. I was trained to not look up unless instructed. I wanted to be sure to follow all the rules, to please him, even though I knew Luke wasn't strict. I think this amused him.

"Stand."

I uncurled myself, eyes lowered, until I was standing in front of him. My nipples hardened under his gaze and pointed straight at him. I felt on display more than I had felt in a while. I was used to be naked most of the time but I was no longer used to Luke taking me in like he was now. I had felt I had become just another object in the room, like a chair, that he saw but didn't really see. But now, I felt seen and it did crazy good things to me.

He traced a finger lightly over my upper chest before running it down my breast, grazing the pert nipple ever so slightly. I took in a sharp breath as I felt the touch everywhere. He repeated the process on the other side, taking his time, touching me, grazing the other nipple ever so slightly, but this time allowing his fingers to go lower until he was grazing my clit.

I tried my hardest to stand still as his fingers slid into me, one at first and then another. His thumb worked my clit ever so lightly as his fingers spread inside me. I knew I was wet, soaking, as his fingers moved in and out, his thumb driving me wild. I closed my eyes against the sensations, feeling the build-up growing, willing myself not to let go too soon since I hoped we were only beginning.

He continued stroking me, his other hand finding his way to a nipple and pulling until I was panting. I had given myself over to him and the sensations rolling through me. Nothing else mattered. I was his to do with however he wanted and I hoped he knew it. I couldn't believe I had considered leaving even for a minute. This was enough. I could be good with this.

Just as I was about to let myself go, he pulled his fingers out and released me. I almost staggered but he caught me.

"Bed," he said, his voice deep and husky. "On your hands and knees, your ass towards me."

I complied, crawling onto his bed on my hands and knees, my ass facing him. I spread my legs apart giving him better access. I heard him unzip his pants and his shoes coming off before he climbed onto the bed behind me. He grabbed my hips before sinking his thick cock into me with one swift movement. I groaned into it as he fucked me from behind, his cock hitting all the right places, filling me.

It only took me a couple of minutes before I was coming all over him and moaning out his name. He fucked me through my orgasm, not letting up, claiming me, until the pressure started building all over again and I came again.

My legs felt like they could no longer support me as I felt limp and liquid but he held me up as he continued to pound me, picking up the pace until he stilled and spilled himself deep inside me.

He pulled out and collapsed next to me on the bed. My body

collapsed without his support and I was grateful for the softness of the bed beneath me. He looked at me, his eyes bright.

"That was incredible," he said, brushing some hair off my face with his fingers. "You're incredible."

I smiled, his words warming me.

"I promise not to let so much time pass by before I fuck you again."

FOUR

I went back to my room to sleep. I didn't want to go but Luke didn't invite me to stay and didn't protest when I got up to leave so I figured it was for the best. I knew I should have felt grateful that he had paid me some much needed attention but there was a part of me that ached for more. I hadn't felt dissatisfied with our arrangement until I met Master Grant and discovered what true submission to a man could be.

I slept fitfully and woke before dawn. I made a big egg bake complete with ham and Swiss, hoping the yummy aroma would rouse Luke and Annabelle. It was Monday, a workday for them, which would leave me on my own. Now that Luke let me wander the island, I considered all the different things I could do with my day while I waited for the egg bake to cook.

Annabelle wandered down first outfitted in a crisp white blouse with most of the buttons undone and a short pencil skirt. Her long auburn hair was pulled up in a high ponytail and she wore minimal makeup.

"Something smells amazing," Annabelle said, all smiles, which made me wonder if she had some morning fun time with Luke. A tinge of jealousy coiled through me. "What are you making?"

"A ham and Swiss egg bake," I said, forcing a smile. "It's almost done."

Annabelle slid onto one of the stools by the counter. I poured her an herbal tea from the kettle. I made a big batch every morning. I refilled my cup.

"Is Luke coming down soon?" I asked since I figured she'd know.

She smiled. "Yea, he's in the shower but shouldn't be too long."

I pulled the egg bake out of the oven and took three plates down. It needed five minutes to sit before serving so hopefully Luke would be down by the time it was ready otherwise I'd need to keep it warm for him. I didn't cook breakfast for him all the time—he didn't mind grabbing an apple out the door—but after last night I felt like I should do something special to show him my appreciation. I also wanted him to recognize my value in the house even if it wasn't always warming his bed.

Annabelle made pleasant small chat with me until Luke descended in a dark suit with a white button-down and a navy tie. The man knew how to fill out a suit with his broad shoulders and well-defined muscles. He smiled at us as he entered the kitchen.

"Yum," he said. "What smells so good? I could smell it all the way upstairs."

"I made a ham and Swiss egg bake," I said. "It's just about ready if you'd like me to serve it."

Luke sat down on one of the stools next to Annabelle.

"Yes, please," Luke said. "Let's eat."

I served three plates, putting them in front of them along with a coffee for Luke. I slid onto the stool next to Annabelle, happy it was the three of us sharing a meal. In a way, I felt like Luke and Annabelle were the mom and dad while I was the somewhat rebellious teenager although I never did anything rebellious. I was a rule follower and pleaser, one of the reasons the island appealed to me. I wanted to be somewhere that had a built-in structure and would allow me to explore my sexuality safely.

When we were about halfway through breakfast, Luke said, "Riley, you'll be coming with me today. Annabelle's needed in my brother's office but I want to take you to the training facility. I need to do some work there and agreed to have you help out with the training."

I nearly choked on the egg in my mouth but did my best to recover and swallowed it without making much of a fuss.

Before I could respond, Luke continued, "Wear one of your dresses with your hair up. I'd like to leave as soon as possible. I'm not sure if you need to shower."

"I'm good to go," I said. I had showered when I woke up. "I'll just need to change and put my hair up."

"Excellent," Luke said. "I'll have Annabelle clean up while you get ready. They're expecting me by nine and I don't want to be late."

I MET Luke downstairs as quickly as I could. I had slipped on a short sheer blue dress that made my blue eyes pop and pulled my short blond hair into a little high ponytail. My ample breasts pushed against the sheer fabric, eager for attention. My heart did funny things at the possibility of seeing Master Grant.

Luke smiled when he saw me which warmed my heart. Annabelle was already gone and the kitchen was clean.

"You look great. Let's go."

We walked to the training facility which was just outside of the business side of town. We passed several men dressed in suits, probably on their way to the office. No one touched me with Luke at my side. I felt protected with Luke, almost like I had an invisible force field around me. I appreciated the reprieve since my heart hammered and my body tingled as we got closer. I didn't want to show up to the facility a complete mess.

Luke led me into the main open room of the facility where he told me to kneel and wait for the day's instruction to begin.

"I'll be in the offices so if you need anything, let me know," Luke said.

"Ok," I said even though I knew there was no way I'd be asking him for anything. He was handing me over to the training facility for the day which meant I was under their control until Luke collected me on his way home.

I knelt on the soft padded floor and waited after Luke left. The space felt enormous around me, making me feel small and insignificant. I kept my eyes lowered as I had been taught, my hands resting on my upper thighs, my knees slightly spread. My heart pounded as I waited. I tried to calm myself by taking in a few deep breaths as I was taught but I was too wound up. I felt like I was about to dive off a cliff into something I didn't know. It both scared and excited me.

Every minute that passed felt like forever. I inhaled the faint aroma of sex combined with lemon cleaner as I waited. I had grown accustomed to being patient while on the island. The women were often thought of as accessories which meant we were left waiting to be used quite often. I didn't mind the wait but it built up the anticipation, making it a challenge to sit still. My body knew something was coming but not knowing what or when put it on edge and more than a little turned on.

I had fallen into a light sleep by the time I heard a commotion around me. I hadn't slept well last night so I wasn't surprised that it didn't take much for me to fall asleep. Thankfully I was able to maintain the pose while I dozed. I didn't want to think about the repercussions of falling asleep while waiting. I should have been running a mantra through my mind to keep me awake.

I heard the shuffling of feet but no talking. I kept my eyes lowered even though I wanted to know what was going on. My heart sped up as I smelled the clean fresh scent of a man getting closer to me.

A hand reached out and grazed my shoulders before pulling away.

"This is the proper waiting pose, sluts," Master Grant said, his voice strong and commanding.

I beamed with pride at his words, letting them wash over me. It had been too long since I had been with him in this way, under his control. I assumed he was talking to a roomful of women fresh to the island. It was the island's new policy to send new women through the training program before auctioning them off. I arrived before they had a training facility but I had gone through their advanced training to help break in the new trainers. I only had an inkling as to what these women were in for.

I kept my eyes lowered, knowing my place, while Master Grant commanded the other women to get into this pose, his voice firm yet accommodating. He wasn't as harsh as Master Owen but he knew how to get his point across. There was something about him that I didn't want to disappoint that went beyond my fear of being reprimanded.

He praised the women once they were in place.

"This is how you will need to be whenever you're not in use or otherwise occupied," Master Grant said. "Your man will expect this of you, to be waiting and ready. It also allows you time to think about your purpose here. You are nothing more than holes to be filled, women to be fucked and used. You are considered property here, nothing more. You released your rights as soon as you agreed to come here. Of course, you may leave at any time but if you do so before your contract is up, you will not be compensated.

"Your owner will decide to what extent others may use you and will show this by the color of your collar. Black allows full use, including pain. Green allows fucking but no pain. Yellow allows groping only and white means you're off limits. If your owner is with you, expect most men to get permission to use you despite your collar color. This shows respect to your owner. But if you're out on your own, your collar will dictate the level of use your owner allows.

"You won't be permanently harmed here—that is against our rules —but you may be punished and experience pain. You may use the safeword red to stop anything happening to you, especially if you feel like you may be permanently harmed. We do our best to protect the women since we want you to want to be here as much as we want you here. You will not be reprimanded for using the safeword but you will be sent home without compensation if it's determined that you weren't under threat of permanent harm."

Master Grant circled the women. He had them positioned opposite me, facing me, but more than a few feet away. I felt like I was at the head of the class, a demonstration, while they sat facing me. I had lifted my eyes slightly to take them in, careful not to look up enough to be noticed. About ten of them occupied the room, all kneeling in the waiting pose, all nude, eyes lowered. I felt suddenly overdressed in my sheer dress. I was surprised Master Grant hadn't made me lose it.

"As a woman on the island, do not initiate conversation with any man, even your owner, unless directed otherwise," Master Grant continued. "Also do not talk with other women when there is a man present. This is considered disrespectful and you will be punished. Also do not make eye contact with a man unless directed. Your eyes should remain lowered at all times.

"You will be trained to be a proper submissive slut before being auctioned off to your new owner. We will provide you with the basics while your owner will instill his own rules for you. Most households have more than one woman so do not expect to be the only woman in a household. There is no hierarchy among women so there's no concern about being in a lower position than any other women here, even those who have been here longer. You are all the same as far as the men are concerned and are all here to fill the same role."

Master Grant stopped in front of them, his back to me, watching them take in his words. Even though I already knew all this—I was told this during my intake—it was a lot to take in. It was a different lifestyle and not every woman made it. The men had set up this training facility to help teach the women what they needed to know about life here before being auction off and to weed out the women who weren't serious about staying. The men paid good money for these women and there were no refunds if the woman left.

"Stand up," Master Grant said, pointing to a redhead.

A flush spread across her chest as she stood. She was thin and willowy with full breasts and nipples that hardened under Master Grant's gaze. She kept her eyes lowered as instructed, her hands at her side. Jealousy snaked through me as Master Grant circled her. She was gorgeous, all smooth pale skin with freckles everywhere. Her lush auburn hair fell in soft waves around her face.

Master Grant didn't speak for a few minutes while he took her in.

"Very good," he said after a minute. "This is the basic attention position, the one you will assume while standing—eyes lowered, hands at your side, showing your submissiveness."

His hand grazed her nipple before pulling it. She gasped but said nothing. I could almost see him smile. He liked getting reactions out of women, this much I knew. He pulled the other nipple, this time harder.

"Very good," he said after he let go. "Nice control. The auctioneer will demonstrate these poses and show your aptitude towards being fondled and used while you're being auctioned. The more tolerance and obedience you demonstrate, the higher the price you'll fetch and the more likely you'll land in a more lucrative household. All the men on the island can care for the women—they're not allowed on the island without being able to—but trust me when I say you'll want to ensure that you go for top dollar."

I swallowed, having never considered this. I had no idea how much Luke paid for me but I doubted it was top dollar. How things had changed in the short time I had been on the island made me thankful that I wasn't coming in with these women. I knew more men were joining the island all the time but I had never considered what it would mean for the women.

Master Grant groped her ass before slapping it, the sound reverberating throughout the room. She didn't make a sound but I watched as her face reddened. She didn't look like the type of woman who'd end up here. She looked like the type who'd be gracing the covers of Vogue or stepping out of a limo with a fur draped around her shoulders. I was intrigued by how she came to be here. What had lured her?

Master Grant bent her over at the waist, moving her like a doll.

"Keep your legs straight and grab your ankles if you can."

She did as instructed, grabbing her ankles with ease.

"This position is called the bent position," he said, his eyes on his class while he caressed the woman's ass. I couldn't see behind her since she was facing me but I surmised he had slipped a finger inside her when she let out a small gasp. "As you can see, and you may look up to view this, this position gives a man full access to your ass and pussy."

The woman started to pant as Master Grant must have pushed his fingers in further, perhaps finding her g-spot or circling her clit with his thumb. He was a master at working a woman up.

I watched as the other women's eyes went wide as Master Grant continued to play with his prize. He pulled her nipples with his other hand, pinching until she squirmed, before releasing them.

"This position also allows easy access to your tits and is a great position for being spanked or flogged."

He pulled his fingers out, wiping her wetness on her ass. I couldn't see her face but I could imagine the embarrassment that must be there. I doubted these women had this kind of treatment back on the mainland and I could see now why this training facility was so important. It was better to be broken in here before being exposed to a room full of men wanting nothing more than to fuck them.

Master Grant smacked her ass again, the sound echoing, before doing it again and again. He smacked her until I imagined her ass turned bright red. I wished I could see it, feeling like I was somehow missing out by not being able to see her ass or her expression. I never thought of myself as getting turned on by watching someone else being used but there was something about Master Grant using her that had me aroused. I wished I was the one he was demonstrating on —and I kind of thought I would be—but it felt more to me than that.

I squirmed a little, grinding my ass into my heels, as Master Grant spanked her a few more times.

"Olivia, I want you to know that you didn't do anything wrong," Master Grant said as he caressed her ass, "but that sometimes a man will spank you because it gives him pleasure. You were a good girl for accepting this without question."

He left her bent over while he played with her ass, perhaps sliding his fingers back inside her. I squirmed as I watched, my eyes higher than they should be as I was taking it all in, mesmerized, until Master Grant caught my eye and smiled. His blue eyes sparkled as he nailed me with his gaze. I was busted and I knew it but I couldn't look away. He continued to toy with Olivia until she started to squirm.

Without breaking his gaze with me, he quickly unzipped his pants and sunk his thick cock inside her. She gasped as he filled her, gripping her hips for more traction, watching me the whole time. I wanted to look away, to look down, to show him the respect he deserved, but I couldn't do it. He had me. I couldn't lower my gaze.

He fucked her slowly at first but then picked up the pace. I wanted to squirm, to rub my clit on the ground, something, as my body remembered the way he had taken me like this during my training.

Olivia let out a moan and started to pant as Master Grant moved quicker, fucking her hard, his eyes never leaving mine. I felt pegged to the wall, immobile, as I watched him fuck her, increasing his speed, taking her, until he stilled and emptied himself in her.

He pulled out without ceremony, smacking her ass one more time before tucking himself in his pants. He gave me one last smile before turning his attention to his class.

"You may sit down, Olivia," Master Grant said. "You were the perfect demonstration of how a woman can expect to be treated here."

I watched as Olivia slowly straightened, come leaking down her inner thighs, and returned to her place with the others, her eyes lowered. I could almost feel her arousal washing through me as my body ached to be filled as she had been. I knew she hadn't come—Master Grant had been too quick for that—and must be beyond turned on. I doubted any of her boyfriends had fucked her like that.

I was lost in thought as Master Grant talked with the class and was startled when I heard Master Grant say my name in a clipped voice.

"Up, Riley," Master Grant said, his voice stern and annoyed. "I shouldn't have to say it twice."

I quickly stood, heat rushing up my face, my eyes lowered.

I felt him walk towards me until he was standing right in front of me. My heart hammered. I was in trouble. I could feel it.

Master Grant quickly spun me around and pulled my hands behind my back, lacing them with rope before pulling them tight until my wrists were linked together, immobile. He grasped my neck, pulling my back to him until his mouth was next to my ear.

"Prepare to be punished, my little slut," he said, his breath hot on my ear.

My body responded, a ripple of pleasure washing through me, as he forced me over at the waist. He kept hold of the rope around my wrists, keeping me from toppling over, as he ran his fingers through my wetness.

"Fully aroused, I see," Master Grant said, loud enough for the whole class to hear, before plunging two fingers into me.

I was so wound up that I came instantly, flooding his hand.

He chuckled before pulling his fingers out.

"So easy," he said, "like a proper slut. This is something to aspire to, class. Keep yourself fully aroused as much as possible so when your owner or any man takes you, you gush freely around him."

Master Grant gave my ass another smack before pulling me up in an upright position.

"But unfortunately for this slut, her punishment has just begun."

Master Grant released his grip on my wrists before slipping a blindfold over my eyes, blocking out everything. I sucked in my breath as I realized I had lost all control over the situation. Not that I had any before but having my sight taken away solidified that I was completely under his control.

Master Grant guided me somewhere, my hands still bound behind my back, until he pushed me over onto something cold and soft that supported my torso. He gave my ass another smack, warming it, before telling me not to move.

"Most men don't want to punish their women," Master Grant said to the class, "but sometimes it's necessary. The men here are trained how to properly discipline and punish their women without permanently harming them. The purpose of punishment is to teach you what is not acceptable and to help keep you in your place. Some men like to punish their women simply because it pleases them but that form of punishment usually differs from the type of punishment I am about to demonstrate for you."

I sucked in my breath as I waited, the anticipation killing me. Master Grant was smart to make me come first because all the arousal had been washed away from me, leaving me open and vulnerable.

Master Grant caressed my ass a moment as if to reassure me.

"The last thing you want to do during a punishment is to tense up," Master Grant said as his hand worked to soothe me. "What you want to do is to relax into the punishment, whatever it is. Don't tense up like Riley's doing. Remaining loose will help the punishment not hurt as much and will allow your mind to accept your punishment easier."

I strived to unclench, to let go, as Master Grant instructed, as his hand smoothed over my ass like I was a pony he was trying to tame.

"Good girl," Master Grant finally said after a few minutes, giving my ass a little pat. "Sit tight. Stay loose."

I took in a few deep breaths, willing myself to remain loose and open, as I waited, the anticipation killing me. I knew all eyes were on me but I didn't care. I was used to eyes on me. In fact, I relished in it. But I had never been punished by Master Grant or really anyone before. Luke wasn't big into punishing and I hadn't done anything wrong with him to warrant it.

I jumped as a spray of leather hit my ass, sending sharp slivers of pain through me. I kept telling myself to be still, to be open, as another spray of leather hit me then another until they were coming in such rapid succession that my mind couldn't keep up. After a few minutes, my body fully relaxed into the pain, opening up to it, allowing it to overtake all my senses, all my thoughts, until I felt like I was floating.

I lost myself as the pain rained down on my ass until it was suddenly over. I heard words, far away words, Master Grant talking, explaining something, before his firm hands found my ass, rubbing a soothing lotion into it, bringing me slowly back to the present moment.

He untied my wrists, rubbing them to help the flow of blood return, before helping me back in a standing position. He slowly turned me around until I was facing him and wrapped his strong arms around me. I allowed myself to bury my nose in his solid chest, inhaling him through his black t-shirt, thankful for his strength because I wasn't sure I'd be able to stand on my own.

"Good girl, Riley," Master Grant purred in my ear, low enough so only I could hear. "You did wonderfully."

I relaxed into him as he continued to hold me, the stinging of my ass reminding me of what I had just been through.

"I got you," he said into my ear, causing my heart to flip. "I've always got you."

FIVE

Master Grant turned the class over to Master Owen as he guided me out of the training room. He kept me tucked in under his arm as we walked, my face buried in his chest, the blindfold still in place. I had no idea where we were going and I didn't care. All I cared about was having a moment alone with him again, to be fully present to whatever he wanted to do.

My heart started to slow as we walked, happy to have him guiding me. He stopped to open a door, walked us through, and shut it behind him. He guided me to what felt like a sofa before sitting and pulling me onto his lap, pulling off my blindfold. I blinked, my eyes adjusting to the dim light. Pale sunlight streamed in through thin grey curtains on one wall, a massive king size bed on the other. My heart skipped as I realized I must be in his bedroom. Master Grant and Master Owen moved in as soon as the facility opened about a month ago.

I cuddled into him, my face buried in his chest, like a small animal seeking comfort. He stroked my back and hair as he whispered soothing words into my ear.

"You did so well, Riley," he whispered, his voice thick with emotion which stirred something deep inside me. "I knew you'd be able to handle it. I know you know you got caught looking at me when your eyes should have been lowered. Part of me was happy that you watched me take Olivia. I saw the fire in your eyes as I fucked her, wanting it to be you. Am I right?"

I nodded into his chest, too afraid to admit it out loud.

"I need your words, Riley. Don't make me flog you again."

"Yes, Master Grant," I said, my face reddening. "I wanted it to be me."

He chuckled against my cheek, his hands in my hair, as he pulled me closer to him until I was curled up on his lap, his strong arms around me. I felt safe. Settled. My whole body relaxed into him as I listened to the rhythm of his steady breathing. He felt solid underneath me. Protective.

"I hope you know I had to punish you," Master Grant said into my hair. "I'm sure the other women saw you looking straight at me. I had to let them know, and you know, that that wasn't acceptable. I don't want any of them getting in more trouble than necessary. It's hard enough for women to find their place on the island. I need to give them every chance to succeed."

"I understand, Master Grant," I said into his chest.

"You've never been punished like that before." It wasn't a question.

"No, Master Grant," I said, my ass still burning.

He smoothed out my hair.

"You took it exceedingly well. You can expect your ass to be sore for a few days but it won't leave any permanent marks. Sitting may be a challenge. I'll send you home with some salve for Luke to administer on you. I'll inform him of what happened. I know this won't be a punishment you will forget anytime soon."

I swallowed. I would never forget this. I had totally forgotten about Luke. He'd probably be collecting me soon to go home. I wished I could stay with Master Grant even if that meant he'd be doing more demonstrations on me to his class. I knew I could handle it and I'd do just about anything to have more time like this alone with him.

"I won't, Master Grant," I said. "Thank you."

He chuckled into my hair.

"You're such a precious gem, Riley," he said, his words deep and soothing. "I'm always happy to see you. I'm happy Luke will be bringing you around more often now that he'll be on-site for a few weeks. Maybe I can convince him I need to take you overnight."

My heart hammered at his words. I had no idea what Luke would say to that but I was happy it was out of my hands. I never wanted Luke to think I didn't want to be with him. He had never been anything but amazing to me. I couldn't ever let him know I'd rather be with Master Grant, especially since Master Grant wasn't an option.

"How are you feeling now?" Master Grant asked.

I wanted to lie and tell him I needed more time curled up on his lap but I was feeling back to normal and a strong part of me didn't want to lie to him.

"Much better, Master Grant. Thank you for taking care of me. I'm not sure where my head went."

"You slipped into subspace. It's common when we throw a lot of pain on a woman in a short amount of time. It's your body's way of coping but it can also feel wonderful. How did it feel for you?"

"I was floating. I felt light as air."

"That's a common response which is why I took you back to my room to come down. Sometimes it can feel like a crash landing and a man needs to do what he can to make it as smooth as possible. We're training the men on the island how to handle this, too. It's part of their care and handling of an owned woman training."

I was shocked to hear this—that the men were being trained, too. I had assumed that only the women needed training but it made sense that the men would benefit, too.

Master Grant kissed the top of my head.

"I'll let you rest here until Luke takes you home," Master Grant said, gently sliding me off his lap and onto the smooth leather sofa. "I'll have one of the kitchen girls bring you lunch and then feel free to nap on my bed. Our session today will have worn you out. I think you've had enough for one day."

My pussy said otherwise, aching to be filled, but I nodded in agreement. What else could I do?

"Thank you, Master Grant," I said. "For everything."

He smiled and was out the door.

I CRAWLED into Master Grant's big bed as soon as he left, wrapping myself up in his scent and falling promptly to sleep. It wasn't until someone was shaking me awake that I realized I had dozed off. I blinked up into startling green eyes and a timid smile, a waterfall of auburn hair obscuring her face but I knew who it was.

"Master Grant had me come wake you," she said, her voice soft with a melodic lilt, her hand on my shoulder.

I blinked at her as she leaned over me, her nipples dangerously close to mine, her lips swollen as if she had been kissed for hours. I wondered if Master Grant had kissed her senseless then sent her to me. My mind fought to reject that thought as she leaned in closer, her soft skin touching mine.

She blinked at me before she leaned in and kissed me, her lips soft and open. Her nipples brushed against mine as she leaned in to kiss me deeper. My mouth automatically opened to her as if trained to open to anyone who wanted to claim me.

She started out tentative but quickly deepened the kiss as her hand cupped my breast, her thumb flicking over my erect nipple, taunting me as she kissed me deeper.

My head spun at the realization that Olivia was kissing me in Master Grant's bed and I wasn't resisting. I couldn't resist. My body gave in to it, molded into hers, as if this was how it was supposed to be. She pinched my nipple, causing me to shudder, my body awakening to her. I had never been with a woman before but I was so turned on by the entire day that my body didn't care who was touching me, it just wanted to be touched.

Her tongue reached out and captured mine, tasting me, as she pinched and pulled on my nipple, causing me to arch my back into her.

As soon as she started, she backed off, releasing me.

I stared at her. Her face reddened.

"Oh my God," she said in a whisper. "I'm not sure why I did that."

I smiled at her. "It's OK. Don't worry about it."

"I'm sure I wasn't supposed to do that but you were lying there and I couldn't resist. It was like my body took over. I'm so sorry."

"I didn't mind," I said, knowing it was the truth. There was something about her that I was attracted to even though I had never been attracted to a woman before. "It was nice."

Olivia's face reddened again.

"Are you a lesbian?" I asked, the thought popping into my head and escaping out of my mouth before I had a moment to process it. But it made sense only it didn't make sense why she would want to come here.

"I don't think so," she said. "I've only ever been with men but maybe. How would I know?"

I smiled at her. "You'd be attracted to women. But maybe you're bisexual. Most women are on some level but rarely act out on it."

Her eyes widened. "Maybe that's it. Either way, gosh, I'm sorry. I shouldn't have done that. Women aren't supposed to initiate sex here."

That was true but I wasn't sure where this fell into the rules. Nothing sexual had ever happened with Annabelle even though we were around each other naked all the time and Luke had fucked us while we were in the same room. I never thought to initiate anything with her but then again, I never felt the desire.

"I won't say anything if you don't," I said, seeing no reason to get us both in trouble. My ass didn't need more reprimanding. "But we should get going if Master Grant is waiting."

"Oh right," she said, her eyes getting wide again. "We should go."

SIX

Master Grant was waiting for us in the main entrance, a smirk on his face. My heart skipped as his eyes focused on mine for a split second before I remembered to lower them. Damn, I wondered if he'd punish me again so soon.

I hoped Olivia remembered to keep her eyes lowered as we closed the gap to him.

"That took a little while," Master Grant said, a touch of humor in his voice.

"I was slow to wake up," I said, wanting to take the weight off Olivia. She didn't need to get in trouble, too.

"I see," Master Grant said as if he in no way believed me. "Luke is ready to leave. I'll take you to him."

"Yes, Master Grant," I said before following him down a hallway to the offices. I didn't dare glance back at Olivia and I hoped she wouldn't get in trouble for delivering me late.

I had never been in the office section of the building and was surprised they looked like offices one would find anywhere else except all the offices had big picture windows facing the inner hallway as well as big picture windows facing out onto the street. Master Grant walked me to one of the furthest ones where Luke sat at a desk working on the computer.

"Stand here in wait pose until he's ready for you," Master Grant said in a low voice in my ear. "And don't think for a minute that I don't know what happened between you and Olivia in my room. There are cameras everywhere in this place."

My face reddened as my heart lodged in my throat. Holy crap, I was in trouble.

Master Grant soothed his hand over my painful ass.

"I'll reprimand you for it tomorrow," he said, his voice low. "No need to let Luke know about this."

I swallowed. "Thank you, Master Grant."

He chuckled before leaving me to wait for Luke to finish up. Somehow I knew I was in for it.

LUKE LEFT me waiting for some time before he shut down his computer and locked up his office. He smiled at me as I stood waiting for him in the hall. He had a clear view of me the entire time but he only looked up momentarily when Master Grant dropped me off. He smiled at me now and I knew he wanted me to look up and meet his eyes. I saw warmth there, the Luke friendliness, and I melted a little. I wished that all that charm would be directed at me at least most of the time but I knew his heart was elsewhere. I didn't think I could compete with Annabelle. They had something special.

"Ready?" he asked.

"Yes, Luke," I said as he guided me down the hall.

We didn't see anyone else as we left the building and walked out into the warm evening. I loved living on the island with its warm tropical breezes and ample sunshine every day. We had the occasional storm but so far nothing serious. The women had no access to news or the internet so I had no idea what was going on elsewhere or if there was ever a major storm headed our way. It was another lesson in trusting that the men had it covered. I knew they were well connected to the outside world even if they kept it behind closed doors.

We walked along, not saying much. I sensed that Luke was exhausted after putting in a long day. He didn't ask about my day except to ask a general "How was it?" I answered fine and that was the end of the discussion. I knew he wouldn't care if Master Grant or anyone else fucked me since he had given me a black collar.

I walked a couple of steps behind him. A few hands reached out and grabbed my ass and pinched a nipple as we walked. I kept my eyes lowered, my expression blank, as if I didn't notice. My pussy ached to be filled while my ass was on fire. I blushed thinking Master Grant must have told Luke about my punishment since I would need help putting the salve on it later. Luke hadn't said anything and hadn't inspected me so maybe Master Grant forgot. I'm sure I'd figure something out at home if he did.

The walk wasn't too long but it felt like it took forever. As soon as we were in the house, Annabelle was there, all smiles, throwing her arms around Luke. He took her up in his arms and gave her a proper kiss as her hands snaked through his hair. I went directly to the kitchen to start dinner, wanting to be busy and also not wanting to watch their obvious affection for each other.

I busied myself in the kitchen, blocking my mind out as much as I could as I heard them go upstairs. I knew what was coming and again I wasn't a part of it. I sautéed some vegetables, making one of my favorite meals that I knew by heart. I should have picked something more complicated so I would really have to focus and could forget about Luke fucking Annabelle while my pussy ached for attention.

I pulled the vegetables off the stove and dumped them into a bowl before starting in on the chicken. I cut them into pieces so they would each get golden brown. The pleasant aroma of pan-fried chicken filled the kitchen and probably drifted up to the bedroom. I knew I shouldn't be complaining—after all, my opinion hardly mattered here —but I needed something more than this. My contract would be up in a couple of months and even though I wanted to stay, I wasn't sure I wanted to stay in Luke's house. I knew I was luckier than a lot of women—most men weren't as nice and accommodating as Luke—but I still yearned for something more.

I finished the sauce, my stomach growling as I plated dinner and brought them out to the dining table. I put little domes over each to keep them warm—something I had suggested to Luke when I first arrived since sometimes other things happened when dinner was served.

I waited on my knees like a proper submissive, my eyes lowered, palms up, as I heard the faint sound of water running and the low murmur of voices.

I didn't have to wait long before they headed down the stairs, freshly showered, both smiling ear to ear. I stuffed down the jealousy that threatened to surface and reminded myself that it wasn't up to me how I was used. Maybe Luke only wanted me for my cooking now that I learned how. I had no control over whether or not he used me sexually and I knew better than to complain.

"The whole house smells amazing," Luke said as he entered the dining room. "I can't wait to dig in. Let's eat."

That was my cue to stand and take a seat at the table with them. Luke liked having us sit at the table when we were in his house. I could have sat waiting but I wanted to emphasize that I knew my place, especially after the punishment I endured earlier.

We popped the domes off the plates and dug in. I noticed that Annabelle looked flushed, her green eyes sparkling. She wore nothing but a smile and heels while I still had on my sheer blue dress. Somehow it had never made its way off me during the day despite everything that happened.

Luke made small talk, sounding his usual chipper self. I figured Luke knew about my punishment but he didn't bring it up. Annabelle talked freely about her day, about the new men that came into Mr. Wood's office and how one talked about fucking her. She wore a green collar so he could have.

Luke smiled at her. "He didn't?"

"No time," Annabelle said between bites. "I think they were headed out to the training facility. I got the impression they might be the new trainers. Did you see them, Riley? You were there today, right?"

I swallowed down the food in my mouth before speaking.

"I didn't see any new men but I did see the new shipment of women. It's a larger class this time, ten total. I sat in on part of their training."

"Who was teaching?" Annabelle asked, her eyes sparkling.

"Master Grant," I said, trying to act casual, like it was nothing. "He's the only man besides Luke and Master Owen that I saw today. It's interesting that they're bringing in more trainers."

"The amount of women wanting to come to the island has increased exponentially over the past few months," Luke said. "Even though Lance set up offices in the mainland to screen potential women and to weed out those who have little chance of making it, the list keeps growing. More men are setting up households on the island, too. This place is booming. It's like word got out and now everyone wants to come. More trainers are a must."

Luke took a bite of food before continuing, "Lance is looking to expand the training facilities, too, and is looking into expanding the building and perhaps even building dorms. It's been insane. That's one reason I'm having to work over there for the next few weeks. There's too much going on."

It took me a moment to connect Lance to his brother Mr. Wood. No one ever used his first name except Luke.

"Wow, that's insane," Annabelle said. "I do have to say that the guys were hot."

Luke shot her an amused look. "How hot?"

"Hot enough to get any woman revved up," she said. "Whoever hired them did a great job."

We all knew who hired them: Mr. Wood. He never let decisions that important go to anyone else. He was building his kingdom here and he wanted full control over who entered it. It was one of the reasons I felt safe here. Even though they didn't have a police force or a government, they were self-regulated with strict rules for the men as well as the women. Anyone caught crossing the line would immediately be shipped off the island and banned forever. Being a privately owned island, Mr. Wood had that level of power.

"You better watch it," Luke said, his voice teasing. His hand disappeared under the table and I knew he was touching Annabelle in some sexy way by the way she squirmed in her seat.

"I'll be good, I promise," she said.

I finished up my meal while Luke played with Annabelle under the table. I sat across from them so I couldn't see what was going on and was happy about that. I started clearing plates as soon as everyone seemed finished. I couldn't wait to disappear into my room and think about everything that has been happening lately and what I wanted to do.

I was in the kitchen finishing washing dishes when Luke came in by himself.

"I heard about your punishment today," Luke said.

I had my back to him, my hands in the sink, so I couldn't see his expression. I kept doing dishes, sure he could see the redness of my ass. It still stung but not as bad. I could see where it'd be sore for a few days. Master Grant hadn't gone easy on me.

"When you're finished here, go lay on your stomach on my bed so I can put salve on your ass. It looks like it's still hurting you."

"It does," I said. "Thank you, Luke."

SEVEN

I finished the dishes and went upstairs to Luke's room. Annabelle's door was closed when I passed but I had no idea if she was in there or not. Again, I wouldn't have been surprised to find her in Luke's room but she wasn't there either.

I crawled into the middle of Luke's bed and laid down on my stomach. I still had my dress on but flipped it up to reveal my red ass. I felt embarrassed more than anything. Luke had never punished me to this extent and I didn't want him to know why I had been punished. I wondered what Master Grant had told him because he had to have told him something. My stomach tensed at the thought.

Luke didn't take long before he came into his room and shut the door behind him. With my face down on the bed, I couldn't see him. I heard him approach and felt the bed sink as he sat down next to my ass. His hand lightly touched the stinging skin.

"Master Grant really did a number on you," Luke said as he started spreading salve over my hot skin. "What did you do?"

I sucked in my breath. I knew I couldn't lie but I didn't want to disrespect Luke by telling him the full truth.

"I watched him fuck one of the new women," I said, my voice small.

"That doesn't sound like a punishable offense," Luke said, his hand soothing against my skin.

"I made direct eye contact with him during the whole thing when I was supposed to be keeping my eyes lowered."

"Ah, I see," Luke said, his hands still working my skin, calming it down. "And what made you do that?"

My face reddened. I was happy Luke couldn't see me. I wasn't sure what to say but I knew I needed to say something.

"I wanted to see," I said, telling the truth but not everything, not how I couldn't look away from Master Grant, how I had wanted to be the woman he was fucking, how my insides turned to mush every time Master Grant looked at me. I hoped what I said was enough. I couldn't get into the rest.

Luke continued to apply salve on my ass, taking his time. I could almost hear him contemplating. Luke was a very thoughtful man. It was one of the things I liked most about him. Everything he did had a purpose. He wasn't careless and he wasn't cruel.

"Was it worth it?" Luke asked after a few minutes as he was finishing up.

Yes was my immediate response but I held back. Every second I didn't answer was a second Luke knew I was seriously considering it which meant that yes, it was worth it.

"I didn't think he'd punish me like this," I said as an answer.

Luke gave an area on my ass that wasn't already red from the flogger a little smack.

"That wasn't the question. Was it worth it?"

"Yes," I said, my voice small. "It was."

Luke sent me back to my room to sleep. I knew I wasn't winning him over by answering honestly but it had been worth it. I didn't want to be punished like that again but I did want to be able to look directly at Master Grant while he had his way with Olivia. It was as if I could feel everything that he did to her. I'd do almost anything for that again. Of course, I didn't tell any of this to Luke. He hadn't said anything else, just sent me to my room, telling me to be ready by 8 AM because we'd be heading back to the training facility. He told me to wear whatever dress I wanted and to not be late. He didn't sound pleased with me and I couldn't blame him. He had to know now that I had a thing for Master Grant.

I was happy not to see Annabelle as I went to my room and closed the door behind me. I was happy to have my little sanctuary away from Annabelle and Luke. I curled up on my bed. Thoughts of Master Grant invaded my mind. I stopped fighting them and let them come.

THE NEXT MORNING Luke barely acknowledged me when he came down to breakfast. I had gotten up early so I could make breakfast for everyone. I wore a sheer pink dress with Lucite heels. I had blown my hair out so it fell softly around my shoulders and put on smoldering makeup. I wanted to think that I had gotten more dolled up for Luke but I had a feeling Luke knew the truth that it wasn't for him.

I served Luke a plate of eggs with bacon and toast when he came into the kitchen. He gave me a little nod but didn't say a word as he took it into the dining room instead of eating at the kitchen counter like usual. Annabelle had left already for work, grabbing a piece of toast on her way out, leaving me alone to deal with Luke. I fixed myself a plate and ate at the kitchen counter, figuring that Luke wanted time alone this morning.

Luke brought his plate in when he was done and loaded it into the dishwasher. He glanced at me as I was finishing up.

"Ready?" he asked, his voice flat. "You can leave the dishes for later. I need to get in a bit earlier today."

"Yes, Luke," I said, putting my fork down. "I'm all set."

I followed Luke out the door and to the training facility. When we entered this time, instead of taking me through to the main training room, he told me to stop and wait inside the entrance.

"I'll let them know you're here," Luke said before disappearing down the hall towards his office.

Shame washed over me as I took in how much I had disappointed Luke. He hadn't mentioned my punishment this morning and hadn't taken the time to put salve on my welts. I had washed them thoroughly but they still burned, a reminder of my disobedience. I knew I deserved it. I hated disappointing people, especially Luke and Master Grant.

I stood still, my eyes lowered, my ass burning. I hoped I wouldn't be made to do anything too demanding today that would make my ass feel worse. What I felt like doing was sitting in a tub of ice water, letting the ice numb my ass as well as the flood of emotions that rushed through me. I wasn't sure how to handle all of what I was thinking and feeling and wished that it would go away. I had hoped by coming to the island that I'd be free of feeling anything for the men here and to be nothing more than a warm body to be used and enjoyed. I wanted to serve and give pleasure and have my happiness derive from that alone. I didn't want my heart tangled up in it.

I felt like I was being punished even more by being forced to wait in the hall to be summoned. I heard voices down the halls, coming from the offices as well as the training room. I imagined that the training sessions had started already and I assumed I'd been forgotten. The thought gutted me as I realized Master Grant hadn't remembered that I'd be waiting again today. He had more important things to focus on and more important women to train. I was sure I wasn't even a blip in his mind after he left me yesterday.

I wanted to cry the longer I waited. Misery washed over me. I held my hands behind my back, thinking that would somehow be more submissive. I knew I was on camera and maybe someone somewhere was watching. There always seemed to be someone watching. I knew new trainers were starting soon so maybe they were monitoring me while Master Grant or Master Owen trained the new women in the main room. I felt like I had been standing there forever.

I held back tears as I felt like a loser. My ass throbbed and my feet ached. I felt abandoned. I felt like I no longer knew where I fit into this world. I had been edged out of Luke's good graces for the moment and I knew I had no way of capturing his heart even if I wanted to. I felt lost in a way I hadn't experienced before. At least on the mainland, I knew who my friends were and where I stood with people. I had never clicked all that much with the guys I dated but I always knew it was only temporary. We were too young and reckless to want anything real and lasting. I knew it happened for some women but never for me. I was always the odd girl out.

I breathed in deeply, taking in all the air I could, willing myself to clear my mind, to release these thoughts. I knew they weren't doing me any favors. It didn't matter if Master Grant forgot about me. It didn't matter if Luke wasn't the love of my life. It didn't even matter if I stayed on this island or not. As much as I wanted to give myself over to this place, it was ultimately my decision whether I stayed and how I wanted to show up here. I could hate it, complain and be miserable or I could accept things as they were and decide to be my best self here, to be submissive and subservient, and to do my best to please the men around me regardless of my thoughts about them.

I breathed this in, willing my mind to shift to this new attitude. I had come to the island with this mindset but somewhere along the way I started to get jealous of Annabelle and wanting that type of relationship for myself. I knew what she shared with Luke was special and not likely to happen again, at least not here. I needed to stop wanting something like that. That wasn't why I came here. I needed to do a full reset and I knew I'd be much happier if I did.

I stood there for what felt like over an hour before I heard footsteps moving towards me. I kept my eyes lowered, not wanting to get in trouble again, so I had no idea who was approaching. I kept my shoulders back, my tits out, while I waited, feeling like I was being judged.

A hand lifted the back of my skirt to reveal the red rawness of my ass.

"Tsk, tsk," Master Grant said, his voice low and gravely. "Looks like you haven't been properly salved today. Didn't Luke do it for you?"

"Not today, no, Master Grant," I said, my voice low. Embarrassment washed over me.

"He didn't punish you more, did he?" Master Grant asked, still behind me, still holding up my dress.

"No, Master Grant. He did smack my ass once last night but not where it hurts. He put salve on me last night. He must have forgotten this morning. I know he was in a rush to get into the office."

The last thing I wanted to do was get Luke into trouble because of me. I wasn't sure how they disciplined the men around here but I knew they had to do something to help keep them in line, too. I knew Mr. Wood took the care of the women on the island very seriously.

Master Grant let the dress fall then walked around to stand in front of me.

"Look at me," he commanded.

I looked up into his deep blue eyes. His expression was serious. I swallowed, nerves snaking through me. I didn't want to be in more trouble.

"What did you do to make him smack your ass?" Master Grant asked, his expression stern.

"I didn't answer his question at first, Master Grant," I said, knowing better than to try to lie.

"What question was that?"

My face went red.

"He asked if my punishment was worth it."

His eyebrow went up. "Was it?"

"Yes, Master Grant," I said, wanting to disappear into the floor.

He held my gaze a couple of seconds before saying, "Follow me."

I followed Master Grant down the hall towards the main training room. I couldn't hear voices but I knew that didn't mean anything. Master Grant could have left the women to wait and there was no way they would be talking amongst themselves without permission.

He passed the main training room but the door was closed. We walked down another hallway until he led me into his bedroom.

"Lay on the bed on your stomach."

I crawled over his grey comforter until I was flat on my stomach in his bed. I inhaled the fresh scent of him and wondered if he ever brought any of the other women into his bed. It made sense that he would—I didn't think I was special—but the thought of someone else in his bed bothered me. I pushed the thought out of my mind, reminding myself of my commitment to my new mindset to be more submissive.

I heard rustling behind me before I felt a dip on the bed and he was beside me. Without a word, he lifted my dress to reveal my ass and started spreading salve all on it. His touch was light but firm enough to ensure the salve was properly rubbed in. When he finished, he got off the bed and disappeared into his adjoining bathroom where I heard him washing his hands.

When he returned, he sat on the edge of the bed near my ass. I didn't dare move.

"I still need to punish you for your indiscretion with Olivia yesterday," Master Grant said. "And in my bed. I really should punish you both but I'll deal with Olivia separately. She's new and still learning. I'm a little laxer with the new women but I've been thinking a lot about how to punish you. Any thoughts?"

I could hear the chuckle in his voice. He was enjoying this. He must have known I was mortified. I knew he couldn't flog me again so soon or do anything with my ass so I was at a loss.

"No, not really, Master Grant," I said. "I'm not sure what would be a suitable punishment."

"Lucky for you, I have some ideas. Follow me. We're going to the training room."

I followed Master Grant into the hallway and to the training room. The women were waiting on their knees, eyes lowered. I wondered where Master Owen was since no one else seemed to be around. I knew better than to ask and followed Master Grant towards the back where they housed bondage furniture.

"Strip," he commanded.

I pulled the sheer dress over my head, letting it drop to the floor.

He slipped leather cuffs around my ankles and wrists, locking them into place with little padlocks, before having me step onto a massive X. He secured my wrists to the X above my head and my ankles to the X below. I thought for sure he was going to flog my front or something but instead he went over to a chest and pulled out clamps that had little weights on him. He pinched and pulled on each nipple, causing me to suck in my breath, before slipping the clips on to each one. The pain shot straight through me, searing, but I fought not to let the amount of my discomfort show.

"You'll keep those clamps on for 15 minute intervals throughout the day," Master Grant said. "If at any time you need to use the bathroom, let me know and I'll have one of the women take you. Otherwise, you'll be on the cross for the duration of the class as your punishment for messing around with Olivia in my bed. Understood?"

"Yes, Master Grant," I said, my head swimming, my nipples aching. I didn't want to think about being on this thing all day but I knew what I did couldn't be tolerated. I shouldn't have let things with Olivia progress as they did.

"Keep your eyes lowered at all times or else I'll blindfold you," Master Grant said. "Got it?"

"Yes, Master Grant," I said, humiliation washing over me.

"Good," he said before turning to the rest of the class. They had their backs to me but Master Grant quickly had them readjust so they were facing me. "I want you to know that Riley will be joining us again today but she will spend the entire class on the cross for her indiscretion with Olivia yesterday. While we encourage women to develop friendships on the island, you are not to engage in any sexual activity unless it's permitted by your owner. Your owner may give you blanket permission to engage with other women in this way or may direct you to do so in the moment. That's up to him. There is no time when it is acceptable for a woman to take it upon herself to engage in sexual activity with anyone without consent from a man. Is that understood?"

"Yes, Master Grant," the class said together.

Heat shot up my face as I felt the depth of his words. I hadn't heard this rule described this way before but it made sense. I wasn't here to initiate sexual contact but to submit to it as commanded by men.

"Olivia, come here," Master Grant said.

I wanted to watch what was happening so badly but I didn't want to be blindfolded so I kept my eyes lowered, fixated on a spot on the floor, while I heard Olivia move towards Master Grant.

"Since you were just as guilty as Riley, you need to be punished as well. Like I explained to Riley, your punishment won't be as severe since you are new to the island and not as familiar with our rules. But I do think you need to be punished so you will be more mindful in the future. Do you understand?"

"Yes, Master Grant," she said in a small voice that I could barely hear.

"Good. Now turn around."

I held my breath as I waited for what I knew was coming. Master Grant's hand smacking Olivia's ass reverberated throughout the room. He smacked her ass in rapid succession. Her mumbled cries filled the room as she tried to hold them in. I knew by the sound of it that he wasn't being gentle with her. He continued for about ten times before he told her to kneel.

"You took that well, Olivia," Master Grant said. "Your owner may punish you in different ways. He'll discover which punishments you hate the most and adjust from there. You don't seem overly fond of being spanked—I noticed that yesterday—so I will add this observation to your file. This will make life with your new owner smoother."

Master Grant directed the class, running them through the different poses he had taught them yesterday, reprimanding as needed. His voice was firm yet kind. I could tell that he cared about these women succeeding on the island.

A timer went off and he came over and released my nipples from the clamps. Pain rushed in as they were released as the blood flowed back to my aching points. He gave each breast a little slap to help with the blood flow. I kept my eyes lowered, not wanting to disappoint him.

"Good girl, Riley," he said, his voice low. He pinched each nipple and pulled, causing me to arch into it. "I'll give your nipples a bit of break but then the clamps will go back on for another 15 minutes. How are you holding up?"

"I'm fine, Master Grant," I said. My arms started to ache but I didn't want to complain. This was my punishment. It wasn't supposed to be easy. I wanted him to be proud of me for enduring it.

"Ok," Master Grant said, "but tell me if you need a break or feel dizzy or anything. This punishment is meant to punish you, not harm you. You won't get in trouble for letting me know, even if I'm in the middle of something with someone else."

"Thank you, Master Grant," I said, my heart warming. "I will."

"Good," he said before returning to the others.

EIGHT

The afternoon stretched on. I took a couple of bathroom breaks and was allowed to eat lunch with the other women in the main dining room. Master Grant directed the women through lunch, telling them how they weren't allowed to talk among themselves when a man was present but how they could if they were alone. I was happy to not have to force conversation with anyone. I noticed that Olivia sat at the other end of the table from me, probably not wanting to get into any more trouble by associating with me. I couldn't blame her. The space between us was good.

After lunch, Master Grant put me back on the cross, securing the clamps on my nipples. I bit my lip as the pain shot through me. I didn't think I'd ever get used to the searing pain. I knew some people got aroused by pain but I wasn't one of them. Master Grant probably knew that. He seemed intuitive when it came to discovering what worked for each woman.

He didn't fuck anyone that I could tell during the afternoon but he did cause many of them to squirm by either fingering them or pulling on their nipples. I heard the intake of breaths and felt the energy in the room. I knew more than one woman had fallen for Master Grant.

It was easy to do. He was dominant without being mean, firm yet accommodating when needed. And he cared.

I wondered how many men on the island cared about the women they owned. I knew Luke did and Mr. Wood to some extent but it seemed like most of the men only cared about the sex and having someone to dominate. I wondered what separated those men from the ones like Master Grant. What made them different?

I had a lot of time to contemplate such things as I stayed on the cross, trying not to be too curious about what was happening in the room. Part of me wished I had been in a room by myself. That would have been easier. Every time a woman took a sharp intake of breath or I heard the undisputed sounds of a woman being penetrated, I wanted to look up. But my sore ass and my sore nipples kept my eyes lowered, kept me obedient. Plus I wanted more than anything to please Master Grant, to be back in his good graces.

By the end of the day, Master Grant released me, unlocking the cuffs and sliding them off before placing them on the table next to the cross. I stepped down gingerly, my legs a little wobbly. Master Grant took my elbow and helped me. He had already dismissed the other women for dinner so we were alone in the expansive room. I kept my eyes lowered.

"You did very well today, Riley," Master Grant said as he helped me. Once I was on the floor, feeling better, he kept his hand on my elbow. "You impressed me."

I wanted to look up at him, to read his expression, but I didn't dare.

He held me a moment longer, like he wanted to say something more, before releasing me. Sadness washed over me from the lack of his touch. I knew I needed to let go of whatever I felt for Master Grant. I was lucky to have this time with him but I knew it wouldn't last. Once Luke finished his business at the facility, I'd be back to cleaning his house and running errands, lucky if I crossed paths with Master Grant.

I stood still, not sure what to do, waiting for a command.

Master Grant walked around me to examine my ass. He ran his hand over it.

"How does it feel?"

"It's sore but nothing like yesterday, Master Grant."

"Good," he said, his hand still on my ass, caressing it softly. "It's looking better. I want to put salve on you before you leave. Unfortunately, it's not here so follow me back to my room."

"OK, Master Grant," I said, my heart hammering at the thought of going to his room. I tried to calm myself as I followed him out and down the hall, telling myself it meant nothing more than him wanting to ensure my ass healed properly.

Once we arrived at his room, he pointed to the bed before disappearing into the bathroom. I crawled on it, face down, and waited. A moment later he sat on the bed next to me and wiped salve over my ass without a word. His hands were delicate yet firm, ensuring that the salve rubbed in properly. I couldn't help getting aroused. It was nonsexual what he was doing but at the same time extremely intimate. I wished I could stick my ass up further as an invitation but I knew better than to do that. A woman couldn't initiate. I had learned that the hard way today.

Master Grant took his time rubbing in the salve. I imagined him examining my ass as he did, working the salve into all the red spots, making sure not to miss any. I felt well cared for and wondered if Master Grant took this level of care with every woman. He probably did. He was that kind of guy which made me like him even more.

When he was done, he returned to the bathroom to wash his hands. I stayed put, waiting for further instruction, not wanting to make any assumptions while also not wanting to leave.

He came back, sat on the bed near my ass, and put a hand on my upper thigh.

"Did you learn your lesson, Riley?"

"Yes, Master Grant."

"What did you learn?"

"Not to initiate sex with anyone, that it's up to a man to decide that for me."

"Very good," he said, patting my thigh. "I don't want to have discipline you again anytime soon. Your body needs time to heal. Your ass will feel better tomorrow but expect your nipples to be sore for a day. I'll let Luke know of your punishment today so he goes easy on them."

Not likely he'll touch them, I thought, but I appreciated Master Grant looking out for me.

"Do you enjoy being punished?" Master Grant asked.

"No, Master Grant," I said. "Not at all."

He chuckled. "Good. You're the easier type of woman to train."

I didn't know what he meant but I was happy to be easier versus challenging. If anything, I came here to please the men, to be what they wanted. I wasn't one who usually got in trouble but here I was suddenly getting in trouble two days in a row. I wasn't sure what had come over me but I hoped I had learned my lesson and would stay out of trouble for the time being. I didn't want to be known as difficult. That sounded like a branding a woman here didn't want.

"I'll walk you back to Luke's office," Master Grant said. "Push yourself up and let's go."

My heart dropped knowing our time would soon be over. I liked these little moments with Master Grant even if we weren't doing anything sexual. I liked being with him. He made me comfortable. Luke made me comfortable, too, but there was something in Master Grant's style and the way he spoke to me that made me feel like he truly cared about me, that I wasn't just another woman he had to deal with.

I followed him out of his room and down several hallways before we stopped outside of the offices. I saw Luke on the phone but his door was closed. It didn't seem like he'd be done anytime soon.

"I need to collect the others from dinner so wait here for Luke to finish," Master Grant instructed. "You may wait on your knees if that's more comfortable. Your legs must be tired from standing all day."

More like my feet but I didn't say that. Instead, I said, "Thank you, Master Grant," and sunk down on my knees. The concrete floor wasn't exactly comfortable but it was better than standing. I sat back on my heels, distributing my weight as much as possible, palms up on my lap, eyes lowered, as Master Grant walked away leaving me to wait.

LUKE DIDN'T TAKE TOO MUCH LONGER to finish up before he collected me and walked me home. He was in a better mood and made small talk, asking how my day went. I knew he must have known about my additional punishment and the nipple clamps but he didn't say anything. He seemed more back to normal and I wasn't about to bring anything up. I trusted that Master Grant told him whatever he needed to know and it wasn't up to me to elaborate. Maybe Luke just wanted to forget about it.

At home I made dinner while Luke went to his office and Annabelle lingered in the kitchen, trying to help. I was surprised she wasn't upstairs with Luke but maybe he needed to work some more. Maybe he'd still be at the office if I hadn't been waiting for him. I knew he had known I was waiting on him. I smiled at his thoughtfulness.

"Have a good day?" Annabelle asked.

She seemed in a chipper mood and I wondered if anyone at the office had fucked her today. Luke had her in a white collar when he first acquired her but she hadn't liked no one being able to touch or fuck her. She had come to the island to experience being submissive to more than one man so Luke had relented and switched her over to the green collar. I still wore black and wondered if Luke would ever move me to a different color. I didn't mind the black but it made me wonder if Luke gave it any thought at all. That's the part that stung.

"It was interesting," I said, not wanting to tell her about my punishment because I didn't want to tell her why I'd been punished. Annabelle saw me as a good girl and I wanted to keep it that way.

"I've been jealous that you get to spend time at the facility," Annabelle said, "while I'm stuck at the office. I'm sure your day was more fun than mine."

I doubted it but I smiled and said maybe while I worked on dinner.

I usually liked the company but today I wasn't in a chatty mood. I hoped Annabelle knew it wasn't about her but I wasn't sure how to explain it so I didn't try.

"How are things at the office?" I asked, wanting to be nice and reciprocate.

Annabelle slid on the stool opposite me.

"They've been good. The new trainers have been in and out so that's been fun to watch. None of them have touched me—I have a feeling Mr. Wood told them not to—which is a little bit of a bummer but it's allowed me to get some work done."

I wondered what type of work she did since I doubted Mr. Wood would give her anything meaty but what did I know. I had never worked in an office. I had no idea what went on there except that Annabelle worked directly under Mr. Wood as his assistant, making her privy to a lot more of what was happening on the island than me.

"I thought you were super into Luke now," I said as I put the dinner in the oven.

Annabelle sighed. "I am but that doesn't mean that's all I want. Luke knows I need to be used sometimes, that it's part of my nature, but it's been a while since he or anyone else has used me in that way."

I was surprised as I leaned on the counter across from her. I assumed Luke used her all the time.

"Have you talked with Luke about it?"

"You know how it is here. Luke's different from most men where I know I can talk with him about it but I'd like it to come from him. I also think he's asked men to keep their distance from me because when I'm out and about, I might as well be wearing a white collar. Unless maybe I've lost some of my shine and attractiveness. Maybe no one's interested anymore."

"I doubt that," I said. Annabelle was gorgeous—all that long auburn hair with pale skin and striking green eyes. "I'm sure you're right that Luke's said something to the men. That can be the only explanation. Or else they've been too busy with the new women arriving on the island. Sometimes men prefer fresh meat."

"That could be it. There have been a lot of new shipments lately."

"I'd talk with Luke about it. At least drop some hints or something. I know he wants you happy and will do whatever it takes to do that."

"I'm sorry if it's been too much him and me lately," Annabelle said, surprising me. "I know we've been leaving you out a lot lately. We're both still navigating what it's like to be in this type of relationship. I've never been in a relationship that involved more than one person."

"Thanks but I get it," I said, meaning it. "I signed up for this knowing that's the way the households worked here. It's new for me, too, but I'm trying to adapt. I'm happy you're here. I hope you know that."

"I do," Annabelle said, her eyes sparkling. "I really do."

NINE

The three of us ate dinner together in the dining room. Annabelle had collected Luke once everything was done while I brought everything to the table. We sat around and ate like a family, something that warmed my heart. I missed easy family time like this, everyone relaxed and comfortable. Of course, I didn't usually eat dinner in a sheer dress or with someone who had her breasts on display but I had gotten so used to all of that that I barely noticed it anymore.

Luke talked about some of the developments happening on the island, including the expansion of the training facility and the new trainers Mr. Wood hired. They were already on the island but going through their own training before they'd be ready to start training the women. I wondered who was training the trainers and assumed it had to be Mr. Wood, Master Owen or Master Grant. Luke was in a talkative mood so I didn't want to pepper him with questions.

"Grant told me you got in trouble again," Luke said to me when we were halfway through dinner. My face reddened. "He told me he didn't physically punish you but put you on the cross for the duration of the class. That couldn't have been comfortable."

"No, it wasn't, Luke," I said, shame washing over me. I thought Master Grant wasn't going to tell Luke about that.

"You seem to be getting in trouble a lot lately," Luke said. "Are you needing more attention from me?"

"No, Luke," I said, my eyes lowered. I felt horrible for him thinking this was his fault when it was all mine.

Luke let out a long sigh. I felt the heaviness in the room. I didn't dare look at Annabelle. I didn't want to see the pity in her eyes because I felt more than pitiful.

"Dinner was very good, Riley," Luke said. "Once you're done cleaning up, I want both you and Annabelle in my room in nothing but your collars in the kneeling position. I'll be in as soon as I finish some work in my office."

With that, Luke pushed away from the table and went upstairs. I didn't dare move until I heard his office door close. Then I let out the breath I'd been holding.

"You've been getting in trouble?" Annabelle asked as I got up to clear plates. She helped, following me into the kitchen.

"Yes," I said as I started to load the dishwasher.

"What happened?" Annabelle asked as she leaned against the counter watching me. "That's not like you."

"I haven't been myself lately," I said, focusing on cleaning the dishes.

"Is this about Master Grant?"

My hands stilled before my brain recovered and I started cleaning again.

"It is, isn't it?" Annabelle asked. "What did you do?"

"I'd rather not talk about it if you don't mind. Master Grant punished me twice now for things I did during his training class that I wasn't supposed to do. That's it. It really had nothing to do with him or Luke but my disobedience. I'm working to be better so it won't happen again."

I wasn't sure Annabelle was buying it but it was the truth. I didn't want to elaborate or tell her how well Master Grant took care of me after each punishment. I knew I'd endure all the punishments again to have that time with him.

I shook my head, telling myself that I was insane, as I finished up the cleaning.

"We should get upstairs," I said. "I don't want to get in more trouble."

Without another word, Annabelle and I went upstairs, stripped off our clothes and kneeled in front of Luke's bed facing the door, lowering our eyes. Luke usually didn't give us such specific commands but with all the trouble I've been getting into lately, maybe he assumed it was the best way to deal with me. I wondered if he'd punish me more himself.

Annabelle and I didn't say a word as we waited. He usually didn't have us wait like this together which made me worry about what he planned to do. We never had sex together and only occasionally have been in the same room while he fucked the other. He seemed to like more one on one despite the nature of the island.

We didn't have to wait too long before Luke entered, standing before us. I blushed as he took us in. Nerves snaked through me. I felt like I was in trouble. I had no idea what Master Grant had told Luke but I felt like Luke wasn't happy with me. I could almost feel him scowling at me.

"Good girls," he said, his voice firm. "Stand up."

We pushed ourselves up until we were standing in front of him, our eyes lowered. I didn't dare look at him.

He pinched and pulled on Annabelle's nipples until she squirmed before coming to me and doing the same. I tried not to let it affect me but the pain went straight to my pussy. Luke lightly slapped one of my breasts and then the other before doing the same to Annabelle.

Luke ran his fingers through Annabelle's wetness before pushing his fingers into her. She gasped as he impaled her, probably flicking her clit to pull her full arousal out of her. I caught her out of the corner of my eye squirming as she tried to stay still.

I gasped when Luke snaked his hand between my legs and dipped into my wetness, pushing two fingers in until they couldn't go any further. His thumb circled my clit, lightly brushing it, while he moved his fingers in and out. I sucked in my breath, ready to explode, wanting to hold back, wanting to last for him, especially since I had no idea what he had in store for the night and I didn't want to peak too soon.

He played with us this way for what felt like forever. I bit my lip, my pussy filled, the pressure building, while I willed myself to hold back. I wasn't sure if he was wanting us to come or was simply toying with us but I had been taught to hold back for as long as possible. Not only did it make it more enjoyable for the man but it also kept the woman more aroused and pliable.

Luke continued to flick my clit as his fingers ground into me. I thought I was going to lose my fucking mind. I felt myself panting, my breasts heaving, as I held back with everything I had, giving myself over to each sensation while not allowing myself to be pushed over the edge.

Luke must have sensed my reluctance to come because suddenly his fingers were gone and he was ordering us to get up on his bed on all fours facing the headboard. We did as commanded until we were on our hands and knees next to one another. Luke smacked my ass before smacking Annabelle's. It stung but not as bad as before.

His fingers plunged back into my pussy, two fingers then three, ignoring my clit this time. He pushed in and out, working up a steady rhythm. I had no idea what he was doing with Annabelle and I no longer cared. I gave in to the sensations rolling through me. My body vibrated and hummed with pleasure, wanting release, wanting more.

His fingers were gone then quickly replaced with his thick cock. He pushed into me in one smooth movement, filling me completely, pushing me forward on the bed. I braced myself as he started to fuck me hard. His fingers dug into my hips, gripping me for leverage, as he plowed into me again and again. I felt my eyes roll to the back of my head as my body orgasmed around him.

He pulled out as soon as I came, leaving me limp and wobbly. He gave my ass a push forward, causing me to collapse onto the bed, my arms and legs no longer able to hold me. I heard him fucking

Annabelle as I laid there, eyes open but not seeing. I felt wrung out. I hadn't come like that in a very long time. The pressure had been building for days.

It didn't take long before Annabelle was panting and Luke was groaning. I heard the quick slapping of his body against hers. He called out her name before spilling inside her. I wasn't sure if she came or not but knew it didn't matter. He had given himself to her, not me, yet again. I pushed down the jealousy as I reminded myself that this was how it was here. It wasn't about me but about him. I needed to accept that or I'd be a very unhappy person.

LUKE TOLD me to wash up in the hall bathroom and to go to bed, that we'd be leaving for the training facility in the morning. Annabelle stayed tucked in Luke's bed where I was sure she would fall asleep and possibly be fucked again in the morning.

I tried not to be jealous as I showered, washing the day off me. I slathered salve on my ass once I dried off, happy it no longer throbbed. It was healing up nicely and I was proud that I was able to take the punishment for Master Grant.

I slept deeply, worn out by my explosive orgasm. I knew I should have been grateful for being allowed to come—Luke wasn't one to have his women hold back or ask for permission—but I felt hollow. I got up early as was my new routine and made breakfast for everyone. I tried not to think about Annabelle tucked in Luke's arms.

They came down together looking happy and well rested. Annabelle glowed. She smiled at me as she entered the kitchen, swiping a piece of toast before telling me she had to run. Mr. Wood wanted her in earlier than usual since he had the trainers coming in for a meeting this morning. Once she was gone, Luke and I settled in for breakfast at the counter. I knew better than to initiate conversation so I didn't say anything, happy for the silence.

"I'm taking you into the facility today," Luke said. "Master Grant informed me that you were invaluable to his lesson plan for today and I don't want to deny him that."

I looked at Luke with surprise.

"I think it'll be good for you, too. I don't want you home alone if I can help it."

"Thank you, Luke," I said, meaning it. I knew he cared. "I promise to be better today."

Luke smiled at me. "I know you will be."

We walked to the facility together, me walking slightly behind Luke. We didn't talk and I was OK with that. I spent the walk lost in thought, wondering what Master Granted had planned for me today. Butterflies danced in my stomach since I wasn't a fan of surprises and anything concerning Master Grant made me jumpy.

Luke left me at the front door, telling me that he'd let Master Grant know I was here. I stood in the waiting position, hands behind my back, eyes lowered, as I waited. I wanted to show Master Grant that I knew how to follow instructions. I wanted him to be pleased with me.

It didn't take long until Master Grant rounded the corner.

"There's my girl," he said, making my heart flip. "I have something fun planned for you today. Follow me."

I followed him to the main training room where the women were waiting on their knees. I kept my eyes lowered as Master Grant led me in, purposely not looking at the women. I didn't want to accidentally catch anyone's eye and get in trouble. I hoped today would be fun and I didn't want to ruin it by needing to be punished again.

Master Grant positioned me at the front of the room so I was facing the women. I kept my eyes lowered, my chest out, as I took in deep calming breaths.

"I'm sure you all remember Riley," Master Grant said with a laugh. "She'll be helping us today as I demonstrate what it's like to live this lifestyle. You have permission to look at me and her and anyone else who comes into this room until I say otherwise. I expect to have your full attention or you will be punished. Understood?"

"Yes, Master Grant," they said in unison.

I swallowed down the nerves plaguing me.

"Good," he said as I imaged ten pairs of eyes on me.

I wore a pale yellow short sheer dress that Master Grant quickly peeled off.

"Expect your owner to tell you how to dress. If you happen to work in an office, you'll be expected to wear a white button-down blouse with a short black pencil skirt. As you already know, undergarments are not allowed at any time. They're not even available on the island so you don't need to worry about that. For today's purposes, I want Riley to be naked except for her heels."

I felt exposed as I stood there. It didn't matter that they also wore nothing. I felt more naked somehow.

"As owned women, you must be prepared to be treated almost like a living doll," Master Grant said, kicking my heels apart, widening my stance. "Allow your owner to position you as he pleases. Be pliable and compliant. Sometimes he'll want to position you in interesting ways simply for his enjoyment."

Master Grant pushed my back forward, causing me to bend at the waist. He pulled my hands in front of my body and had me brace myself by my knees.

"Consider this part of your submission. Allow yourself to give in to it. Even allow yourself to become aroused by it. That's OK. Ideally, you'll be in a constant state of arousal. It will make whatever's happening easier to accept, even punishment."

Master Grant pinched and pulled on one dangling nipple and then the other as if he were milking me. Arousal flooded me as he continued to pinch and pull. With my legs parted, I had no control over my pussy. It felt open and exposed, the cool air of the room circulating around it, offering me nothing.

After he was satisfied, he ran a hand through my wetness, making an appreciative sound.

"See, she's wet already. It didn't take much to get Riley aroused but don't expect your owner to even do this much for you. It's in your best interest to get into a submissive headspace and stay there as often as you can. It will probably take practice for most of you but it's well worth the effort. We'll be teaching you some mantras that you can repeat to yourself to help get you there. For now, I want you to understand the importance of being in this receptive state of mind."

Master Grant squeezed my ass before he walked a few steps away from me, giving me space like a piece of art in a gallery. I felt his eyes on me as I tried my best not to move, to stay in the position he had put me in, wondering what was pleasant about this.

Before I could give it much more thought, I heard a commotion as doors flung open and heavy footsteps moved towards me. They stopped in front of me so I couldn't see who it was. I held my breath as anticipation rolled through me.

"Women, I would like you to meet two of our new trainers, Master Austin and Master Brooks. They will be assisting me with the rest of your training. You will obey them as if they were your owner. Actually, since you all are currently not collared, expect to be used and enjoyed by any man on the island, including the master teachers here."

I wished I could see them. I felt ridiculous in my pose but knew better than to move.

Master Austin and Master Brooks circled me until they were standing behind me. I could see the bottom of their black jeans and black shoes through my legs. I was careful to not let my eyes wander further up.

One of them reached out and ran his fingers through my wetness before plunging his fingers into me. I opened myself to it, knowing that was expected, wanting to please them. The other one slapped my ass before pinching both my nipples. I felt Master Grant's eyes on me as the two men started to work me up. Arousal washed through me. I gave myself over to it completely, reminding myself that this was why I was here. I wanted to be available like this, to be used.

Master Grant said something to the women but I wasn't hearing it as the fingers in my pussy started to build up a steady rhythm that left me panting. A thumb brushed against my clit over and over again as fingers plunged into me. The one who was pulling my nipples pulled my head up so I was aligned with his thick cock. I opened my mouth automatically, letting it slide into my warmth.

The fingers disappeared a moment before another thick cock

pushed into my wet pussy. They fucked me from both ends and all I could do was open myself up to it. My body hummed as I let myself give in to it. I heard Master Grant talking, maybe encouraging them, but I wasn't hearing it. I had disappeared into a fog of sensation, floating along, not caring about anything.

One of them pulled my nipples as they picked up the pace. I felt the pressure building as my body felt overworked and overstimulated. I clamped down on both cocks as the orgasm exploded through me, causing them to pick up the pace and come deep inside me.

Once it was over, they pulled out and one of them helped me into a standing position. My head spun. My limbs felt like wet noodles. I wasn't sure I'd be able to stand on my own. One of them sensed this and held onto me while helping me over to a bench so I could sit down.

He lifted my chin so I was looking into deep brown eyes. He smiled.

"You did amazing, Riley," he said. "I'm Master Austin. Nice to meet you."

I smiled back, my heart warming.

Master Austin draped a blanket around my shoulders.

"Rest here until lunch," he said. "You earned it."

I watched as Master Austin joined Master Grant and Master Brooks as they talked to the women. Master Grant said something about being open to being used by multiple men like I was and how I handled it with ease. My head was still spinning as my body started to come down from being used like that and finally releasing. All I wanted was to curl up for a long nap and wished I was at Luke's place so I could do just that.

I kept my eyes lowered as I sat on the bench, catching my breath, but I couldn't help sneaking a peek at the men, whose backs were to me, as they directed the women. Master Brooks had called one of the women forward to suck his cock. She hesitated only a moment but enough for Master Grant to call her out and let her and the rest of the women know hesitating could get them punished.

To demonstrate and to teach her not to hesitate in the future,

Master Brooks bent her over at the waist with her hands on her knees while he spanked her several times. She didn't let out a sound but I sensed she wanted to as his hand landed hard on her ass. I wondered if she had ever been spanked before. I knew some women got off on it but it didn't look like she was enjoying it.

Once he finished, Master Brooks commanded for her to kneel in front of him and suck his cock. She didn't hesitate this time. It was amazing what a little spanking could do.

I watched the rest of the morning's class with interest as the three men demonstrated different positions to the women, stopping to discipline as needed with rapid spanking. By the time lunchtime rolled around, I sensed the women were feeling rung out. I had finally settled down and no longer felt the need for the blanket around me.

Master Grant indicated I should join the women as they lined up to walk to the dining hall with a little nod. He gave me a knowing smirk as he caught me watching again and my whole body responded as if his hand had already begun to smooth over my ass.

I was the last woman in line with Master Grant right behind me. Master Austin and Master Brooks were in the lead, walking us like we were baby chicks or something. I felt the weight of Master Grant's presence the whole way. I tried not to make it obvious that I knew he was right behind me but I couldn't help walking with a little more sway. My body reacted to him in a way I wasn't used to. Even being fucked by Master Brooks and Master Austin didn't distinguish the fire I felt when Master Grant was near me.

Much to my disappointment, Master Grant didn't touch me during the walk. I wondered if that was deliberate.

I sat at the end again, far away from Olivia, and inhaled the mush-like food they put down in front of us. It barely had any flavor but I didn't care. I could cook whatever I wanted at Luke's so eating less than desirable food while I was at the facility didn't phase me. I knew it was part of the women's training and had endured it during my week-long advanced training with Annabelle.

The men left us to eat on our own which made me wonder if we were allowed to talk. I was dying to talk with the other women today, to ask what brought them to the island, to find out their stories. Everyone had such different reasons for being here and it was reassuring to hear their reasons.

My eyes shifted to Olivia more than once while we ate despite our distance. I never caught her eye—she kept hers lowered—but I wondered if she felt my eyes on her. I knew she'd go quickly at auction and wondered what type of man she'd end up with. Part of me worried that she'd end up with a man who was too harsh or had too many other women in his household to pay her much attention. I hated to think she'd end up in a situation similar to mine where she'd become a second thought.

The men returned as we finished up to escort us back to the main training room. They had us stand in a straight line facing them, hands behind our backs, eyes lowered.

"This afternoon we're going to take you out around town," Master Grant said. "Since you're unowned, except for Riley, and don't have collars yet, we're going to give you black collars to wear during your time out. These are special black collars that have the training facility's initials stamped into them letting the men know that you're in the training program. Otherwise, if we let you go out without collars, a man can claim you as his own and we don't want that to happen."

Master Austin and Master Brooks appeared with a handful of black collars and went about sliding them around each woman's neck, fastening them with a little lock similar to mine. Once they were done, Master Grant attached a long leather leash to each one, including mine.

"Since this is your first time venturing out," Master Grant said, "we have decided to keep you leashed so you don't wander. It will also help you to get used to the idea of being leashed in case this is how your owner plans to take you out. Each of us will lead several women since there are only three of us and eleven of you. Be careful not to step on each other and to keep up. We will walk at a normal pace but I understand that our legs are longer than yours. This is something you'll need to deal with so you'll want to get used to it.

"Expect to be groped, manhandled and possibly used while we're out. Your black collars indicate to the men that you're available for any type of use, including the infliction of pain, so be prepared and open to that. Remember to obey any command without hesitation or you may be punished. Also, remember to not look at any man in the eye unless directed and to not speak unless directed. Do you understand?"

"Yes, Master Grant," we said in unison.

I hated the idea of being paraded around town but knew I had no choice. I had a feeling that they'd purposely walk us around until they found men who were more than happy to play with us.

"Good," Master Grant said. "Now let's go."

TEN

The sun caressed my skin as we walked outside, the sunlight blinding me after being inside all day. Since the training facility was located in the business side of town, the streets were quiet for early afternoon. Master Grant led me with two other women while Master Austin and Master Brooks both led four women each. Olivia was with Master Austin.

I found it challenging to walk without tripping over the two other women. The leashes were maybe six feet so we were forced to keep close. I considered suggesting to the women that we hold hands to help keep us in sync but knew better than to say anything. I kept my eyes lowered and focused on keeping up.

It wasn't until we made it over to the men's side of town where all the restaurants and bars were located that hands started to find us. Random men slapped and groped our asses, pinched and pulled our nipples, and were vocal about their appreciation of our assets.

I knew it wasn't every day that three men walked down the street with so many women on leashes. I kept my eyes lowered as I accepted it all, knowing that in some small way it made Master Grant happy to parade us around like this.

Master Grant pulled us into one of the rowdier bars.

"Mingle," Master Grant instructed us as he unhooked our leashes. "Keep your eyes lowered and be prepared to be used by anyone. You're here only to serve. And who knows, maybe you'll meet your new owner this way. Some men like to take the women for a test drive before buying them."

A thick tension hung in the air as the women absorbed this. This was probably their first experience like this. A frisson of excitement rolled through me at the thought of some random men using me however they pleased. It had been a while since I was out without Luke. I was still turned on from being fucked earlier and could use another release or two.

Just as I was about to turn to get lost in the crowd, a strong hand gripped my arm and spun me around. Expecting to come face to face with some random man, it surprised me to find Master Grant staring back at me with dark intense eyes. He didn't say anything at first but held my gaze as if willing me to speak first so he'd have reason to punish me. I felt tempted but bit my lip instead.

"You're not going anywhere," he said in a low growl. "Come with me."

I hurried behind Master Grant as he practically dragged me out of the bar and down the street before pulling me into a deserted side alley. Before I could question what he was doing, his lips crashed down on mine. One hand found its way in my hair while the other cupped my ass, pulling me closer to him.

I felt his long erection against my center, straining to be free. My hand itched to squeeze it, to direct it to where I wanted it to go, but I didn't dare. My thoughts scattered as Master Grant claimed my mouth, my body going on overload. Sensations rippled through me as he deepened the kiss, pushing me up against the cool brick wall until I could no longer think. I gave into it all, wanting more, wanting something I couldn't comprehend, as his hand found its way between my legs and pushed its way in.

His fingers entered me effortlessly. I was already drenched for him. My body hummed with need as he broke the kiss only to nip at my neck and find his way down my body until he pulled each nipple into his mouth. His tongue circled and sucked each nipple while his fingers worked me and I couldn't hold back any longer. I let out a scream as my body convulsed around him. I came with such a fierceness that I thought I might pass out.

Master Grant chuckled in my ear, "That's my girl," before claiming my mouth again. My mind went blank as he ravaged me. I felt desired on a level I had never experienced before. My body hummed with need, ached for more, as he replaced his fingers with his thick cock.

He entered me with one hard push, impaling me, filling me completely, and I was coming again. I came completely undone as he fucked me, my back rubbing against the harsh brick, but I didn't care. Somehow this was everything and all I needed all at once.

It didn't take long until Master Grant was coming deep inside me. I wanted to drink all that glorious come in, to clean him off, but I didn't do anything but take what he had to give.

Once he finished, he pulled out and tucked himself into his pants, a big grin on his face.

"I've been wanting to do that all week," he said, "but I didn't want to do it in front of everyone. We're not supposed to give any of the women special treatment during their training and I didn't want to single you out."

I blinked at him, not sure what to say, not sure if I should say anything. My heart hammered as I digested his words. He thought I was special. He wanted me.

He was holding me up, bracing my back against the brick wall, as he took me in. I was grateful for the support or else I would have been a puddle on the ground. I opened my mouth to say something but quickly closed it. I didn't know what to say and he hadn't asked a direct question so I felt safer not talking.

He leaned in and kissed me. This one was more gentle, almost loving, as he drank me in. I opened to him, relishing his lips on mine, wishing this moment would never end. There was a spark between us that hadn't been there with anyone else on the island and I wondered if he felt it, too. I knew the men here didn't fall in love but maybe it was possible to fall in lust with a woman. Maybe that's what he was feeling.

I let my mind go blank as he deepened the kiss, giving myself over to it, allowing myself to enjoy it fully. Who knew when or if he'd kiss me like this again. He did say he couldn't show me special treatment in front of anyone and I wasn't sure when we'd be alone again.

He pinched and pulled on one of my nipples, sending a zing of pleasure through me, before he came up for air. He smiled at me, warming me, his face close to mine.

"You're spectacular, Riley," Master Grant said, his voice low. "So beautiful but more than that. There's something special about you."

I let his words sink in as my heart opened and blossomed. I felt like a flower getting water after weeks in the desert. I had always considered myself ordinary and unremarkable despite my blonde hair that men seemed to gravitate to. I wasn't gorgeous like Annabelle or Olivia. I didn't turn heads.

"I hope you don't mind this," he said, indicating us with a slight nod.

I shook my head. "I don't mind at all."

He kissed me again before taking my hand and leading me back.

"We should get back before Austin and Brooks discover us missing," he said as we walked towards the bar. "I want this to remain between us."

I nodded as he pulled me into the bar. The crowd was thick so the chances of being missed were slim although they could have been looking for Master Grant. My head filled with his words, turning them over, trying to comprehend them, as hands found my ass and my nipples as we walked. I barely felt them as Master Grant led me through the crowd towards the back of the bar that had several pool tables. The women from the training facility were being fucked and used in various positions on and around the pool tables. Some were bent over them, taking it from behind, while one was spread eagle on one, taking a man in her mouth while another fucked her.

My eyes roamed until they landed on Olivia who was being fucked from behind as she grasped the table in front of her. Her wide eyes found mine. I saw lust along with euphoria there and I was happy she was enjoying herself. She must have come to the island wanting to experience all of this, like we all had, and it looked like she had given herself over fully to it.

Master Grant released my hand as he moved further into the room. It only took a moment before hands were on me, groping and pulling. One snaked between my legs from behind, dipping into my wetness.

"This bitch has been used already," a man said behind me.

"Doesn't matter," another man said. "Fuck her anyway."

A hand pushed me forward before a cock pushed into my pussy from behind. I was so wet and loose that it slid in easily. He gripped my hips and started fucking me wildly in a sporadic rhythm that left me off balance. It felt nothing like Master Grant's cock but I was so wound up that I took it all the same.

Hands found my nipples and pulled. The pain was exquisite and shot straight to my aching pussy.

"Suck my cock, slut," a man in front of me said as he unzipped himself, revealing a meaty cock.

I leaned forward to take him in while the man behind me continued to fuck me senseless, pushing me deeper and deeper onto the cock in my mouth. Both men groaned as they came, spilling themselves inside me, before leaving without another word.

I stayed bent over for a minute, trying to catch my breath, before another pair of cocks pushed into me, one from behind and one in my mouth. They grabbed and pulled on my body as they buried themselves in me, fucking me hard. I opened myself up to it, knowing that was why I was here, to be used in this way, to be open to all of this.

While the cocks fucked me, I felt further and further away from Luke. I wondered what his intentions towards me were and what he hoped my role would be in his household now that he and Annabelle were more or less a couple. He still let others fuck her but only because it's something she needed. If he had his way, she'd be in a white collar. But with me, there'd never been a discussion to move me to a different color collar. It's always been black and felt like it'd always be black.

The cocks finished with me, pulling out, and I barely noticed. I was exhausted, my limbs ached and I just wanted to curl up in my bed and sleep. Come dripped down my legs as I started to straighten up, my back aching.

"Not so fast," a larger man said as he stepped in front of me. "I want that sweet mouth around my cock. On your knees, slut."

He slapped me hard, shocking me, before I sank to my knees and opened my mouth. He pushed his long cock in without mercy until it was fully lodged down my throat, practically strangling me. I took a few deep breaths in through my nose, happy to know I could still breath, as he started fucking my mouth. His hands were in my hair, gripping it, pulling, as he fucked my face. All of it felt rough and unnecessary but I stayed open to it, hoping it'd be over quickly. I did my best to roll my tongue along his shaft, hoping for a quick release.

He slapped my face a few more times while he fucked me before pulling out to spray my face with his hot come.

"That's how a slut like you should look," he said with a satisfied look on his face, "covered in come."

I lowered my eyes, still on my knees, as he walked away, wishing this afternoon would be over already. It had started so promising but now I was nothing more than holes to filled, a woman to be used. Maybe I would end up leaving the island when my contract was up. I always thought I'd stay but now with Annabelle and Luke being what they were, I wasn't sure how I fit into that household any longer. I hated feeling like an outsider all the time. I knew it wasn't their fault but it was just how it was.

Hands reached down and clipped a leash onto my collar. I looked up into Master Grant's deep blue eyes before blushing and quickly looking back down.

"Come on, Riley," he said in a low voice close to my ear. "Time to go."

I walked back to the training facility with the other women, all trailing behind the masters on leashes. They were all covered in various degrees of come. Some of their asses were red while some of their nipples looked raw. I had forgotten about them while I was being used and wondered how they enjoyed their first true experience on the island. It wasn't an easy life for a woman but I knew that for some, it was the only life that made them feel whole.

When we returned to the facility, Master Grant brought us into the main room and told us to kneel facing him, Master Austin and Master Brooks.

"Congratulations on your first afternoon out on the town," Master Grant said. "I suspect you were all well used. Your time on the island probably won't always be like today but I wanted to take you to one of the rowdier bars so you'd have a full experience. Of course, your owner will decide where to take you, how you will be used and if you'll be allowed to venture out on your own. You may end up in a white collar which doesn't allow anyone to touch you."

Master Grant paced in front of us. I felt his eyes on me and I suddenly felt shame wash over me.

"If you don't think this is the type of life you want," Master Grant said, "now would be the perfect time to let us know so we can send you home. Of course, you will be able to leave at any time but know that if you leave before your contract is up, unless it's a legitimate emergency, you will not be compensated. It's better for everyone if you leave now or before your training is complete if you don't think this is what you want."

Master Grant stood before us and waited. I held my breath. I knew I wasn't going anywhere but I wondered about the others. I wished I could see them, to read their thoughts, but I kept my eyes lowered and waited.

Master Grant shifted his focus, causing me to stiffen.

"Yes, Ashley," he said, directing his attention to her. "Please stand."

Master Grant paused a moment before asking, "Is it your wish to leave?"

"Yes, Master Grant," she said in a small voice.

"You do understand that once you leave before your contract is up, you will not be permitted back on the island for any reason?"

"I understand, Master Grant," she said, her voice barely making it to my ears.

"Very well," Master Grant said. "Master Austin, will you please see Ashley out?"

"Sure thing," Master Austin said before moving towards Ashley and escorting her out the door.

I felt stunned. If we had been allowed to talk, I'm sure there would have been a low murmur among the women. But instead, there was nothing but dead silence.

"Anyone else?" Master Grant asked, turning his attention back to us.

No one else spoke up.

"Very well," Master Grant said. "There is no shame in leaving. It's better to leave now than later. We want to ensure that we only put the women up for auction that truly want to be here and be part of this lifestyle. Even though your contracts are for six months, it's in our best interest for you to want to stay longer. We're striving to build a robust community here and the women are a major part of that. We want everyone to thrive and be happy here."

He paced in front of us, as if eyeing each of us down, waiting for someone else to leave but no one did. I was happy Olivia stayed. I wondered if she'd make it through her contract.

"Good," Master Grant said. "Go shower then go directly to the dining hall for dinner. Except for Riley. You stay here."

My heart sank as the other women left with Master Austin and Master Brooks, leaving me alone with Master Grant. I knew I must be in trouble but I wasn't sure why. Master Grant waited until everyone left before he stood directly in front of me.

"Please stand."

I uncurled myself slowly until I was standing. For a split second, I wondered if he'd kiss me but then I remembered there were cameras everywhere and I doubted he'd want to be caught doing that.

"I'm sending you home like this," he said. "I want Luke to see how well used you were today. It'll give him something to think about. At least that's what I'm hoping."

I wanted to ask him what he meant but stayed silent. It wasn't up to me. I knew that Master Grant had my best interest at heart even if I didn't understand it. And if he felt like I needed to know why, he'd tell me.

"Come on," Master Grant said. "Follow me."

He led me out into the hallway and toward the offices. He positioned me outside of Luke's office and told me to kneel. I knew I looked a mess with come dried on my face and in my hair but I didn't care. This was my place and I was going to settle myself into it.

"See you tomorrow," Master Grant said before he was off.

ELEVEN

Luke barely noticed my condition until we got home. He barely looked at me as we left the office, only telling me it was time to go, and I followed a few steps behind him. Once we were inside his house, standing in the kitchen, he turned to look at me.

"What the hell did they do with you?" Luke asked, his words scalding like I did something wrong.

I kept my eyes lowered as I answered. "Master Grant and the new trainers took us to one of the rowdier bars in town. They wanted to show the women what life would be like living here. They were hoping to weed out the ones who couldn't take it. One woman left."

I felt Luke's eyes on me. I knew I must be a mess—come in my hair, running down my inner thighs, caked on my face. I hadn't looked in a mirror but I felt it all over me. I almost felt like I wore it as some sort of twisted badge of honor, like letting Luke know that there were men that wanted me. Maybe he'd be better off letting me go to someone who actually wanted to use me.

"How many men fucked you?" Luke asked, his voice sharp.

"I don't know. I lost count."

Luke sighed as if he were disappointed in me, like I had come home past curfew reeking of alcohol.

"Did you enjoy yourself?"

"Not particularly," I said. I swallowed back mentioning anything about my time with Master Grant and prayed he wouldn't push. I knew I'd tell him if he did.

"Ok," Luke said, his voice cold. "Go clean up. We're going out tonight for dinner."

I hurried up the stairs, not letting myself wonder about dinner. I stepped into the hot shower, grateful to be able to wash away all the men that had used me today. I was a little sore but not too bad. More confused than anything. I loved the time I spent with Master Grant and still couldn't believe that he had pulled me outside like that and taken me in the alley. My head was still spinning from that and I had to stop myself from overthinking it. Master Grant was a man just like any other on this island and for whatever reason, he wanted me specifically today so he took it. There was nothing more to it. There couldn't be. And even if he had a soft spot for me, it'd never work. Luke owned me and the trainers at the facility were too busy training the new women that they didn't have time to establish their own households.

I washed my hair twice, wanting to be sure I washed every ounce of come off me, before towel drying and getting ready for dinner. I slipped on a short sheer blue dress and silver high heels before perfecting my hair and makeup. I hadn't heard or seen Annabelle yet and wondered if she was still at work. We hadn't talked as much as we used to lately and I wondered if that was my fault. I had backed off since she came back into Luke's house, wanting to give them space, and I've yet to let myself back in. I was so happy to have her back—she truly belonged with Luke—but now I wasn't sure where that left me.

I came downstairs about half an hour later to find Luke dressed in tan dress slacks and a blue sports jacket. He smiled when he saw me which went straight through me. I was happy that I seemed to have pleased him for once.

"You look beautiful, Riley," he said once I was standing in front of him.

I smiled. "Thank you, Luke. You look nice yourself."

"Thanks," Luke said, linking his arm through mine before heading towards the door. "We're having dinner with my brother and a few of the investors I haven't met yet so I want to make a good impression. Having you on my arm will help."

The walk over was uneventful. With Luke's arm looped through mine, no one touched me. I had to think it was a tactical move on Luke's part since he probably didn't want me messed with before dinner.

Anxiety pulsed through me as we got closer. I knew there wasn't much if anything for me to do but I couldn't help feeling nervous. I prayed that I wouldn't be used as some sort of example for the investors and that wasn't the reason Luke wanted me to tag along.

Mr. Wood and men I didn't recognize sat around a large round table when we arrived. The men stood when we approached, leaning over to shake Luke's hand. They introduced themselves to Luke one after the other before sitting back down.

Mr. Wood had a beautiful naked dark-haired woman sitting at his side, her eyes lowered, hands in her lap. Luke indicated I sit in the chair next to him with a small gesture of his hand. I sat, grateful I didn't need to kneel on the floor the whole evening.

The men I didn't recognize didn't have women with them which made me think they were the investors. They hadn't indicated as such when they introduced themselves but I knew Luke would know exactly who they were. I felt their eyes on me and Mr. Wood's woman and wondered if additional women would be joining us. I had an empty seat next to me and Luke had a couple of empty seats on the other side of him, putting us almost directly across from Mr. Wood and the other men.

The waitress came around to take drink orders for Luke and me. Luke ordered a beer while he ordered me a glass of something white. I rarely drank but was happy to have some wine on the way. Maybe it would help calm my nerves that were getting out of control for no good reason.

The waitress returned quickly, setting the drinks in front of us, before disappearing into the crowd. I snuck a peek around the restaurant while keeping my eyes lowered, taking in the breathtaking views of the water on two sides. The restaurant opened up to it, letting the warm evening breezes in. Piano music drifted into us but I couldn't see who was playing. The whole place was loud, male voices talking over each other mixed in with sporadic moaning and the sound of skin slapping.

The men at the table talked but I wasn't listening. My mind wandered off as nerves continued to snake through me. It had been a rough day but I couldn't get Master Grant out of my mind. I wanted to know what he meant when he said he wanted to give Luke something to think about. What did he want Luke to think about? That I was worth using? I knew Luke knew that but rarely had the time. It was amazing how in the span of a few weeks I had somehow lost my footing here and no longer knew where I belonged. The thought of returning to the mainland left me cold but the thought of staying in Luke's household made me feel empty. I needed more but I didn't know what that more was.

I practically jumped out of my skin when a deep voice leaned in and said, "Good evening, Riley," in my ear. Without thinking, I turned and looked at dark blues eyes taking me in, a small smirk on his lips. I quickly lowered my eyes, my heart beating like mad, as I hoped he didn't make a big deal out of my indiscretion. I felt my face go red as his eyes lingered on me. His hand made its way on my upper thigh, all warm and solid, and squeezed.

Our food arrived, helping to relieve my mortification somewhat. Plates of steak, baked potatoes and asparagus went in front of most of the men while plates of fish and other various seafood landed in front of the women. My plate looked like some sort of fish filet topped with parmesan and pistachios. I inhaled the amazing aroma, happy to have something to distract me from Master Grant sitting next to me.

He removed his hand to dig into his steak while he conversed easily with the other men. I kept my eyes lowered as I savored each bite of fish, wishing my mind would shut up for a little while and give me a break.

I glanced over to see that Annabelle and Master Austin had sat down on Luke's other side. Annabelle wore a long sheer iridescent gown that shimmered in the low light. She looked happy as she ate with her eyes lowered and Luke's hand brushing against her thigh every now and again.

Master Grant mostly ignored me while we ate, his hand occupied with eating and gesturing rather than touching me. I knew I should be relieved since I didn't want to upset Luke but I missed his attention. He seemed to be the only one who went out of his way to be kind to me lately. Sadness washed over me at this realization and I did my best to brush it off. I knew I was lucky to be with Luke—it could be so much worse—and I needed to understand that it wasn't up to me how I was treated here. My only recourse was to leave and I wasn't sure I was ready to do that yet.

Once dinner concluded and the cordials were brought out for the men and tea for the women, Mr. Wood held up his glass and thanked everyone for coming out this evening.

"I continue to be amazed that what started as an idea of mine has flourished into all that we have here today on the island," Mr. Wood said. "I want to thank all of you for your contribution to making this island and community a success. I had faith in it from the beginning but without all of you, including the gorgeous women with us tonight, none of this would be possible. We have come a long way and I hope you will continue your dedication and efforts towards making this island amazing."

We toasted to that, the men adding their congratulations while the women remained silent. It warmed me to be recognized for my small part in helping to make this community what it was even while I struggled to discover what it meant to me.

"As a thank you, you are all invited to my house for the evening," Mr. Wood said. "I've made a few modifications over the past few months that I'm sure you will enjoy as well as a few additions to my household. Once we finish up here, we can be on our way."

I took in a deep breath at the realization that the evening was far from over. I had started to relax as I visualized my warm bed waiting for me and being able to lose myself to it for the night. Now I had no idea what was in store.

I WALKED behind Luke with Annabelle at my side as we made our way to Mr. Wood's house. I had never been but Annabelle had been acquired by Mr. Wood when she arrived on the island. I wondered how she felt going back to where it all began.

I sucked in my breath as his massive house came into view. It sat perched on a small hill overlooking the marina and most of downtown. He didn't have a gate but a long driveway that set his house apart from the rest. Every light in the house twinkled at us as we approached, making it sparkle. Mr. Wood had said he made additions to his household so I assumed they were home waiting for us to arrive. The men on the island were encouraged to keep more than one woman in their house so they wouldn't form attachments to them as Luke had. I wondered how many women Mr. Wood had in his.

We entered a grand foyer with a bifurcated staircase and a massive crystal chandelier hanging from the two-story ceiling. Music drifted in from the back of the house. A gorgeous blonde wearing nothing but heels and a black collar led us through the house and out the back where a pool glistened in the pale moonlight. A bar sat off to one side, tended by a naked woman with a yellow collar.

I stuck close to Luke with my eyes lowered, grateful I didn't need to take the initiative to mingle. Men seemed to be everywhere, much more than had been at dinner, along with several women that must have been part of Mr. Wood's household or with the other men. Most of them wore black collars and all of them were drop-dead gorgeous.

One woman with luminous ebony skin was blindfolded and fastened to a large cross in the middle of everything. I wondered if this was part of a punishment for her or simply because Mr. Wood wanted to show her off. She wore a black collar and was an obvious invitation for men to explore. Her nipples stood at attention and she squirmed slightly. I knew she wouldn't be left alone for long.

A few hands found my ass as we walked through the party. Luke stopped to talk with a couple of men from dinner that I assumed were the investors. They made no qualms about taking in all the naked women milling about as if it were nothing. I wished I could look around, too, without being obvious. My heart hammered at the thought of Master Grant being here. I knew he probably was since he was at dinner and a major part of the training facility's expansion. I knew he couldn't show me any favoritism, especially here, but some part of me still hoped he would.

"Let me introduce my household, Annabelle and Riley," Luke said, introducing us to the investors. I wasn't sure if I was supposed to say hi or shake their hands so I did nothing, keeping my eyes lowered. The last thing I wanted was to get in trouble. Annabelle didn't do anything either so I felt a little relieved.

"They're gorgeous," one man said. He reached out and ran his hand along the underbelly of my breast before pinching the nipple. "It's hard to believe a place like this exists. If I weren't married, I would be packing my bags tomorrow."

"I know what you mean," Luke said even though I knew he didn't fully buy into this lifestyle. He had moved here to help his brother.

"Maybe you can convince Silvia to adopt this lifestyle," the other man said, laughing.

"That will be the day," the first man said, "but you never know. Do the men always show off their women so much?"

"Most do but it's the man's choice," Luke said. "The office women are more covered with typical office wear. It'd be up to you how you'd want her to dress. You could also have her wear a white collar which would let other men know they can't touch her. I had Annabelle in a white collar when I first acquired her but she didn't like it."

The men laughed and I could almost feel Annabelle blush. I didn't think I would have liked a white collar either. That wasn't the point of being here but it was nice that it was an option.

"Well, it would take a lot of convincing," the first man said, "but if I didn't have to show her off and she knew she wouldn't be touched by anyone, maybe she'd be up for it."

Luke started talking about the benefits of the island, how the economy worked and how these men could profit from it.

"As investors, I'm sure my brother would be more than happy to put you up somewhere on the island whenever you want," Luke said. "You wouldn't need to have a permanent residence here."

The men looked around, taking it all in, as the party gained momentum. The woman on the cross had started to generate a lot of attention. Several men were caressing her, pinching and pulling on her nipples. Annabelle had been sent to the pillories as a punishment once where the men came at her one after another for several hours. I had been fortunate enough to never have been punished in that way but I could see myself enjoying it.

Another woman was being fucked over one of the chaise lounges. The men took as they pleased, like the women were simply appetizers to be sampled.

One of the men reached out and started playing with my nipples, flicking them, pinching and pulling, having his fun. I tried not to react, keeping my eyes lowered, knowing that's why I was here. Usually, the men would have asked Luke if they could touch me but seeing that these men hadn't gone through the initial intake like most of the men on the island, they weren't familiar with the island's rules and etiquette. Luke didn't say anything which made sense since he was trying to get them to invest.

The other man started playing with Annabelle in the same way. I couldn't see Luke's expression but I knew he wasn't a fan of men playing with her. She wore a green collar since she had wanted to have more of a full experience here. Otherwise, Luke would have had her in a white collar, allowing no one to touch her.

"Mind if we indulge?" the man who was fondling me asked. "That's how this works, right?"

"Of course," Luke said. "Be my guest. There are cabanas on the other side of the pool if you prefer more privacy or you can indulge right here."

The man who was fondling me didn't need any further invitation. After thanking Luke, he grabbed my wrist and led me to the other side of the pool by the cabanas. I was guessing this was his first time performing in public and it made sense he didn't want to do it in the middle of everyone.

I kept my eyes lowered as we walked despite how much I wanted to look around for Master Grant. Part of me hoped he was watching me being dragged away by one of the investors, forced to entertain him. I knew Master Grant wasn't a jealous man, and he'd have no reason to be jealous anyway, but I couldn't help fabricating a story in my mind where he saw me from across the room and ended up saving me from the investor and claiming me for himself.

The investor looked a little lost once we made our way to one of the cabanas. An outdoor sofa sat against one of the cream fabric walls with a coffee table in front of it and a spanking bench off to the side. I figured this man must have some experience in the kink world since he was here but it felt like this was his first time exploring it. Nerves snaked through me as I kept my eyes lowered.

"Kneel, bitch," he said once we were inside the cabana with the flap closed.

I kneeled without hesitation, a frisson of fear washing over me at no longer being in Luke's sight. Usually, when I was used by other men, there were a lot of other people around. I always felt safe knowing others were watching but being alone with this man made me feel edgy. No one was around to stop things if he got out of hand.

He unzipped his slacks and popped out his erect cock. It was shorter than most but thick. I opened my mouth figuring that was what he wanted. I kept my hands on my lap, palms up, as I waited.

He seemed to be taking me in, sizing me up, before he moved forward and slid his thick cock in my mouth. He pulled on the back of my head ensuring that I took all of him in one swift movement. Luckily his length barely touched the back of my throat and I easily took him in.

He groaned as he started fucking my mouth, an unsteady rhythm that felt like it was taking a lot of effort. He was an older guy, maybe in his late fifties, with grey hair at the base of his dick.

I closed my eyes as he fucked my face, his hand at the back of my head guiding me. He pulled out suddenly. I expected him to spray himself over my face but instead, he pulled me up by the wrist and told me to bend over the sofa. I did as I was told, happy to no longer have to suck him, as he pushed his way into my pussy. I was wet despite myself and he slid in easily. He grabbed at my hips as he pushed himself in and out, fucking me like he was riding a bull. I felt detached from what was happening. I knew in my small way I was helping win over the investors and that made me happy. Other than that, I checked out.

It didn't take long before he was grunting and coming inside me. He pulled out without ceremony before rejoining the party without another word. I waited until I knew he wasn't coming back before I slowly straightened up.

His come leaked down my legs and since I wasn't told not to clean myself, I grabbed a washcloth that was sitting on the table and wiped myself quickly. I didn't want to spend the rest of the party with this guy leaking out of me.

I was about to pull back the curtain to rejoin the party when Master Grant entered. Stunned, I just stood there looking into his intense blue eyes. He looked angry mixed with concern. It took me a moment before I remembered to lower my eyes. My heart hammered as he approached me, getting ready for some sort of punishment, but instead, he gripped my upper arms and said, "Look at me."

I raised my eyes to meet his and it was like he was seeing deep into me. I wanted to collapse in his arms but knew I couldn't. I held his gaze as his eyes searched mine.

"Are you OK?" he asked, concern in his voice.

"Yes, Master Grant. I'm fine."

"I saw you go off with one of the investors but then he came out and you didn't..." he let his words trail off. "I got worried."

"I'm fine." I blinked at him, amazed by his intensity.

Master Grant didn't loosen his grip on my shoulders as he looked at me as if trying to read something more, something I wasn't saying. He could have asked me what happened but he didn't. I was about to open my mouth to say something, to offer some sort of explanation, when his mouth crashed down on mine.

I was stunned as he pulled me to him, my breasts pushing up against his solid chest. His hands were still gripped tightly around my upper arms as his mouth devoured mine. My heart was hammering so quickly I thought I might pass out as I allowed myself to melt into him. He tasted like bourbon and warmth and something else. My head spun as he deepened the kiss, as if trying to take me all the way in, until I wasn't sure if I was breathing or not anymore.

He pulled away just as quickly, his deep blue eyes on mine looking a bit stunned.

"What is it with you, Riley?" he said in a whisper, his voice rough and gravely. "I can't keep myself from doing that."

I wanted to tell him not to keep himself from doing that, that I loved it, but I said nothing, not sure what I could possibly say at that moment. My mind was spinning. My body was on fire. I wanted him to take me, to lift me up and fuck me senseless, to show me how much he wanted me. I was already naked and ready to go. He had to know I wanted him. I knew it must be obvious in the way I looked at him.

He loosened his grip on me until he was barely touching me. His hands hovered over my skin. I felt the electricity pass between us and wondered if he felt it, too. Were we somehow magnetic to each other? I hoped so.

His eyes didn't leave mine.

"I need to get back out there," he said after a minute. I felt his reluctance. "Find me if you need me. And try to stay in more public areas."

I wanted to tell him it wasn't my choice to come in here and he had to know that—nothing was a woman's choice here—but I didn't say that. Instead, I said, "Yes, Master Grant."

He gave me one more look before he pushed open the curtain shielding us from the rest of the party and pushed me back into the crowd. I wanted to turn to ask him another question, anything to keep the conversation going, but I knew he was already gone.

TWELVE

I felt lost and a little stunned as I wandered back into the party. I wasn't sure what just happened. More people filled out the party and the music was louder making everything feel more intense. I passed several women being fucked, accepting whatever it was the men wanted to give. A few hands reached out for me but none pulled me in. I told myself I was looking for Luke since that was what I should have been doing but I scanned the party for Master Grant. I knew I couldn't approach him but I knew I'd feel safer if he was nearby.

The woman on the cross squirmed as men played with her pussy and nipples. I wondered how many times she had come already and how many times she had been come on. She wore a blindfold, oblivious to how many men surrounded her. I had never been the center of attention like that but part of me yearned to be. I wanted to lose myself in that, to not care anymore, to give myself over completely to being taken.

I averted my eyes, lowering them, as I walked away from that scene. Even though part of me wanted the attention, I didn't want to become part of what was happening to her.

A few hands reached out and caressed my ass and brushed against my nipples as I moved through the party. My mouth felt raw from Master Grant's kiss and I wondered if the other men could tell. Most of the men weren't big on kissing the women, like it wasn't necessary for their satisfaction. I hadn't missed it—there was something about not kissing that kept me distant from the men using me even when their cocks were buried in me—but now that Master Grant had kissed me, I couldn't get enough.

I passed more women being fucked in various positions including Olivia being taken by two men, one in front and one behind. I hoped she was enjoying herself and would decide to stay. It was an interesting place for women but I was beginning to understand how it held its appeal. A woman could lose herself here and give herself over to the fantasy of being taken and being fully cared for. There wasn't romance here, not usually, but after many failed relationships, some women had given up on finding love and would rather give themselves over to sex instead.

I wasn't sure what I believed or wanted any more. I had yet to have a serious relationship and knew I had no idea what I was missing. I didn't consider myself a romantic but when Master Grant kissed me, he stirred something inside me. I wasn't sure what it was exactly since it was new to me but it still lingered, swirling through me like a quiet storm waiting to overtake me.

I found Luke talking with someone I didn't recognize with Annabelle at his side looking fresh and untouched. I wondered if he'd told inquiring men that she was off limits or if it just so happened that no one wanted to take her for a spin. Luke smiled when he saw me approach and reached out a hand to me to pull me in closer.

"This is my other girl, Riley," Luke told the man as he positioned me next to him. "She's my free spirit and enjoys a bit more autonomy."

I kept my eyes lowered as I felt the man's eyes roam over my naked body. He reached out and pinched each nipple, slowly pulling each one, causing a rush of pain through me, before letting go.

"She's gorgeous," the man said. "They both are. You're a very lucky man. How does one obtain such beautiful women?"

"I am a lucky man," Luke said. "First off, you need to become a resident here. You wouldn't need to live here full time but the majority of the time would be preferable. You wouldn't be able to take any woman off the island unless she agreed and, as I'm sure you know, you wouldn't be able to live this lifestyle most anywhere else. But once you're a resident, you would be able to attend the auctions and bid on anyone you want there."

I assumed this was one of the investors since they didn't seem to let men on the island that weren't residents.

The man asked Luke some more questions, including the limits, if any, of using the women.

"Once you own them, they're yours to do with what you want," Luke said. "The only limits are no permanent bodily harm. And the women can leave the island at any time so you'd want to keep that in mind. But the women who come to the island know what they're getting into and we've set up the training facility to help make their transition to island life easier. Most of the women here tonight are in their initial training period at the facility and will be auctioned off in the next week or so."

"What if I wanted someone that was already owned?" the man asked. I felt his eyes on Annabelle.

"You'd have to take that up with her owner. Men have been known to sell their women to other men. It's not uncommon."

I knew that was how Luke acquired Annabelle—that he had convinced his brother to sell her to him. I knew he wouldn't be letting Annabelle go. This man would be disappointed if he tried to acquire her.

"What special advantages would the investors have?" the man asked as he reached out and played with my nipples. "Even if we're not residents yet."

Luke considered this.

"As I mentioned to Bill, I'm sure my brother would be more than happy to put up the investors anytime they wanted to visit the island. We don't have a hotel since everyone here has their own homes but it wouldn't be a bad idea for us to have a place where investors could stay if they weren't able to be here full time. You would have full access to the women on the island who wore black collars with limited access to those in green and yellow.

"You'd probably need to go through a training similar to the ones we're putting the new residents through so you'd have a full understanding of our rules and etiquette. My brother is striving to make this place a thriving society for both the men and the women which means there is zero-tolerance for rule breakers. You'll want to have a full grasp on what's acceptable and not before indulging."

The man stopped playing with my nipples as he took Luke's words in. Luke didn't say anything to the man about touching me without his permission but that was the kind of man Luke was. He let little indiscretions slide.

"I'm excited to look over the rest of the proposal," the man said. "I believe we'll be able to work together in some way."

The man reached out and shook Luke's hand before turning and making his way to the bar across the yard.

Luke pulled Annabelle and me in closer to him, one arm around each of us, as he whispered, "That man has the power to take this island to the next level. He owns hotels and casinos all over the world and wants to bring casinos and even showgirls to the island. The thing is he's married with grown kids who probably wouldn't understand this place so I'm thinking he'd be reluctant to move here. But if he invests his money here, I could see why he'd want to come as often as he could."

"Couldn't he have a part-time residence?" Annabelle asked. "It sounds like he's financially independent enough to support a household here."

"Everyone who's a resident here is mostly full time," Luke said, "although maybe Lance needs to start opening it up to part-timers. I'm not sure how that would work with the women in the household but it's an interesting idea."

"The women could have jobs like I do," Annabelle said, "or be given tasks to do or directions while the men are away. They could easily be kept occupied while their men were away. Some might appreciate that more than having their man around all of the time."

Luke gave her a little smack on the ass as if to say hey watch it but he was smiling and this was just how they played with each other. My stomach knotted at their closeness, leaving me feeling left out. I tried reminding myself that it wasn't up to me to determine my relationship with Luke. It was up to him. I needed to get OK with their dynamic since this was how it was and I didn't want to be miserable all the time.

I did appreciate Luke sharing this information with us. I liked knowing about the changes happening on the island. It felt ripe for a boom with an influx of new people. It was an exciting time and it's own little revolution as both men and women began to flock to the island and its unique lifestyle.

THE NEXT MORNING Luke took me to the training facility which has been our new routine. He told me to wait at the front entrance to be collected. I kept my eyes lowered and waited. I wore a sheer white dress today that barely covered my ass. My nipples strained against the sheer fabric in anticipation of seeing Master Grant. He had been the one to collect me and I expected him to round the corner any minute.

My anticipation grew with each passing minute. I heard male voices down the hall, perhaps in the training room directing the other women, but I couldn't make out what they were saying. As the voices drew closer, it became clear that it was two men having a conversation. I recognized Master Owen's voice but I didn't know the other one. Their footsteps echoed down the hall as their voices grew louder until they were standing in the entranceway with me.

"What about this one here?"

"This one is already taken," Master Owen said, "but we have a fresh shipment currently in training that I would love to introduce you to."

Master Owen approached me, clicking a leash to my collar.

"Let me take you there now," Master Owen said to the man as he started to lead me towards the main training room. "You'll get to see some of the training in action."

I was happy to be spared from spending too much time with the other man. I recognized him from the party, the one that took me to the cabana. It made sense that the investors would want to check out the facility but I didn't want to spend any more time with the man than I needed to. He gave me the creeps.

Master Owen continued to talk to the man as he led us to the main room. My heart skipped as my eyes landing on Master Grant. He was at the head of the class looking sexy as hell in tight black jeans and a black t-shirt with the women in their kneeling position before him. His eyes locked on mine. I blushed and quickly lowered them, fearing that he might punish me again.

"Mr. Martin, this is one of our other trainers Master Grant," Master Owen said.

Master Grant came forward to shake Mr. Martin's hand, a smile on his face.

"It's a pleasure to meet you," Master Grant said. "I trust you've been enjoying your time on the island."

"Very much so," Mr. Martin said. "I was just talking with Owen about acquiring my own woman or two. I've already taken this one for a spin but I've been told she's not available. Maybe I can try out another or two while I'm here."

Heat crept up my face. I kept my eyes lowered so I couldn't see the looks passing between everyone but I felt the tension rise in the room.

After a minute, Master Grant said, "Be my guest. These women are new to the island but are available for use. I take it you were at the party last night."

"Oh yes," Mr. Martin said. "What a fun time. I've never had such a great time at a party. You're making it easy for me to want to say yes to investing here. I can see why the men love it so much."

Master Owen chuckled.

"Yes, it is easy to see why the men love it so much," Master Owen said, "but we strive to make sure that the women love it, too. Without them, it'd just be an island full of men playing with themselves."

"Right," Mr. Martin said as if he didn't quite believe that. He didn't strike me as the kind of man who considered what the women thought at all. One of the reasons I liked this place was that despite the women being submissive to the men, we were treated with enough consideration to make us want to stay. I liked that it was meant to be a win/win for everyone. I wasn't sure Mr. Martin got that.

"Who would you like to play with?" Master Grant asked, gesturing to the women waiting patiently on their knees. "I would be more than happy to help you set up a scene. We can make it part of their training for today if you want."

Mr. Martin wasted no time circling the women. I kept my eyes lowered but could see him making his way around them, circling like a hunter going after his prey. My heart pounded as he stopped by Olivia. Her pale skin and long auburn hair made her stand out from the rest.

"Her," Mr. Martin said, pointing to Olivia. "And her."

My heart nearly stopped as he pointed at me.

"She's wearing a black collar, right?" Mr. Martin asked even though it was obvious I was. "That means she's available for anything I want, right?"

Master Grant paused a moment before saying, "Yes, that's what it means. What type of set up would you like?"

I held my breath as I waited for the man to answer.

"Not here," Mr. Martin said. "I'd prefer somewhere more private. I'm staying at Lance's place. How about bringing them by this evening? Say at seven o'clock?"

Fear ran through me at the thought of being alone with this man again but at least I'd have Olivia with me. I knew Luke would have to say yes to this request. He wouldn't want to say no to a potential investor. I'd have to do whatever he wanted.

"That can be arranged," Master Owen said after it was clear Master Grant wasn't going to respond. "We'll bring them by this evening at seven. Is there anyone else you'd like to take for a spin now? Perhaps a quick blowjob?"

Mr. Martin looked over the girls but shook his head.

"Naw," he said, "These are the two I want. I'd rather save my energy for them."

"As you wish," Master Owen said. "Let me show you the rest of the facility before you leave. Riley, you can stay here with the class."

I let out a sigh of relief as Master Owen left with Mr. Martin, feeling like I had been saved for the time being. I wished he had used us right then so it'd be over with and it would be under the watchful eyes of Master Grant and Master Owen. That I could have handled. Being taken to Mr. Wood's place and left with this man, I'm not sure how I was going to do it. I trusted that ultimately I'd be safe but the idea made my stomach churn.

"Please join us, Riley," Master Grant said after the two other men left. "We were about to demonstrate the best way to suck a cock."

THIRTEEN

I spent the rest of the day with a pit in my stomach, not wanting seven o'clock to come but knowing there was no way to avoid it. Master Grant showed us various techniques to increase a man's pleasure while sucking cock using a variety of dildos that we forced down our throats. I was happy to numb out for a while, allowing myself to focus on how I could increase a man's pleasure while opening up my throat. Part of me wanted Master Grant to demonstrate on one of us, preferably me, with his cock but he kept it neatly tucked in his pants the whole time.

After dinner, which I ate in silence with the other women, Master Grant dismissed the class to their room before attaching leashes to Olivia and me. He had assured me earlier that Luke had been informed of Mr. Martin's request and wouldn't be expecting me home anytime soon. I wished I had a chance to talk with Luke but knew it wouldn't have made a difference. What could I have said to change things? I knew Luke needed to please this man and unfortunately, I was part of that happening.

"Ready?" Master Grant asked. He hadn't used us in any way today so we were both clean. I wondered if he purposely kept things minimal during class so we would be better able to handle tonight.

"Yes, Master Grant," we said in unison.

"Good," Master Grant said. "I'll be taking you to Mr. Wood's place so Mr. Martin may enjoy you for the evening. He's been given instructions on what is and isn't acceptable when using you. Riley, since you wear a black collar, and Olivia, since you wear none, understand that pain along with penetration is acceptable."

My heart hammered at the thought and not in a good way.

"I will be on the premises the whole time," Master Grant continued, "so I will be able to escort you back when your time with him is complete. I do not expect you to be made to stay the night but that could happen. Luke has given his consent for this if Mr. Martin wishes. In that case, I will also stay the night to ensure that you're both well cared for.

"If at any time you feel in jeopardy, please signal to us. You can do this by either tapping on something three times, raising three fingers or shaking your head three times. Mr. Wood has security cameras in every area of his house so you will be fully monitored during your time with Mr. Martin. He is aware of these cameras and understands the consequences of going past the limits he was given."

I felt myself sway as a wave of dizziness washed over me. I was happy about the safety precautions but it concerned me that Master Grant felt the need to explain them to us so thoroughly. It sounded like he expected us to be in jeopardy with this man.

"Permission to speak," I said in a small voice.

"Yes, of course, Riley," Master Grant said. "You may look at me."

I met his dark blue eyes. They gave away nothing.

"Are you afraid we won't be safe?"

Master Grant looked at me a moment before saying, "I will make sure that you're safe, Riley. I promise you that. That's why I'll be there the whole time. I won't let anything happen to either of you. Usually, I wouldn't feel the need to take as many precautions but since Mr. Martin hasn't been on the island long, he doesn't know how it operates yet. I want you both to know what you need to do if you feel in jeopardy. You won't be punished or sent home if you signal and it turns out he wasn't going to harm you. I'm giving you that permission now as your trainer. Do you understand?"

"Yes, Master Grant," we said.

I felt better, reassured, but something still felt off.

"Is there anything else, Riley?" Master Grant asked as if reading my mind.

Since I didn't know how to verbalize it or even exactly what was bothering me, I shook my head. "No, Master Grant. Thank you for explaining."

Master Grant led us to Mr. Wood's house up on the hill in silence. No one touched us as we walked, making me feel like we were marked with huge hands-off signs. The ebony woman from last night answered the door, her eyes lowered, as she let us in. She didn't say anything to us which shouldn't have surprised me.

"Is Mr. Wood at home?" Master Grant asked her.

"I'm sorry, Sir, he is not but how may I assist you?"

"Mr. Martin requested I bring these two women for his entertainment. Would you happen to know where I can find him?"

"I believe he's out by the pool, Sir," she said. "Please let me escort you."

Master Grant followed her through the house and out to the pool behind the house with us trailing behind. The yard felt more spacious without the crowd of people. Mr. Martin sprawled on one of the lounge chairs taking in the dwindling evening light. He jumped up as we approached, a huge smile on his face.

"Ah, my sluts are here," Mr. Martin said, taking our leashes from Master Grant. "Thank you for delivering them. I can't wait to try them out."

"It's my pleasure," Master Grant said. "I will be waiting in Mr. Wood's guest office if you need anything or to let me know when you're done. It's number four on the intercom."

Mr. Martin gave out a laugh. "Yes, of course. I'll let you know when I'm finished with them."

Master Grant gave Mr. Martin a little nod before disappearing into the house. The other woman had already left us and part of me wondered if it was because she didn't want to be any part of what Mr. Martin had planned for us. I couldn't blame her. He wasn't an unattractive man but there was something about him I didn't like. Maybe it had to do with how he treated us like we were nothing more than playthings created only for his amusement. I knew that I had come here to experience exactly that but since being here, it had turned into so much more.

Mr. Martin wasted no time turning his attention to us, pinching and pulling each of our nipples while he took us in. I wasn't surprised when he didn't say anything to us while his hands explored our bodies. He shoved a finger into my pussy while I watched him do the same to Olivia. She let out a little gasp while I purposefully didn't show any response. I knew I wasn't wet for him and that I felt tight around his finger as he worked it in.

"What's wrong with you, slut?" he said to me as he pushed his finger in further. "You're as dry as the Sahara."

He roughly pulled his finger out of me, turning his attention to Olivia.

"At least this bitch is wet," he said as his fingers remained buried in her and he played with her nipples.

Olivia kept her eyes lowered as one hand pulled and pinched her nipples before slapping each one. I stood there happy to not have his attention but feeling bad for Olivia. He slapped Olivia's face and then slapped mine. I was momentarily stunned.

"I want you bitches upstairs in my suite," he said. "Follow me."

We followed him into the house and through the living room before he opened double doors that led to his suite of rooms. There was a little sitting area right when we walked in that opened up to a patio overlooking a garden. The doors were open, letting in the warm tropical breeze. The sun was setting, casting a warm glow throughout the room. At any other time, this might have felt romantic but with Mr. Martin, it felt anything but.

"On your knees, sluts," he said the moment we were in the living room and had shut the doors behind us.

We sank down without hesitation. It was evident this man didn't mind dishing out pain and I didn't want to see what his worst could be.

He slipped his cock out from his pants. It was short but thick. He went over to Olivia first. She opened her mouth, anticipating him, but he smacked her cheek with his cock instead, leaving a bead of pre-come.

"You need to earn this, slut," he barked. "I need you to beg for it."

She kept her eyes lowered but said nothing. It wasn't a direct question and not exactly a command so I felt her uncertainty as to what to do. When it doubt, it was always best to say nothing.

He came to stand in front of me. I kept my eyes lowered, waiting for him to tell me what he wanted. I didn't open my mouth after how he responded to Olivia. This man wanted to be fully in control. I could do that.

"Open your mouth, slut."

I obeyed, opening my mouth. He slid his hard cock in until my lips rested at the base. He gripped my head as if I might want to back off. He wasn't that long—I was used to longer—so he didn't even hit the back of my throat. I kept my mouth open to him but didn't suck or do any of the things one might expect from a blowjob. I didn't feel like he wanted that anyway. He seemed to simply want to stick his dick as far back into my mouth as possible simply to have his way with me.

After a moment, he popped himself out, his cock bobbing before my face.

He slapped my face, startling me. He slapped me again but from the other side. Both cheeks stung.

"That's not for being wet," he said. "What slut here doesn't get wet when being fondled?"

I didn't respond. There was nothing I could say that would please him.

"I'm a big deal to this island and your owner. Your owner would be very disappointed if I wasn't able to give him a glowing review of you. It could affect the whole deal."

My heart sank. I couldn't screw up the island's prospect of expanding.

"Do you understand me, slut?" he asked before slapping me again.

"Yes, Sir," I said, my eyes lowered. "I will do better."

"You bet your ass you will or you can expect to be punished."

He grabbed my arm and pulled hard until I was standing.

"Take everything off, including those ridiculous shoes, and go lay on the bed with your ass at the edge with your heels by your ass."

I sprinted to the bedroom, not wanting to give him any more reason to slap me. A king-size bed dominated the room. Without looking around, I stripped, tossing my dress and the shoes on the floor, and positioned myself as commanded. My ass was facing the doorway leading in so I couldn't see what was going on. I heard him say something to Olivia but I couldn't make it out. A moment later, he dragged her in through the door.

"I'm happy to see you can at least follow orders, slut." I didn't know if he was talking to me or Olivia but it didn't matter. At least he was momentarily happy with one of us.

I heard him approach the bed, probably taking me in. My hands were down by my ankles, holding them in position, my legs spread for easy access to my pussy.

He slid a finger through my folds. I knew I wasn't wet and cringed as I waited for his reaction. He pushed my legs wider and stuck his face between my legs. He didn't lick me like I thought he might. He didn't hit me either. After a moment he went to the dresser. When he returned, he slipped a rope around my wrist and my ankle, tying them together tightly. He did the same to the other side before standing back to take it in.

"Lick her, cunt," he ordered which I assumed was to Olivia.

Heat rose up my chest as I felt her settle between my legs.

"On your knees, bitch. I need you to get this bitch wet for me."

Olivia didn't say anything—what could she say?—and after a moment I felt the heat of her mouth between my legs before her tongue reached out and tentatively licked me. I wanted to buck off the bed at how amazing it felt. My body immediately reacted to her as she gained more confidence and started licking up and down my slit. My juices started to flood her as she increased the pressure, circling her tongue, licking me up and down.

After a moment she found my clit and teased it. I thought I was going to lose it. I didn't want to give Mr. Martin the satisfaction of knowing how amazing it felt so I tried not to react. I knew he'd tell her to stop if he discovered how well she turned me on. I bit my lip as I willed myself not to react, wanting the insanity to continue. Olivia flicked my clit with her tongue, sending waves of pleasure through me. I closed my eyes and willed myself not to come as the pressure started to build, the pleasure threatened to overtake me.

"Enough," Mr. Martin said and then Olivia was gone.

I felt his fingers push into me, sliding in without resistance.

"About time," he said, pulling his fingers out.

A moment later, he pushed his thick cock into me, bracing himself on my legs. He grunted and groaned as he fucked me hard. My pussy opened to him, well-lubed now, and I took it in. I knew this was why I had come to the island—to be used and controlled. I tried pretending he was someone else but I couldn't do it. My mind refused to cooperate.

He seemed to strain as he fucked me, his thick cock stretching me with each push. I wondered what Olivia was doing, if she was watching, and if he planned to fuck her, too.

I felt myself grow cold as he continued pushing into me. With the sweetness of Olivia gone, I was no longer turned on.

After a few more grunts, he pulled out and sprayed himself on me. His hot load hit my bare pussy as well as my inner thighs and pubic bone. He slid a finger inside me and hooked it, painfully hitting my g-spot.

"Not one to come, eh, slut?"

"I've been taught not to come unless instructed, Sir," I said, hoping that would satisfy him.

He pushed his finger in deeper. A sharp pain radiated through me as I gritted my teeth. He pulled out, wiping my juices on my thigh.

"Not the best fuck of my life but I can see your appeal," he said. "Clean me off, slut."

Since I couldn't move, I assumed he was talking to Olivia. I felt sorry for her having to clean him off and laid there as I listened to her sucking him. It didn't take long until he seemed satisfied and told her enough. I heard him zip up his pants.

"Clean her up, too. I want to see her come. Don't stop until she does."

I sucked in my breath as I felt Olivia's tongue on my inner thigh, licking up the come he had squirted there. She licked one thigh clean before moving to the other one. I couldn't imagine this was fun for her but I reminded myself that she signed up for this, too.

She sucked on my pubic bone, cleaning me with her tongue, before she made her way to my slit. She licked up and down as if licking an ice cream cone, in long soft strokes. I felt my arousal return as her tongue teased me, stopping to flick my clit every second or third lick, keeping me guessing. I knew Mr. Martin was somewhere in the room watching but I no longer cared. I gave myself over to the sensations between my legs and the arousal that was building.

Olivia circled my clit with her tongue before she sucked it into her mouth. I just about lost it as my hips bucked to meet her, wanting more, my breathing becoming ragged and shallow. She increased the pressure, playing with my clit, flicking her tongue over it before sucking it some more.

"She's almost there," Mr. Martin said through the haze.

I had my eyes closed as Olivia continued to play with my clit with her tongue before pushing her tongue into my pussy. I gasped at the intrusion, my body humming with desire, as she slipped a finger in while she continued to lick me up and down. Hands found my nipples, pinching and pulling, practically milking an orgasm out of me. Olivia sucked in my clit as my nipples were being pulled, causing me to scream as my body jerked and I came with a fierceness that made me almost pass out.

As soon as I came, her mouth was gone but my nipples were still being pulled, a ripe pain blossoming from them.

"Very good," Mr. Martin said as he let go of my nipples. I kept my eyes closed, not wanting to see his victory, my body spent. I didn't want to move but doubted I'd be offered that luxury.

"Now it's her turn. I want you to lick her off while I play with her tits. Make her come or you'll both get whipped."

I opened my eyes, not sure what to do since my hands were still bound. He must have noticed my predicament because he quickly untied me. I slowly pushed myself up while Olivia crawled on the bed looking concerned. I had never licked a woman before so I wasn't sure what to expect but knew I didn't have a choice.

As soon as she was on her back on the bed, I made my way between her legs, pushing them open as I took her in. Mr. Martin was already at her breasts, pulling and pinching her delicate nipples. She squirmed, probably from the pain of it, her hands gripping the comforter.

I had never seen a pussy up close before. She was fully waxed, like all the women on the island, including myself, and musky. I leaned in, not wanting Mr. Martin to reprimand me, and slowly slid my tongue through her delicate folds. She squirmed more. I wasn't sure if it was from me or Mr. Martin but I proceeded to move my tongue through her silkiness. She was slightly wet as my tongue glided over her.

I pressed my hands against her thighs, opening her to me, as my tongue found her clit. I brushed over it lightly, understanding the sensitivity of it, causing her to buck her hips to meet me. Mr. Martin pinched and pulled her nipples, calling her a good slut as she squirmed. I wanted to do what I could to bring her pleasure, knowing it would benefit us both.

I worked my tongue over her, flicking her clit as often as I could, letting myself get into it. She tasted sweet and musky and I was surprised by how much I enjoyed it. Her breathing became shallow as she grew closer to erupting. I wanted more than anything to coax an orgasm out of her. I knew it was me who was building one in her, not Mr. Martin, and this knowledge gave me great pleasure.

I slipped two fingers inside her wet pussy as I continued to lap at her clit. She bucked her hips once more before coming all over me. I worked my fingers through her orgasm, wanting more, suddenly greedy for it. She came again, crying out, flailing all over the bed. I slowly pulled my fingers out, satisfied, and looked up to see Mr. Martin looming over her.

"That was amazing," he said, giving her nipples one more pinch. "What I would do to acquire both of you. It's like you belong together."

My heart hammered at his words. I was Luke's. I didn't want to be with this man. I shuddered at the thought, knowing my life wouldn't be easy with him. There was a possibility that Luke would give me over to this man to solidify the investment. The thought made me shiver. I knew I had the option to leave but I didn't want to be forced to in this way.

Unsure what to do, I kneeled in front of Olivia's open pussy, wanting to show respect while also wanting to signify a moment of completion. Olivia didn't move, probably unsure as well. Mr. Martin probably wasn't used to directing women like us who were trained not to do anything without instruction. I kept my eyes lowered, grateful not to have to look at him, as I waited.

"Go wash yourselves up," he said after a minute. "There's a bathroom through that door. Shower together to save time but don't waste time. I want you back here within five minutes."

Not having a lot of time, we jumped up and scurried into the adjacent bathroom. It was lush with white tiles, cream counters and fluffy white towels. The shower was massive, lined with light tan tiles that were rough to the touch. We turned the water to hot and got in, lathering ourselves up without haste. I didn't want to get reprimanded and I'm sure Olivia felt the same.

"Is this always how it's like?" Olivia asked me in a whisper as we washed our hair.

"Hardly," I said. "It depends on who you're with. When you're out on the town, it can be more crass like this, but with an owner, it's something different. Not like a boyfriend would be, at least not for most of us, but there's more respect. Well, for me anyway. Every owner is different."

"I've always dreamt of being used in this way," Olivia said as we rinsed, "but it's different than I imagined it'd be."

"Do you think you'll stay?" I asked, suddenly afraid that this may have her wanting to leave.

"I think so," she said as she turned the water off and we stepped out to towel ourselves off. "I want to. I guess it'll depend on who acquires me and what that's like."

I got it. That was a major deciding factor for many of the women here. We didn't get to choose who acquired us. In some respects, this was part of why we came, to fully surrender, but it also could be scary and pushed us to our limits.

We stopped talking as our five-minute deadline inched near. I also didn't want Mr. Martin to hear us or, worse, burst into the bathroom in some sort of fury. I already knew this wasn't a man I wanted to push. He didn't seem to have a lot of empathy for women and it made me wonder what type of woman had married him.

Back in the room, Mr. Martin stood by the bed with several cuffs in his hands. My heart sank.

"Come here," he said.

We approached him without hesitation until we stood in front of him. Without a word, he slipped cuffs around our wrists and our ankles, locking each into place with a little padlock. I'd been locked into cuffs before but this time it made me feel unsettled. I reminded myself that we were being monitored and that Master Grant was somewhere in the house waiting to rescue us if needed. That thought helped my breathing return to normal as I took in a few deep breaths.

"I've always wanted to restrain a woman," Mr. Martin said once he was done with the cuffs, "and how lucky is it that I get to restrain two?"

We didn't say anything, keeping our eyes lowered.

Mr. Martin grabbed Olivia's arm and directed her to a spanking bench on the other side of the room. It sat in front of the windows leading out to the garden. I hadn't noticed it before but I'd been in a hurry earlier.

I watched as she leaned her over the bench until her torso rested on it, her breasts dangling in the open space between the cushion bracing her shoulders and her abdomen. He secured her wrists and ankles to the bench, making her immobile. He gave her ass a good smack that resonated throughout the room before sliding a couple of fingers into her.

"Still wet, I see. I may need to do something about that."

He left her and came over to me. I kept my eyes lowered, not sure what to expect. I tried to blank my mind, to become nothing more than my body, knowing it'd be easier that way. This was what I had signed up for.

"As for you," Mr. Martin said, taking my arm as he led me to the other side of the room, "I want you on the cross."

I hadn't noticed the cross either that sat opposite the spanking bench. He attached my arms and my ankles to the cross so I mimicked its shape. The cross leaned back a little, helping to support my body and not leave me hanging by my wrists. I could see Olivia from this position, even with my eyes lowered, and wondered if that was part of the point.

Once I was attached, Mr. Martin returned his attention to Olivia. He ran his hand over her ass, caressing it gently, before slipping his fingers between her legs. She let out a soft gasp as I imagined his fingers slipped into her. He pushed into her, almost pushing her forward but she had nowhere to go. She was stuck just like I was, unable to do anything except take whatever he had to give. He pulled on her nipple with the other hand, almost as if he were milking her, pulling and pinching, as he worked between her legs.

Her breathing got shallow until she was almost panting. He quickened his pace between her legs, his other hand fondling and groping her breasts, until she erupted in an orgasm. He pulled out immediately and gave her ass a good smack. He smacked her ass a few more times until it turned a light pink. He smoothed his hand over it before giving it one more good smack, looking satisfied.

He didn't say anything as he moved his attention to me. I kept my eyes lowered but since I was raised up a bit, I saw him move towards me.

He smacked my breasts, watching them bounce, before smacking them again. Each slap stung and vibrated through me. My nipples hardened from the impact. It wasn't hard but it wasn't gentle either. He kept slapping as if playing, watching them sway, watching me react with each strike.

He pushed his fingers into me. I was still wet from earlier and this seemed to satisfy him. He slapped my breasts again as he fingered me, playing, not having a clue what he was doing. I closed my eyes and allowed my body to respond as it wanted, detaching from the scene. My body enjoyed the attention while my mind wished it was someone else giving it to me.

The fingers did nothing for me but I squirmed a little to give him the indication that he was hitting the right spots.

"Come, bitch," he barked out as he increased the pace and pressure between my legs.

I never came on demand and knew I wouldn't be able to do it now, but wanting to please him, I started to pant and squeezed down around his fingers, letting out a scream as my body convulsed.

Satisfied, he pulled out, wiped his hand down my thigh.

"Good slut. It's about time you started to listen."

He stood back to take me in, his eyes roaming over me. I kept my eyes lowered, not wanting to make eye contact, not wanting him to have that part of me.

"If you were mine, I'd keep you like that all night," he said. "Both of you. Comfortable enough but unable to move. Or like this during a party where my guests could view you and use you as they chose. Of course, you'd both be in black collars. I'd have no restrictions. You're only purpose is to be used and I believe all women need to be used as much as possible."

He went over to Olivia and smacked her ass. She jumped since he had come from behind. He smoothed his hand over her ass before smacking her again.

"I don't think I'd ever get tired of this. I want you both as part of my household. I'll need to wait until I have a residence established here but that won't be too hard to do. I'll let Lance know that we can finalize the deal once I have his word that I can acquire the two of you."

FOURTEEN

Mr. Martin left us bound after he gave his speech and left without another word. It didn't take long for Master Grant to come in and release us.

"I heard every word," he said while he unhooked me from the cross. I wanted to look into his eyes but didn't dare. My ass stung just thinking about it. "As you may know, he's a very important part of Mr. Wood's expansion plans and Mr. Wood wants him as a key investor. Mr. Wood has directed everyone at the training facility to keep him happy which is why Luke agreed to let him have you for the evening."

Once Master Grant had me down, he went over to Olivia and started unhooking her. I still had the cuffs on but that didn't matter. I sunk to my knees, grateful to be off my feet. My limbs ached from being stretched and I was happy to be able to relax for a minute.

Once Master Grant had Olivia unhooked, he helped her up and started unlocking and taking off her cuffs. He didn't say anything more and I felt the heaviness in the room. It felt like this was no longer in his hands or even in Luke's. We all seemed to be at the mercy of Mr. Martin and I didn't like it one bit.

When he finished with Olivia, he left her standing, not giving her a command otherwise, and came over to me.

"Stand up, Riley."

I complied, uncurling myself until I stood in front of him. He unlocked and pulled off my cuffs, his hands lingering just a moment, making me want to look up into his deep blue eyes. My heart hammered at his proximity but I knew better than to say anything. We were still being monitored and I didn't want to get any of us in trouble. Who knew if Mr. Martin or even Mr. Wood were somewhere watching. I knew Mr. Wood prided himself on how well the training facility was working to shape the women here and the last thing I wanted to do was go against that.

"It's been a long evening," Master Grant said. "As a thank you, Mr. Wood would like the two of you to stay the night. Luke has been informed so you don't need to worry about him. He understands the importance of you being here."

Master Grant tucked the cuffs into a drawer before turning to face us.

"You'll share a room and a bed. There's something about the two of you together that Mr. Martin finds appealing. Don't be surprised if your sleep gets interrupted. Mr. Martin is staying with Mr. Wood while he's on the island. He specifically requested that you stay the night."

I took in a deep breath, not liking the sound of that but knowing I had no say in the matter.

"I will remain on hand and will be monitoring any activity throughout the night along with Master Owen. Again, don't hesitate to let us know via your signals if you feel yourself in danger. You will not be reprimanded if you do so and it's discovered that you weren't in any danger. This is a special situation."

I hated that Master Grant felt that we could be in danger with Mr. Martin. It seemed like Mr. Martin was interested in using us how he pleased but I no longer felt like he'd permanently hurt us. Still, I wasn't looking forward to tonight.

"I'll escort you to your room," Master Grant said, "where a late-night snack is waiting for you. Feel free to shower again if you wish. There is an adjoining bathroom for your use. The only rule you have tonight is to not leave the room unless there's an emergency. Do you understand?"

"Yes, Master Grant," we said together.

"Do either of you have any questions?"

"No, Master Grant."

"OK, good. I'll take you to your room now."

Our room for the night was on the small side with a queen-sized bed in the middle covered in a white comforter. A dresser and armchair completed the room with a window overlooking the pool. There was an adjoining bathroom as promised with a shower but no tub. White fluffy towels were tucked into the towel rack while several white washcloths sat on the counter.

As promised, a tray of fruit, cheese and crackers sat on the bed like an oasis. Bottles of water were lined up on the dresser beaconing us. I was suddenly starving and couldn't wait to dive in.

"All set?" Master Grant asked. "Do you need anything else?"

I needed a lot of things but nothing he could give me at the moment.

"No, Master Grant," I said with Olivia saying the same a moment later.

"Very well. I'll see you both in the morning. Sleep well."

I let out the breath I was holding as soon as Master Grant left. I felt like Olivia did the same. We looked at each other as if to ask what now. We were technically allowed to talk with no men present but I was painfully aware that we were being monitored. I knew our conversation would not be private so we needed to be careful about what we said.

"Do you want to shower again?" I asked.

She shook her head. "I honestly just want to sleep. Especially if we're going to be used again at some point."

I nodded. I had to agree.

"Ok," I said. "Let's go to bed."

We snuggled like girls having a fun sleepover, our noses almost touching as we pulled the comforter up around us. The bed felt amazing, soft and comforting. I liked the idea of having a friend I could talk with again. Annabelle had been that somewhat for me before she and Luke become a couple. I missed being able to talk freely with someone about this crazy place, someone who understood my point of view.

I pulled the comforter over our heads, essentially burying us in it, before whispering, "Are you liking it here so far?" I hoped I was quiet enough to not be heard by whatever microphones might be in the room.

"It's interesting," Olivia said in a whisper. "Different than I thought it'd be. I knew I'd be used for sex and not much else but I didn't realize how much control I'd be giving up."

"Yea, your life is not your own here. We are truly property."

"But you like your owner, right?"

I considered her question a moment. "I do. I'm lucky. Not all men here are as nice as Luke or even the trainers."

"I wished we could pick who we're with," Olivia said. "I also wish the trainers acquired women, too."

I smiled. "Any trainer in particular?"

I swear she blushed but it was too dark to tell.

"Master Grant," she said in a squeak. "I know he'd always protect me."

I felt a rush of jealousy, thinking maybe Master Grant preferred Olivia over me, but I also felt something else I couldn't put my finger on.

"He is super protective," I said. And gorgeous, I didn't say. There was also no way I would share any of our private encounters with Olivia. "We'd better get to sleep. Who knows when we'll be woken up."

"Good idea," Olivia said. "And I'm happy I'm here with you."

WE MADE it through the night without being disturbed. I woke up entangled with Olivia, my arm draped over her shoulder and my leg between hers. It felt comfortable, like we did this all the time. I wanted to pull her into me, to cuddle more, but I didn't want to wake her. I also didn't want to give anyone watching any indication of my desires. I felt like they could be used against me.

The sun streamed in through the window, making me wonder what time it was. Not that time mattered—I rarely knew what time it was—but somehow it seemed important today. I didn't even know what day it was. Was it a workday? Would these men be heading into the office? I had no idea.

I had the sense of waiting to be collected as I laid there, realizing that that was my only purpose. I had no other reason to be here than to be used by these men. In a way, it was a liberating thought. In another, it could easily shift into terrorizing. Thankfully I trusted the security here and the measures taken to ensure that the women remained essentially unharmed. I couldn't imagine being like this anywhere else. The island allowed me to be open in ways I had never imagined.

When I had first arrived on the island, I was naïve in thinking that it would be some sort of adult Disneyland with sex all the time and everyone getting pleasure from every interaction. Since then I've learned that there are a lot of dynamics going on between the men and women. Each one is as unique as each individual but I've recognized consistent themes emerging.

Love relationships like Luke and Annabelle shared rarely happened. The men didn't come to the island for that, or at least as far as I've seen, but sometimes it snuck up on them. Most men preferred the owner/property type of relationship, wanting full control over the woman, and she was more than happy to submit. Emotions stayed out of this type of relationship. I've heard more than one woman who had fallen for her owner but it was rarely reciprocated. The men were encouraged to own more than one woman to help prevent this from happening and also to remind the women that they were replaceable.

More frequently the men wanted to not only own the women but to break them down so they were more compliant and receptive to their every want and desire. These men were the scariest because it robbed women of the ability to think for themselves so they'd never leave even if it was in their best interest to do so. I wondered what Mr.

Wood and the others were doing to keep these men from infiltrating the island. I wondered if it was possible to keep them out.

My mind wandered into dangerous places, places I didn't want to think about, until Olivia moved next to me. She blinked at me as she woke up, looking at me as if she had no idea where she was.

"Morning," I said in a low voice. "Sleep well?"

"Yea," she said, her voice sleepy. "Better than I have since I got here."

My heart warmed. I hoped I was part of the reason.

Before I could give it much thought, the door opened and the gorgeous ebony woman pushed a tray piled with food, juice and milk into the middle of the room. She kept her eyes lowered and looked a little apprehensive as she came in. I wanted to talk with her, to ask her questions about herself, but knew better than to push.

"Thank you," I said from the bed. I lifted myself on my elbows so I could see her better. "I'm Riley. This is Olivia."

"I'm Ruby," she said in a whisper as her eyes darted around.

"Are you Mr. Woods?" I asked, my curiosity getting the better of me.

"Yes."

I waited a moment, hoping for more, but nothing came. I couldn't see her eyes since she refused to look at me. I wanted to tell her that we were the same as her, just women, and she had nothing to fear but maybe she knew something we didn't. A frisson of fear ran through me at the thought and I knew it'd do me no good to work myself up over things I didn't know.

"I need to go," she said in a whisper and then she was gone.

With nothing else to do, I got up, used the bathroom and returned to the wonderful spread of food. Olivia had already started in on it, shoving in pancakes and eggs like there was no tomorrow. I joined her on the bed and went at it. There were pancakes, eggs, bacon, sausages, orange juice, milk, biscuits and fruit. It was hard not to want to shovel in everything at once but I knew I'd be sick if I did.

I took my time as I ate, savoring every bite, while Olivia ate like she had no idea where her next meal was coming from. I knew they were served tasteless gruel at the training facility so I couldn't blame her. I was lucky that Luke let me dictate the menu most of the time.

Thinking about Luke made me miss him and the simplicity of my life with him. It was hard to believe that I had considered anything else. I was one of the luckier women on the island and this whole experience with Mr. Martin helped to reinforce that for me. I had nothing to complain about. Now that Luke let me leave the house without him, I could experience random use whenever I wanted or I could stay home and curl up with a good book instead. I had no idea why I had been unhappy.

My head filled with these thoughts as I started to get full. Olivia started to slow down, too. I took another swig of orange juice then pushed my plate away. Olivia took a few more bites then did the same.

I opened my mouth to ask Olivia what she thought was on tap for us today when the door swung open. I was half expecting Mr. Martin but to my delight, it was Master Grant. I practically salivated at the sight of him, a puppy with her tail wagging, but quickly reeled myself in and lowered my eyes. It wouldn't do either of us any good if he knew how much I was infatuated with him.

"You're needed downstairs," Master Grant said. He approached us with two leashes which he quickly attached to our collars.

I tried not to pout as he led us down the stairs and out into the main living room. We had nothing on but our collars and heels. Mr. Martin was already there, dressed more casually in khakis and a polo shirt with a smirk on his face. I kept my eyes lowered but managed to catch it. My skin squirmed. I knew I'd have to leave the island if this man managed to acquire me. I knew I wouldn't be able to take it for long.

Master Grant led us to Mr. Martin and handed him our leashes. I felt tethered in a way I have yet to feel on the island. I no longer felt like myself but just some other woman, any woman, that needed to do what this man wanted.

"Ah, the lovely ladies," Mr. Martin said as he took our leashes. "We're going to have fun today."

Dread ran through me as I realized we'd be with him longer than just the morning.

Master Grant gave us one last look before he left us alone with Mr. Martin. No one else was in the main living room which made me wonder if anyone else was in the house. I wondered where Ruby and Mr. Wood were this morning. Maybe she went into the office with Mr. Wood, kneeling by his side all day. I could picture it.

I almost jerked my head up with I felt a strong tug on the leash. Mr. Martin pulled on the leash, expecting us to follow, expecting our full obedience as he walked us to the front door and out into the warm morning sunshine. We trailed behind him as he walked down the long driveway and out into the men's side of town. Even though it was early, people were everywhere. Hands found their way to us, groping as we passed, pulling and tugging on us as if we were puppies to be petted.

Mr. Martin said hello to some of the men as we walked but didn't stop to chat. He seemed to know exactly where he was headed and wasn't going to stop for anyone. He kept up a quick pace, literally keeping us on our toes as we tried to keep up behind him. He didn't look back to check on us and he didn't talk to us. It felt like he was taking his bitches out for a walk, parading us around town, showing us off to everyone he knew.

I fell in line, eyes lowered, happy for the moment that I didn't need to do anything else. My thoughts wandered to Olivia, wondering how she was holding up. I worried that her first impressions of the island weren't good ones. For all she knew, this was what life was like with an owner. I had no doubt Mr. Martin would acquire her if he moved here. Maybe she'd be kept under the training facility's care while he was away or maybe she'd be left on her own at his place, probably with other women. I doubted she'd be lonely. I knew she'd figure this place out.

As for me, I wasn't sure what I wanted anymore. Life with Luke felt like living with a couple but I knew I didn't want a life with Mr. Martin. Ideally, I'd find some way to be with Master Grant even if that meant being owned by the training facility. I wouldn't mind him using me for demos while he trained the new women. He had mentioned that there had been an influx of inquiries from women wanting to come here and they were having a challenge keeping up with the demand. I needed to figure out a way to show him I could be useful in that capacity. Maybe going along with Mr. Martin today would help prove that.

Mr. Martin pulled us into one of the nicer restaurants. It was surprisingly full for midmorning with men in suits and some dressed more casually in khakis and polos. Mr. Martin breezed by the hostess stand and led us to a large round table situated in the middle of the room that had a raised platform in the middle. He pulled us onto the platform, securing our leashes to a post in the middle.

He pinched and pulled both of our nipples before slapping us across the face. My cheek stung as I closed my eyes, hoping he wouldn't do it again.

"You sluts will be our entertainment during our brunch," Mr. Martin said. "You'll probably be fucked many times but while you're not being used, I want you to entertain us by enjoying each other. There should be at no point that you're not in use, do you understand?"

"Yes, Mr. Martin," we said.

My heart hammered as I thought about what he was asking.

"If you don't comply, you will be punished. I don't tolerate disobedient sluts. You're both mine for the day so I can test you out. Be the good bitches that I know you can be."

With that, he left to take a seat around the table. A few men quickly joined him as a waitress flitted around taking drink orders. She wore nothing but a waist apron and men enjoyed fondling her tits while they ordered.

Not wanting to get punished, I turned towards Olivia and started running my hands over her pale skin. I was always shocked by how soft she felt as I let my hands run over her shoulders and down her arms. She picked up on what I was doing and started running her hands over me as well, down my sides, over my hips, over my ass. We were standing close, our nipples almost touching.

I blocked out the men around us, knowing they were watching, as I allowed myself to get lost in my exploration of Olivia. I was happy to be touching her and knew this could very well be the last time.

Her hands explored my ass, gently massaging me, as I allowed my hands to skim down her sides. I was careful not to give into my inclination to follow the curve of her breast, to test her nipple with my fingers, since I had a feeling today was going to be a long day and I didn't want to move too fast. My goal was to keep the men entertained while enjoying my opportunity to explore Olivia's body. She seemed to take her cue from me and stayed clear of my sensitive areas.

I gently squeezed her ass as she leaned into me, her nipples brushing against mine, sending a flurry of sensations through my body. I closed my eyes, blocking out everything but her, as I let my hands move to her hips and down her outer thighs. I felt her start to move against me, her skin silk against mine, causing my body to react in surprising ways. My nipples were hard, brushing against her stiff peaks, wanting more attention while knowing it would be too much.

She let out a soft groan that went straight through me as she pulled me closer to her. Her lips found my shoulder and kissed it, slowly working its way down my chest. My breath caught as her hand cupped my breast and her mouth found my hardened nipple. She sucked it in, her tongue flicking over it again and again until I thought I might pass out. I could hear the men in the distance cheering her on as she continued to suck and pull on my nipple, my whole body giving into her.

I arched my back so she could take it in more. Her other hand came up and pinched the other nipple causing a ripple of ecstasy to rip through me. My breathing got shallow as she moved her hot mouth from one nipple to the other, her tongue playing with each one, teasing me, making me consumed with lust.

The men cheered, loving the show, but I blocked them out as I gave myself over completely to Olivia. I ran my hands up her sides until I found her heavy breasts, running my thumbs over her erect nipples, causing her to moan. I loved the feel of them against my thumbs, their responsiveness to my touch. I pinched on one and then the other until her mouth left my nipples and suddenly found my mouth.

She kissed me like I had never been kissed before, her lips soft and forgiving as her kiss demanded everything from me. I was still gripping her nipples, squeezing and pulling, as her hands found mine, doing the same, until I was spinning from all of it. The ecstasy was unreal as her mouth devoured mine, claiming me in a way no man ever had, her hands pawing at my nipples, her determination fierce and unyielding.

New hands caressed my ass before dipping between my legs and running fingers through my wetness. I knew I shouldn't have been surprised by the sudden addition but I had forgotten where we were and that we were putting on a show. I kept my eyes closed as Olivia continued to kiss me, the fingers pushing themselves inside me. I automatically spread my legs, my body wanting the friction and not caring who was giving it to me.

The fingers were rough, pushing in deep, flicking on my clit without a hint of finesse, until I couldn't hold back anymore and exploded into a million pieces. The fingers worked through my orgasm, a deep chuckle in my ear, and suddenly they were gone, leaving my pussy vacant as Olivia's hands roamed the front of my body. Before I could give it another thought, hands were spreading my cheeks and a thick cock slammed into me, causing my pussy to shudder around it. The cock buried itself inside me until there was nowhere else for it to go.

He gripped my hips as he fucked me, Olivia's lips still on mine. Her breathing became shallow, matching mine, making me think she must be getting fucked, too. My pussy gripped onto the cock buried deep inside me causing it to push in quicker, almost frantic, sliding easily and quickly in and out of me, my wetness dripping down my legs.

I felt on fire, my body humming with waves of pleasure, as another orgasm began to build. The fucking became more frantic as I felt the cock begin to shudder then still as it spilled itself inside me. My nipples were pinched and pulled, the pain radiating through me. I no longer knew who was doing it and I no longer cared.

The cock slipped out, quickly replaced by another. It pushed into me without ceremony, the man's hands on my hips for leverage as he began to fuck me hard. I kept getting pushed into Olivia who had stopped kissing me as she began to pant in my ear, her hands braced against my shoulders, probably helping to hold herself up. I opened my eyes briefly to see a man behind her, probably buried deep inside her. We clung to each other as random men fucked us from behind one after another until I lost count.

At some point, someone turned us around so Olivia and I were back to back.

"On your knees, sluts," a man I didn't recognize said.

We immediately complied, sinking to our knees. A few men surrounded us, their cocks out, pointed directly at us. I opened my mouth without thinking and was slapped.

"Aren't you a greedy one?" one man said. "Don't open your mouth unless you're told, slut. You need to earn our cocks in your mouth."

I shut it, feeling reprimanded, as I sat there with my eyes lowered, waiting for further instruction.

The men circled us, their cocks in their hands, as if debating whether or not we were worthy to suck their cocks. My mind flashed to Mr. Martin and I wondered if he was enjoying the show. I knew this would be my life if Mr. Martin acquired me and while it could be exciting some of the time, I wasn't sure I wanted it all of the time. Not that I had the choice unless I wanted to leave and I wasn't ready to do that yet.

One man stopped in front of me, his cock large and foreboding.

"Open up, slut."

I opened my mouth without hesitation. He slid his thick cock in until it pressed against the back of my throat. I had been taught how not to gag so I opened my throat for it, accepting it, tasting its musky saltiness. He pumped in slowly at first, hitting the back of my throat every time. He was so large that my tongue almost had nowhere to go. I tried sucking him but it felt impossible. He didn't seem to notice or care as he started fucking my face with more force, grabbing the back of my head with one hand for leverage.

I let my mind go blank as he fucked me, my throat already raw from him, open and obedient. It didn't long before he came down my throat, emptying his cock in me. I opened for him, taking it, happy to be accommodating. Once he slipped out, another entered and it went this way until I lost count, my mind spinning. I felt like a mouth simply existing to be used. Some came down my throat. Some came on my face. Some slapped me before they started and some slapped me once they finished.

By the time the last cock pulled out and another one wasn't there to replace it, my mouth felt raw and my jaw ached. My mind had slipped to somewhere else and I didn't feel completely inside my body. It took me a moment to remember where I was and what I was doing. I sat back on my heels, my legs aching, my mouth closed, as I waited for the next use of me.

FIFTEEN

Someone clicked a leash to my collar. I didn't even bother trying to see who it was. I knew it didn't matter. I was covered in come, exhausted and no longer cared. I had a vague sense of Olivia behind me, the click of her leash, before a man told us to stand.

I slowly uncurled, my legs aching, as I struggled to stand. I knew I was a mess but I didn't care. I felt like I had somehow transitioned into a woman whose only purpose was to accept cock and be whatever the men here wanted me to be. My opinions and desires didn't matter. I felt like I had given myself over fully, accepted my fate, knowing I wouldn't be able to return home without some deep part of me missing. I felt numb and blank and followed the leash without caring where it was taking me.

We walked through the restaurant and out onto the street. The sun blazed hot over us. No one bothered touching me and I wasn't surprised. I had come everywhere.

I kept my eyes lowered as we walked, focused on the work boots in front of me leading me to wherever he wanted us to go. I didn't pay attention to the surroundings, knowing it didn't matter. I had fully given in to my place here, knowing this was probably how it was going to be, especially if Mr. Martin acquired me. I didn't doubt that Luke would let me go to him if it meant closing their deal. Although Luke liked me, I didn't have the bond with him like he had with Annabelle. He would have fought for Annabelle. I didn't see him fighting for me.

My heart cracked a little at this thought. I wasn't in love with Luke but I had felt cherished and appreciated by him. I knew Mr. Martin wouldn't treat me the same way. My days would probably be more like today, displayed and used as he wanted, just another woman in his household there solely for his pleasure. I knew I could do it—that's why I came here—but for some reason, it wasn't enough.

I was surprised when I realized we were entering the training facility's main entrance. I assumed we'd be going back to Mr. Wood's house or maybe to another venue. Mr. Martin hadn't even fucked us today. Or maybe he did and I hadn't noticed.

I followed the work boots in front of me as they led us down various halls. I heard a male voice talking, as if lecturing, and I wondered if there was a class in session. It made sense considering a fresh batch of women were going through training. I didn't know how long they trained the women before they went up for auction. A new shipment could have arrived, too. They've been saying how high the demand has been for both men and women wanting to come to the island. I knew I should have felt privileged to be here. Instead, I felt defeated.

I almost ran into the man leading us when he stopped and turned to face us. I kept my eyes lowered, afraid to look at him, not wanting to get in trouble. He approached me and my heart hammered, not sure what to expect. He slowly lifted my chin until I was staring into deep blue eyes. My heart nearly stopped as I found myself looking at Master Grant. His expression was serious and unreadable. He captured my gaze and wouldn't let go. I couldn't look away.

"Riley," he said, his voice almost a whisper, "how are you holding up?"

"I'm fine, Master Grant," I said because what else could I say. I couldn't begin to describe the turmoil I was feeling.

He didn't look like he believed me. He asked Olivia, who was standing next to me, the same question.

"I'm good, Master Grant," she said, her voice steady and clear.

He looked at her then returned his gaze to me as if trying to decide what to do.

"I told Mr. Martin you both were needed back here for the rest of the day," he said, "so you'd be able to get a break. I know life on the island isn't always easy for the women but I believe in giving the women some downtime to recuperate. You've both had an intense couple of days and deserve a rest. I want you to know that you both did beautifully yesterday and today and I couldn't be prouder."

My heart beamed at his words. I wanted nothing more than to please him.

"I've been permitted by Mr. Wood to let you both rest here with me for the rest of the day. I want you to know that Mr. Wood is also pleased with your performance and that's why he's allowed you this break.

"The first thing I want you to do is shower. You can use my private bathroom. The shower is big enough for both of you so I want you to shower together but don't play with each other and don't come. I have plans for you."

My eyes widened as I let his words sink in, my heart hammering but this time with happy anticipation. I hadn't even noticed that he had brought us into his private bedroom.

"Go," he said after we stood there a moment too long.

We scurried to his bathroom, leaving the door open because we weren't worried about privacy here. We took off our heels before stepping into the warm spray, scrubbing ourselves down from head to toe, each taking care of ourselves and not worrying about the other. We didn't talk since Master Grant was somewhere within hearing distance. Not that I thought he would have minded but I didn't want to ruin whatever he had planned with our disobedience. I sensed Olivia felt the same way.

Olivia and I made lots of eye contact, communicating through that alone, telling each other how relieved we were to be back with Master Grant and away from Mr. Martin. I wondered what Olivia thought of all this and if she planned to stay.

Once we were cleaned, we shut off the water and stepped out, drying ourselves with the plush white towels Master Grant had hanging in his bathroom. I liked the idea of using the same soap and shampoo that he used. Even though it had a neutral clean scent, I liked the idea of smelling like him.

I had no idea what Master Grant had planned but I was bursting with excitement when we returned to his room all clean and glowing. He sat in a chair in the corner of the room when we entered, smiling like two eager school girls. I kept my eyes lowered but allowed myself a peek. He caught me looking and gave me a lopsided grin that made my heart skip. I didn't even care that Olivia was standing next to me and I wouldn't be having Master Grant all to myself.

Master Grant slowly pushed himself up and walked over to us until he was standing in front of us. I felt like squealing and had to bite my lip to keep from doing it.

"You have permission to look at me while you're in this room," he said, his words warm and low. "I like being able to see all of you and your eyes are a major part of that."

I looked up at him, catching his gaze. He was staring right at me. My heart hammered as we stared at each other. His expression was intense, as if he were trying to figure me out. I had no idea what my expression said except I was overjoyed to be with him. I hoped I didn't come across as too eager. I knew men didn't always appreciate that. I should be exhausted from the morning but I was surprisingly rejuvenated after the shower and knowing we'd have time off from Mr. Martin.

Master Grant gave me a small smile before turning his gaze to Olivia. I felt a little jealous as he took her in, knowing I was being ridiculous. Of course, he wasn't here for me. He knew we needed a break from Mr. Martin and that's all that was happening. I needed to remind myself that Master Grant and I could never be a thing. That didn't happen here unless you were Annabelle.

He put his hand under Olivia's chin before leaning in and capturing her lips with his. Jealousy coursed through as I watched out of the corner of my eye as he kissed her. He didn't touch her in any other way and she didn't touch him. We were trained not to touch unless instructed and somehow she managed to maintain this as he deepened the kiss.

I tried not to watch but it was hard not to. I was drawn in by them. Jealousy snaked through me but something else started to blossom, like a little pull towards them, towards their connection. I had never experienced anything like that before and was curious what it was about.

Master Grant broke off the kiss with Olivia, pulling back to look at her. Her shallow breathing echoed around us. I wondered when was the last time she'd been kissed like that. Most of the men on the island didn't bother kissing us.

Master Grant held her gaze a few minutes. The silence filled the room and something else I couldn't name. I felt like I held my breath as I waited for what he'd do next. I felt like Olivia and I were in this together, like we were a unit now, not to be separated. I wondered if Master Grant knew that Mr. Martin would be acquiring us to help seal their deal and this would be the last time he'd be alone with us like this.

When he turned his gaze back on me, my heart stopped. His gaze was intense mixed with heat. He wasted no time leaning in and capturing my mouth with his. My instinct was to reach out and touch him, to put my hands around his neck, to pull him in deeper, but I resisted and kept my hands at my sides. He cupped my face with his hand as he pulled me in towards him, his lips hot on mine, his tongue exploring the depths of my mouth.

My body exploded with desire for him, aching to be taken, aching to please him in any way. At that moment if he had told me that going to live with Mr. Martin would please him, I would have done it without another thought. As long as Master Grant was happy, that's all that would have mattered to me.

He deepened the kiss, drawing me in, until I was breathless and floating. My whole body tingled, ready to explode, wanting nothing more than to be his, for him to claim me completely. I forgot about Olivia as his mouth moved over mine, his tongue sweet and savory, exploring me in a way I had never been explored before. Just when I thought I might pass out from it all, he broke off his kiss and stared at me.

My eyes were wide as he took me in. I felt stunned and more turned on than I'd ever been. He had me. I was his whether or not he knew it or would do anything about it. No matter who owned me, I'd always be his.

"On your knees," he said, his voice hoarse and deep.

We both immediately fell to our knees, looking up at him as we waited for his next command. He looked all-powerful standing before us, a man who could easily command us to do anything but who I knew would always protect us. I felt safe with him. Secure. I knew nothing bad would ever happen to me as long as Master Grant was around.

He pulled out his glorious cock from his dark jeans. He was hard and long and ready for us. I instinctively opened my mouth even though he hadn't instructed me to and he took it as an invitation. His cock slid in smoothly as my mouth wrapped around his impressive length. He didn't push himself all the way in like some men but instead only gave me half of himself, just enough to tease me.

He must have known I wanted all of him because he chuckled before pulling out.

Olivia must have been also waiting with her mouth open since he turned to her and gave her a taste as well. This time I wasn't jealous as I watched her take him in her mouth. Again, he only gave her half of himself, just enough for her to taste and nothing more. He pulled out after a minute, still hard, still ready to go.

"Stand up and get on the bed."

We lept to our feet and scurried over to his king-sized bed. Since he didn't tell us how to get on the bed, we piled in as if we were going to sleep, pulling the covers back and climbing onto the cool white sheets. We looked back at him as he stood watching us, a slight smirk on his face. He looked delighted at the sight of us which warmed my heart. He had no idea how happy he made me feel.

"My gorgeous girls," he said, his eyes warm and inviting before he moved towards us.

My body vibrated with need. This man had no idea what he did to me. Olivia squirmed next to me and I assumed she felt the same way. We had both fallen for this man we could never have but I quickly pushed that thought away as I reminded myself to focus on the moment. I needed to make the most of it.

He climbed on the bed until he was looming over us. We sunk back into the soft bed, on our backs, looking up at him, as if he was about to devour us. He held himself up by his powerful arms, his muscles flexing, showing us his power and authority.

He leaned in and kissed me on the lips, soft at first and then more demanding. I kissed him back, wanting to wrap my arms around him and pull him in closer but I didn't dare. Instead, I laid back and enjoyed the sensation of his lips against mine and the arousal it stirred deep inside me.

Just as I was sinking into it, all thoughts forgotten, he broke the kiss and smiled at me before moving on to kiss Olivia. My lips felt plump from his kiss and instead of peeking over to watch him kiss Olivia, I stared up at the ceiling and wondered how I got here.

A friend had shown me an ad in the college paper talking about a well-paying opportunity for college-aged women. There weren't a lot of details in the ad but it was intriguing enough to make the call. The money itself was substantial. That's the first thing the woman on the other end of the phone told me before going into more detail about the island and what would be expected of me. She said it was only for six months and I would be free to leave whenever I wanted minus the compensation.

I had always wondered about this type of lifestyle and had often fantasized about being taken, kidnapped perhaps, and forced to do all sorts of sexual things. I thought it could be a dream come true and signed up immediately. I had just dropped out of college and had no idea what I was going to do next. It felt like synchronicity and I didn't question it.

Master Grant broke the kiss from Olivia, snapping me back to the present moment. He looked at me then her, a sly smile on his lips.

"I want you to kiss each other," he said. "I'll watch."

Olivia and I were lying side by side. We turned to each other, smiles on our faces. I felt giggly and a little unsure. I had always felt a little something with Olivia. We had kissed before, obviously, but here in Master Grant's bed, it felt different. More intimate. More real.

She reached out and touched me first, trailing her fingers across my bottom lip. I opened my mouth slightly giving her better access, my eyes never leaving hers. Her eyes were hooded but intense as they watched her fingers move over me. I wanted to suck her fingers in, to taste them, but I also wanted her to take full control. I didn't want to interrupt what she was doing because I felt mesmerized by it.

Her hand moved lower until it brushed against my erect nipples. I sucked in my breath at her touch, gentle like a whisper. She feathered her fingers across them again and again, sending arousal through me. I wanted to arch into her hand, to do something, but I bit my lip and allowed her to tease my delicate buds.

I felt Master Grant's eyes on us. I didn't dare look at him. He had pushed himself back so he was watching us from the edge of the bed.

Olivia pinched one nipple and pulled and I couldn't help groaning in ecstasy. I felt raw and exposed. A rush of emotions and sweet sensations poured through me, my head blank. I felt lost and found and like I never wanted her to stop touching me.

She pinched and pulled the other one. This time I leaned into it. I started to pant, short shallow breaths, as she took both nipples between her fingers and pulled.

Just when I didn't think I could take it anymore, her lips found mine, soft and plush. She kept a firm grip on my nipples as her mouth melted onto mine. Our tongues mingled, tasting and exploring. She tasted sweet and fresh. She felt soft and pliable.

I reached out and found her erect nipples and brushed over them. She sighed into my mouth at the touch. I gripped and pulled on her nipples as she continued to grip mine. She sighed into my mouth as I deepened the kiss, euphoria washing over me. I had never been with a woman like this, with such passion. Earlier it had been about putting on a show. I had enjoyed it but this was something else. This was more like a moment, a true connection, something I would remember for the rest of my life.

As we kissed and explored each other's nipples, pulling and pinching, causing exquisite pain and delight, I felt my legs being spread and a thick cock slipped easily into me. I bucked my hips as the cock filled me, my mouth still on hers, almost coming apart from it all. I was on my side so Master Grant had maneuvered behind me as his cock started to plow into me, hitting my G-spot in a way that made me scream. My body convulsed around him as I nearly lost consciousness as the biggest orgasm of my life overtook me. I swear I passed out for a second.

Master Grant continued to fuck me through it, pushing me over the edge again, until I was lost and came all over again.

He chuckled as he pulled out, his cock still hard. I had my eyes closed, my mouth on Olivia's, the kiss continuing. I felt her stiffen as I assumed Master Grant slid into her. I felt the rhythm of him fucking her through the kiss. Her mouth didn't leave mine but she stopped kissing me, all thought probably seeping out of her head as he started to pound into her.

I pinched and pulled on her nipples until she bucked against me. Master Grant quickened his pace until Olivia was screaming against my mouth, her whole body shuddering.

"That's it," Master Grant said. "Come for me, Olivia."

Master Grant fucked her through her orgasm before he stilled, releasing himself inside her. He smacked her ass before collapsing on the bed behind her.

I opened my eyes and met his over Olivia's slumped body. They were intense and pierced right through me. His lips curled into a smile. My heart hammered like mad. He pulled Olivia's limp body towards him and rested his chin on her shoulder, his eyes never leaving mine. Olivia had her eyes closed, her breathing settling into deep steady breaths, oblivious to the palpable tension rising between Master Grant and me. The air turned electric. I felt like everything changed. My head spun with it, confused and excited.

He reached around Olivia and pulled on one of her nipples. She groaned but didn't open her eyes. It looked like she had fallen into a light sleep. He squeezed her generous breast, fondling her, as his eyes stayed on me. Even though he wasn't touching me, I felt like he was. I felt like he was looking right through me, seeing deep into my soul.

A small smile formed on his lips as he studied me, his hands wandering over Olivia's sleeping body. She was curled up against his chest and for once I wasn't insanely jealous. Somehow she felt like she was meant to be here with us, curled up, part of us. I wanted to reach out to touch her, too, share her with him but I didn't want to disrupt the moment.

"Mr. Martin wants to acquire both of you," Master Grant said after a minute in a whisper. "He wants you both to be part of his household here. He wants to have the paperwork drawn up as soon as possible."

My stomach clenched as his words sunk in. A frisson of fear passed through me.

"I told him that it'd be in his best interest if he allowed Olivia to finish her training at the facility," Master Grant continued. "I also told him that Luke would allow you to come here to freshen up your training. He doesn't know that you were just here doing advanced training."

I wanted to scream or cry or do something but I could only stare at Master Grant, my heart sad and defeated. I knew Mr. Martin wanted us. He'd made it clear. I knew there'd be other women, of course there would be, and I also knew that Luke wouldn't be able to put up much of a fight considering how much he had to lose if he said no. I was in a no-win situation. The only thing I could do was leave the island and I wasn't sure I was ready to do that.

"I see your mind spinning," Master Grant said. "I'm not happy about this either. I managed to buy us another week and I'll figure this out. Do you trust me?"

"Yes, Master Grant," I said, my voice small. I did trust him but I doubted he could do anything.

"Good," he said. "Don't you worry about it. Let me take care of everything."

SIXTEEN

Master Grant woke me up the next morning with a kiss. He was positioned over me, his lips hard on mine, and I automatically yielded to him. My body jumped to life as he deepened the kiss. I opened my eyes and he was staring straight at me, his eyes filled with heat and something else. His hand came up and cupped my breast, his thumb rubbing lazy circles over my erect nipple.

He kicked my legs apart before slipping into me, his cock filling me. I raised my hips to meet him, wanting all of him. He broke the kiss to smile at me.

"You're being a little greedy this morning, aren't you?" he asked in a teasing way as he increased his pace.

I gripped the sheets as I gave myself over to the rolling sensations of pleasure washing over me as his cock filled me again and again. I felt myself edging towards bliss, threatening to spill over while wanting to hold back as long as possible.

He must have sensed my reluctance to let go because just as I thought I couldn't hold back anymore, he said, "Come for me, Riley."

I exploded, bucking with my release, my body shaking around him, as he fucked me through a powerful orgasm. He pushed in a few more times before he stilled and spilled himself inside me. His eyes were on mine the whole time as if drinking me in. I knew this could be the last time he fucked me and my heart plummeted at the thought.

He leaned in and kissed me before pulling out and collapsing on the bed next to me. He pulled me into his arms and rested his chin on the top of my head. I wrapped my arms around him, inhaling his fresh scent, wanting nothing more than to be with this man forever. There was something about him that made me feel safe and secure. I knew he always had my best interest at heart and I couldn't help thinking about what life would be like if he was allowed to own me. I knew there'd be no way I'd leave the island if Master Grant was able to make me his.

Tears formed in my eyes at the thought since I knew it could never happen. Mr. Martin had staked his claim on us and I knew he wouldn't let go. He also didn't seem like the type of man who was willing to compromise. I was surprised that Master Grant had convinced him to allow Olivia and me to stay at the facility another week. I'm sure Master Grant had thought up something clever to stay to ensure Mr. Martin that it was in his best interest.

Master Grant wiped away my tears as he gently kissed my lips.

"I'll figure this out," Master Grant said. "Trust me."

The funny thing was I did.

MASTER GRANT WALKED with me to the dining hall after taking a quick shower with me where he washed my hair and soaped up my body. I clung to him like a little girl, his muscles hard beneath my hands. The sight of him fully naked took my breath away. I had only seen glimpses of his cock but never all of him all at once.

I hadn't asked where Olivia was because honestly, I didn't want to know.

When we walked into the dining hall, all the women from Olivia's class sat at the long table eating. I remembered at the last second to keep my eyes lowered. Master Owen was in the room along with another man I didn't recognize. I didn't want to get in trouble. I wanted to spend this last week under Master Grant's care as freely as possible.

I scooted in next to one of the women where there was an opening at the table without being directed. I hadn't been able to do a full sweep of the women so I didn't know if Olivia was among them. Even though I felt pangs of jealousy that she had somehow become part of what I had with Master Grant, I also felt oddly protective of her. I had been on the island much longer than her and I knew it wasn't always an easy place for a woman.

I ate with my head held low, eating without tasting, my head muddled with too many thoughts. It was disconcerting not knowing what was in store for me. With Luke, at least I sort of knew what my days would look like but now, I felt like a boat shipped out to sea without a sail. I felt lost, scared and uncertain. I didn't want to leave the island yet but I wasn't sure I could handle being under Mr. Martin's care. He didn't seem like the kind of man who would give much consideration to his women.

We cleared our plates as soon as we were done. One after the other, we lined up and handed them over to the kitchen women. I had no idea how they became kitchen women but they weren't collared. Perhaps they were the property of the facility. I didn't have long to consider this when Master Owen pulled me aside.

"You and Olivia are going back to Mr. Wood's house to entertain Mr. Martin," he said.

My heart plummeted. I knew I shouldn't be surprised but I was.

"I will take you over there since Master Grant is needed here."

I had a feeling there was more to that than Master Grant being busy but of course, I didn't say anything. I kept my eyes lowered, accepting my fate for the day.

Master Owen led me over to where Olivia stood. He clipped leashes onto our collars and walked us out the door. The sun was shining as usual but I wasn't able to appreciate it. I kept my eyes lowered, concentrating on Master Owen's shoes as he walked in front of us. I didn't bother looking at Olivia. I wondered where she had been this morning but knew it didn't matter. If Mr. Martin ended up acquiring us, I felt like not much in my life would matter anymore.

We didn't pass many people as we walked to Mr. Wood's house. Only a few men were out. Some men groped us but that was it. I didn't mind. I barely noticed. It was interesting how quickly things became commonplace and started not to matter.

The walk to Mr. Wood's house felt like the march to my execution. Perhaps not that dramatic but I knew my life on the island as I knew it would be over. I knew my one on one time with Master Grant was definitely over. I missed him already. He already felt lost to me as Master Owen pushed open Mr. Wood's front door and led us inside.

Mr. Martin stood waiting for us. He practically squealed with excitement when he saw us, snatching our leashes from Master Owen.

"I see you brought back my sluts," Mr. Martin said. "It's only a technicality until they're officially mine."

"They're all yours for the day," Master Owen said. "I'll be back to collect them this evening. I understand Mr. Wood has you otherwise engaged this evening."

"Yea, some meeting or something," Mr. Martin said. "The sluts can come with me, sit at my feet and keep me company."

"They're required back at the training facility," Master Owen said, "but I assure you we'll do everything we can to ensure they're yours very soon."

With that, Master Owen left us alone with Mr. Martin. My heart hammered. Anxiety crawling up my skin but I was relieved to hear we wouldn't be with him all night. Having a time limit made it more bearable.

Mr. Martin pulled us in close by our leashes as if he couldn't be bothered to step towards us. We stumbled on our heels at the sharp tug but moved closer as commanded. Mr. Martin circled his hands around our asses, pulling us in hard against him.

His mouth was between our ears as he breathed out heavily. "We're going to have a fun time today, sluts, and before the week is out, you're both going to be mine."

I swallowed, willing myself not to think about it, as his hand slipped around my backside until he found my asshole. He slipped a finger in, startling me, impaling me there. I assumed he had done the same to Olivia because she sucked in her breath. He slipped his finger out and slapped my ass before slipping his finger between my lips. I opened automatically, trying not to think where it had just been. I sucked it clean, knowing I had no choice, and swallowed it down, trying not to gag.

"Good sluts," he said. "Willing to eat shit. Good to know. Now kneel."

We slipped to our knees, positioned side by side, palms up on our thighs. Mr. Martin undid his dress slacks and popped out his cock. He approached Olivia first, sliding it into her mouth. She took him in as he fucked her face, his hand on her head for leverage, grunting with each thrust.

After a minute, he slipped out and approached me. I obediently opened my mouth, allowing his cock to enter. He grabbed my head and started to fuck my mouth. I kept it open but didn't use my tongue like I normally would. I didn't want to make it any better than it already was. I hoped that there was some chance that he'd find some other woman he liked better than me and would let me remain with Luke.

He popped his cock out before slapping me hard across the face.

"There was no effort there, slut. Next time I put my cock in your mouth, you will suck it. Got it, slut?"

"Yes, sir," I said, my eyes still lowered.

He slapped me again as if for good measure. My face stung but I knew it could be worse.

"Stand, sluts," Mr. Martin commanded.

We immediately stood before him, arms at our sides.

His eyes raked over us as he examined us. He reached out and pinched one of my nipples before slapping my breast. He did the same to Olivia.

"We're going to stay here today because I want to experience what life will be like once you're mine. Lance has given me his place for the day and he assured me that we won't be interrupted."

I swallowed. Was there anyone monitoring us? It didn't sound like it.

"You will do whatever I command or else you'll be punished. And you won't like the punishment. Do you understand?"

"Yes, sir," we said in unison.

"Good. Now to get started, from here on out, I want you bitches on your hands and knees at all times unless I tell you otherwise. You are to walk this way, too, on all fours like the pathetic sluts you are. Now get down."

I sank to my hands and knees with Olivia beside me. I felt like I was being transformed into someone's pet and I didn't like it. I reminded myself that I only needed to tolerate him for a short time today and that would help get me through. I could manage anything for a limited amount of time.

He came around us and smacked our asses one after the other several times until I felt the heat of it. He seemed to delight in this because he continued longer than necessary, slapping me then Olivia again and again. He slipped a finger inside my pussy without warning, hooking his finger inside me. I wasn't particularly aroused but more agitated. He pushed it deeper as if that was going to do something.

He pulled out then slapped my ass. I jumped slightly and he slapped me again.

"I want both of you sluts to be wet for me at all times," he said as if this was something we could do. "If not, expect to be punished. Now follow me."

He walked ahead of us as we trailed behind on all fours over the hard marble tile and out onto the back patio. The pool sparkled, reflecting the dazzling sunlight, and I wished I had the luxury of diving in and going for a cool swim. Part of me yearned for my old life, for being able to do whatever I wanted and not being at the command of some man I didn't like. I knew if I stayed, this would be my life, being led around and used in ways I might not be happy about.

He walked over to one of the loungers and plopped down. Not knowing what to do, I kneeled next to him and waited. Olivia took my lead and did the same. He proceeded to ignore us as he flipped through his iPad for the next hour. The hot sun baked down on us and I wondered if our fair skin was burning. I kept my eyes down, happy for the break, letting my mind wander to happier things.

Master Grant popped up first thing. I wondered what he was doing at that moment. He was probably finishing up the training of Olivia's class, instructing them how to be proper sluts, subservient and obedient to the men here, telling and showing them exactly what was expected of them. I assumed he thought Olivia was getting enough life experience not to need to finish up the class. I knew Mr. Martin was anxious to acquire us and I doubted Master Grant would want to delay the inevitable.

My heart plummeted at the thought. It may be time for me to leave. I wasn't sure I could handle being in Mr. Martin's household for long. I knew this was what I wanted to experience when I signed up to come but after having been with Luke and Master Grant, I wasn't sure I could go back to just this. I needed more and I knew that was my downfall.

Time slipped by, shade finally finding us. My stomach growled. It had to be well past lunchtime. Mr. Martin finally put his iPad on the side table and looked at us. My eyes were lowered but I had become adept at sensing movement around me. I wondered if he heard my stomach growl or, more likely, he was hungry himself.

He pushed himself up and wandered inside. We sat there waiting, not wanting to move unless instructed. I wondered for a moment if he had intended for us to follow and had simply forgotten, not being used to needing to tell us our every move, or if he intentionally left us sitting outside.

It didn't take him long to come back with a plate full of food and a couple of drinks. I tried not to be hopeful as he approached and settled back down on the lounge chair while my stomach growled in protest. I could take not eating until dinner. It wouldn't be the most challenging thing I've done since coming here.

He opened a bottle of water and handed it to Olivia. She took it without a word, almost unsure what to do with it.

"Drink," he finally said.

Without hesitation, Olivia drank the whole thing down.

He handed me the other bottle of water and told me to drink, too. I was grateful for the nourishing water as it made its way down, cooling me as it went. I hadn't realized how thirsty I had become.

I handed the bottle back when I finished. He took it without a word before he dug into his plate of food. After a few minutes, he looked back to us and handed each of us a quarter of a turkey sandwich piled high with avocado and cheese.

"You'll need your strength for later," he said. "I've been told to be sure to feed and water you, like proper pets. You may use the bathroom inside once you're done. I have fun plans for the afternoon."

Olivia and I went inside, crawling on all fours, after we finished our sandwiches. I was grateful to have a moment away from him but knew if we talked, we'd need to be careful what we said. The house was monitored and even if no one was there now, the tapes could always be reviewed.

We found the bathroom next to the kitchen. It was all white and opulent with light streaming in from the large unadorned windows. We used the facilities and washed up. I splashed cool water over my face and arms, unpleased with the spread of red against my skin. Olivia had the same reddish glow. I gulped down more water while I had the chance, unsure when my next chance would be.

"Is this how life is here?" Olivia asked in a whisper.

"I have a bad feeling for us this is how it will be if Mr. Martin has his way. I know he wants to acquire us."

Olivia didn't look happy at this revelation. I had no idea how she didn't know where this was heading.

"Luke, my current owner, is nothing like this. I have a lot of freedom with him. But he came to the island a bit reluctantly. He's Mr. Wood's brother and only came because of him. I doubt he'd have any women except his brother insisted. Now he's in love with Annabelle, his other woman, and I've been left to kind of just hang out. Until now."

I knew I shouldn't feel sorry for myself but I did. I did have it good. Why couldn't I have been happy with that? I knew I had it easy compared to most of the women here. Most of the men on the island were more like Mr. Martin, wanting nothing more than sex slaves and possibly house cleaners and cooks.

"Are most of the men like Mr. Martin here?" she asked, her eyes huge.

"I'm starting to think they are."

SEVENTEEN

The afternoon happened in a blur. I zoned out during most of it, imagining myself elsewhere or nowhere at all. Mr. Martin toyed with our bodies out by the pool, slipping his fingers inside us, pinching and pulling on our nipples, making us kiss and grope each other. I didn't mind kissing and groping Olivia. Her skin was soft and receptive. Being with Olivia helped me get through the afternoon and helped arouse me enough to satisfy Mr. Martin when pushed his fat cock into my pussy.

He fucked us both, alternating, while we had our asses and pussies in the air, presented to him. Thankfully we were positioned on an outdoor rug that kept our knees from scraping against the concrete tiles. He pulled out and came across our backs, marking us in a way that seemed to please him. He smacked our asses several times until the heat spread through them.

He slipped his fingers inside me, flicking my clit with his thumb, probably trying to coax an orgasm out of me. I felt aroused enough to be wet but I was nowhere close to being able to climax. He must have figured this out quickly because his fingers left me before sliding into Olivia.

After several minutes and some intense nipple pinching and pulling, he managed to get an orgasm out of her.

He smacked her ass before saying, "Finally," under his breath. "You sluts are a lot of work."

I wanted to giggle but didn't dare. Maybe he wouldn't be so eager to acquire us now. I knew a lot of the women didn't care who they ended up with and expected this sort of treatment, actually getting off on it. I felt too spoiled now after living with Luke to want this base level of submission. I hated myself for wanting more.

Master Owen came back in the late afternoon to collect us as promised. Mr. Martin looked disappointed but didn't protest. Master Owen clicked leashes to our collars and led us out of the house without a word. We walked back into town. A few hands found us but no one bothered to stop us. I wondered if that had to do with Master Owen. I assumed men knew who he was by now.

Instead of leading us back to the training facility, Master Owen walked us to Luke's neighborhood. My heart hammered. I couldn't remember the last time I saw Luke. Was Master Owen going to tell Luke about Mr. Martin's plan to acquire me? My head spun as we got closer to Luke's place. I was also surprised that Olivia was being taken with me.

Master Owen had barely knocked on Luke's door when Luke opened it with a huge smile. Luke engulfed me in a hug, surprising me.

"I feel like I haven't seen you in forever, Riley," he said as he pulled back, his hands gripping my shoulders as he took me in. I kept my eyes lowered even though I knew Luke didn't mind me looking at him. I did it more due to Master Owen's presence than anything else. I didn't want to show Luke any disrespect in front of him. "Come in. All of you."

Master Owen looked hesitant but stepped into the house with Olivia behind him.

Luke unhooked my leash which spurred Master Owen to unhook Olivia's. I felt freer already. I wished there was some way I could stay with Luke and not be handed over to Mr. Martin. I knew I couldn't stay on the island if Mr. Martin ended up with me and I wasn't ready to leave.

"You need to stay for dinner," Luke said. "Annabelle is cooking something to celebrate Riley's return."

His words shocked and warmed me. I knew Annabelle wasn't one to cook but she must have been making an effort since I wasn't around to do it.

"Should I help her, Luke?" I asked, knowing he didn't mind me initiating conversation. I felt Olivia's shock at my asking him. I was happy to show her a different side of how things could be on the island.

"Oh no, don't worry about that," Luke said. "I'm sure you've been through enough the past few days and could use a rest. Why don't we move into the dining room. Dinner will be served shortly."

Master Owen looked reluctant but followed Luke into the dining room. The table was set for six which surprised me. I dreaded thinking Mr. Martin or Mr. Wood could be the sixth guest. Maybe Annabelle wasn't sure how many there would be and added an extra just to be sure. That would be like her.

Luke directed us to the chairs, pulling out chairs for me and Olivia while motioning to Master Owen which chair to take. Luke had positioned me next to him with Olivia on my other side and Master Owen next to her. The chairs on Luke's other side and next to that one remained open.

A warmth washed over me as I took in the scent of roasted chicken coming from the kitchen. I hadn't noticed it until I sat down. My mind had been overloaded with seeing Luke again.

Luke reached under the table and squeezed my leg. It was more reassuring than sexual. I turned to him and smiled.

"It's good to have you back," Luke said. "Unfortunately I'm not sure how long I'll be able to keep you."

My heart plummeted.

Before he could say anything else, Annabelle appeared with a platter of roasted chicken and an assortment of vegetables. Luke hopped up to help her bring it to the table. Annabelle was dressed in a sheer Kelly green dress that highlighted her eyes. Her nipples were erect and pointing directly at Luke. She looked happy. If the island hadn't injected all of the women with powerful birth control shots, I would have suspected she was knocked up. She glowed.

Just as Annabelle settled in next to Luke, the doorbell rang. I jumped to my feet without thinking and went for the door. I swung it open and my heart stopped as I saw Master Grant standing there. I felt so overwhelmed, I didn't know where to look. I took in his black t-shirt that hugged his well-defined muscles and his black jeans, my heart hammering. I ached to lean into him but lowered my eyes and moved aside so he could enter.

"Riley," he said, his voice low and husky, sending tingles through me.

He moved passed me, his voice trailing over my bare stomach, sparking something deep inside me. I wore nothing but heels and my black collar. Clothes didn't matter to me anymore. He gave me one last look before moving towards the dining room. I followed, my eyes lowered, my heart threatening to beat out of my chest.

Luke stood to greet Master Grant, shaking his hand as he said, "I'm so happy you could join us. I wanted to thank you for taking such good care of my girl."

I swallowed hard as I sat. If he only knew how true that was.

"It's good to be here," Master Grant said before settling into the chair between Annabelle and Master Owen. "It's been a pleasure taking care of Riley. She's been nothing but a delight."

Master Grant's words warmed me. A blush crept up my chest and flooded my face. I prayed no one noticed.

Once everyone was settled, Annabelle served, scooping piles of chicken and vegetables on everyone's plates, starting with Luke then the men then us. I felt bad for not helping but knew this was Annabelle's show. It was like she was the woman of the house and Luke was the man of the house. I wondered if couples got married here. I wouldn't be surprised if they did.

Annabelle sat down and everyone dug in once Luke started.

"I understand Mr. Martin wants to acquire Riley," Luke said after a minute.

I knew I shouldn't have been surprised but it startled me. This was real. I kept my eyes lowered as I tried not to react.

"Unfortunately, yes," Master Owen said. "He's taken a liking to Riley and Olivia and has gone as far as to say he won't invest in the new casino if he's not guaranteed them as his first acquisition."

My heart dropped.

"I see," Luke said, his voice serious. "I didn't realize he had made that ultimatum."

"He's expressed it several times to us," Master Owen said, indicating himself and Master Grant. "I'm surprised he hasn't discussed it with you. After all, he can only acquire Riley if you agree to sell her."

I kept my eyes lowered and stopped eating, hanging on every word.

"True," Luke said. "I can only speculate that he's waiting for the deal to be closer to being finalized before he springs this on me. He seems like that kind of guy."

"I wouldn't put it past him," Master Owen agreed.

"Do you plan to sell her?" Master Grant asked. His voice had a hard edge to it.

"My brother needs this deal to go through," Luke said. "I don't want to do it but I don't think I have much choice."

Luke turned to me, his hand back on my thigh.

"I'm sorry, Riley," Luke said. "This deal could make or break the success of the island. It would open up more opportunities for the men and women here. It's out of my hands."

I swallowed, my heart in my shoes. I couldn't believe this was happening. I hated that Luke didn't think there was anything he could do. He had given up on me and that stung. I doubted he'd let Annabelle go like this.

I swallowed down the jealousy that threatened to overtake me and said in a small voice, "I understand, Luke. It'll be fine."

He squeezed my leg again before returning to his dinner. I kept my eyes lowered, afraid I was going to cry. There was no way I could look at Master Grant. I felt my heart breaking over all the silly possibilities

I thought I could have with him. I had always been kidding myself. There was no way I could be with Master Grant, especially now. I would be stuck with Mr. Martin and could only pray that he'd give me up when someone shinier and prettier came along. Or I could leave the island. That was always an option but not one I wanted to take. I knew I'd miss everyone too much. I felt out of options.

Luke discussed the impending changes happening on the island with Master Owen and Master Grant, including the new casino Mr. Martin was planning to bring the island and exactly how it would benefit everyone. It sounded like it would offer more job opportunities for the women. Even though they were compensated for being here and wouldn't be given a salary at whatever job they held, it was a way for them to socialize and feel useful. Not a lot of women wanted to sit around the house all day waiting to be used.

Luke talked about how these added jobs would help retain women on the island by making them feel more useful and giving them an additional sense of purpose. The casino would also generate additional income for the conglomerate that supported the island, including the women's compensation. It was a way for the island to generate income for itself to be fully sustainable. Up until now, Mr. Wood had bankrolled much of the island's expenses with the restaurants and shops making up a small portion. He had started the training facility as a way to help increase the women's retention rate as well but he was currently paying for most of that himself.

The more I listened to the men discuss it, the more I realized Luke had no choice but to let me go. He couldn't let me be the one thing that stood in the way of the island becoming self-sufficient. I could always leave but besides not wanting to, I didn't want to do that to the island. I could stick it out another six months if I had to in order to make everyone happy. Then I could decide from there what I wanted. Maybe it wouldn't be so bad.

THE EVENING ENDED with the men sipping cordials in the living room while the women cleaned up. I didn't mind. It was nice to focus on something other than my impending acquisition by Mr. Martin. We cleared the dining table as soon as the men moved to the living room, their conversation moving to how well the training facility was doing. It sounded like another shipment of women was due to arrive and the current class was ready to be auctioned, Olivia included.

I stacked dishes in the dishwasher while Annabelle put the leftovers away. Olivia looked at us wide-eyed as if she was unsure what to do.

"You can speak freely in Luke's house," Annabelle told Olivia, "but keep your voice lowered so Master Owen and Master Grant don't overhear. I'm not sure they'd like it."

"Oh, OK," Olivia said as she sagged against the counter. "How can I help?"

"Just relax," Annabelle said. "Riley and I have this. There's not much to do."

I continued to stack the dishwasher, not wanting to think about Olivia and my predicament. I didn't want to discuss it but part of me felt I should reassure Olivia in some way. The problem was I wasn't feeling very reassured myself. I knew life with Mr. Martin would be difficult, probably worse than what we've already endured.

"You seem really happy," Olivia said in a whisper to Annabelle.

Annabelle smiled. "I am. I'm one of the lucky ones. I don't like the idea of you being handed over to this Mr. Martin to seal the deal. I'm guessing he's not that great."

Olivia let out a heavy sigh. "He's not. I assumed the men here wouldn't be overly sympathetic to the women but Mr. Martin seems like he doesn't care at all."

"That sounds awful," Annabelle said. "Is there any way to get out of it?"

"You know how it works here," I said, feeling irritated. "The women don't have a choice. We can either stay and do what they want or leave. That's the only choice we have."

I finished with the dishwasher and closed it with a slam. I was upset at myself for not dealing with this better but I was bubbling over with injustice. I knew coming here that I wouldn't have a choice, that was how this island worked, and I had agreed to that. I knew what I was getting into. But now it felt unfair and I wasn't sure how to handle it.

"Sorry," I said after a minute. "I knew what this place was about and I wanted to experience it. I just wasn't prepared for the reality of it."

Annabelle put her hand on my shoulder.

"I get it," she said. "I had a rough time in the beginning, too. I was lucky, I know, with Luke but my life with Mr. Wood before Luke wasn't easy. I endured a lot but I feel like it was worth it, all part of the experience of being here. It made me stronger, more adaptable and more ready to live this lifestyle for the long haul. I know it's hard now but trust that everything will work out. Chances are you won't be with Mr. Martin forever. He sounds like the type of man that has a short attention span. That could be to your benefit."

Olivia looked slightly relieved but didn't say anything. I knew what Annabelle was saying was probably true, that I had to trust this or else give it up completely. The real challenge was wanting something I couldn't have. Even though it worked out for Annabelle, that didn't mean it would work out for me. Life wasn't like that.

Annabelle wiped down the counters, finishing our chore. The men's voices drifted in from the living room but we couldn't make out what they were saying. I felt like we should entertain them but I wasn't sure what to do. What I wanted to do was crawl into my old room and fall asleep for several days. Exhaustion washed over me.

"Let's bring the men some sweets," Annabelle said after a minute. "We can each take them a plate. I'll bring one to Luke. Olivia, you bring one to Master Owen and, Riley, you bring one to Master Grant."

Heat crept up my face as I accepted a little plate filled with two chocolate chip cookies and a decadent-looking fudge brownie from Annabelle. She handed one to Olivia and took one for herself before leading us into the living room.

Luke and Master Owen sat on the leather chairs while Master

Grant had the sleek leather sofa to himself. He sat at one end as if he was expecting company. The men smiled as we joined them, each woman going to the man Annabelle assigned her.

My nerves jumped as I approached Master Grant, my eyes lowered, my steps slow and steady. I kneeled before him, presenting him with the little plate of treats. I could almost feel his lips curl up into a smirk, amused by my submission before him. It felt personal in a way I hadn't experienced before. My back was to the others which helped me block them out. The other two men thanked Annabelle and Olivia but Master Grant said nothing.

He took the plate without a word. I kept my eyes lowered even though I ached to look at him. Anywhere else, maybe I would have risked it but here, with Luke present, I didn't dare. I felt that would have been a great disrespect to Luke and I didn't want to give him any additional incentive to get rid of me. I knew my time with him was precarious enough.

I sat back on my heels and waited, my eyes lowered, focused on Master Grant's boots, as conversation swirled around me. The men made positive comments about the treats, Luke especially raving about how much Annabelle had been spoiling him in my absence.

"She's a quick learner," Luke said. "Since Riley has been at the training facility recently, Annabelle has been studying some of the cookbooks and making great progress on her cooking skills. I couldn't be prouder."

A lump formed in my throat and I swallowed it down. It couldn't be more obvious that I wasn't missed. Annabelle quickly took my place as the cook of the house, making me unnecessary. Even though I knew Luke wasn't pushing to get rid of me, I felt more expendable than ever. My heart sank at the thought. I wanted to disappear into the floor. A wave of sadness washed over me, threatening to take me down.

"Riley cooks?" Master Grant asked, his voice smooth.

Luke let out a little laugh. "Riley's a fabulous cook. She didn't know how when she first arrived but with a lot of determination and studying, she's become amazing at it. I'll have to have you by for one of her meals."

"I'd like that," Master Grant said, his voice low, like a caress. "Let's make that happen soon."

"Why don't you come tomorrow night?" Luke said. "I'll keep Riley with me for the day so she can shop and prep. I need to run into the office but she'll be fine on her own. What do you think, Riley? Does that sound good to you?"

"Yes, Luke," I said, my heart hammering at the thought of cooking for Master Grant. "I'd like that very much."

"Good," Luke said. "It's settled. Come by around seven and we'll do dinner. Master Owen, you're more than welcome to join us. We can make a night of it."

"I'm afraid I must help entertain Mr. Martin," Master Owen said, "so I won't be available but I appreciate the offer. I'm sure Riley's cooking is as wonderful as you say. She's a woman of many talents."

"Will Mr. Martin want the girls back tomorrow?" Luke asked. I could hear the concern in his voice.

"I'll make sure he doesn't," Master Owen said. "I'll bring him some of the other women to play with. He might not be happy but I'll explain that he doesn't want to settle on these two just yet, that perhaps some of the other women would be better suited for him. Don't worry. I'll convince him."

I let out the breath I'd been holding.

Master Grant shifted in front of me. I wanted to look into his eyes, read his expression, but I kept my eyes lowered. Master Grant placed the plate down on the coffee table next to me, his hand lightly grazing my shoulder before he sat back, sending a shiver through me.

Master Grant stood.

"We should go," Master Grant said. "Thank you for dinner. It was wonderful."

"You're always welcome," Luke said. "Thank you for taking care of Riley for me."

I couldn't believe my luck that I was being left at Luke's for the night and all the next day. I was excited to get back to a bit of normality.

"Would you like to keep Olivia for the night?" Master Grant asked, surprising me. "She could use some time away from the training facility. Plus she's bonded with Riley so it might be nice for Riley to show her around a bit tomorrow."

"Of course," Luke said. "Olivia is more than welcome."

"Good," Master Grant said. He was still standing in front of me, his power somehow comforting me. "I'll leave the black collar on her so she'll look owned. I'll take her back with me tomorrow night after dinner."

"That sounds perfect," Luke said. "See you tomorrow."

EIGHTEEN

I was practically bursting with excitement after Master Grant and Master Owen left. I stayed kneeled, in my place, but I couldn't believe my luck at being able to spend the next day doing basically whatever I wanted. I'd have to make dinner for everyone, probably shop and then prepare for that, but that was nothing after the last few days of servicing Mr. Martin. I wanted to squeal with joy but smiled to myself instead.

"Welcome back, Riley," Luke said when he came back to the living room after showing the masters out. "And welcome, Olivia. Please stand so I can see both of you."

I pushed myself up and joined Olivia in front of Luke. Annabelle started clearing plates and glasses, knowing this conversation didn't concern her.

"Very good," Luke said. "As Riley knows, you can relax and pretty much do what you want while you're in my house. You can talk to me and each other while I'm around. You have permission to sit on the furniture and to sleep on the beds. You can look me in the eyes. I'd actually prefer it."

I looked up at him. Luke smiled at me then moved his attention to Olivia.

"Since Annabelle's been sleeping with me, Olivia can take her room. Riley will get you settled. Please let me know if you have any questions. The only thing I won't permit is you leaving the house by yourself since you're new to the island and I'm responsible for you. But you both may go out tomorrow together. I'm sure Riley will want to get groceries for dinner. However, I want you to stay on the woman's side of town. Do you understand?"

"Yes, Luke," we said in unison. I was excited to be given so much freedom again. I had almost forgotten what it was like.

"Good," Luke said. "Annabelle will clean up while you two are free to spend the evening how you wish. Riley, show Olivia to Annabelle's room. And tomorrow, while you're out shopping, feel free to wear dresses. You don't need to be nude at all times around me, although I can't say I mind."

Luke gave us a little smirk. For a moment I thought he was going to reach out and graze our nipples or touch us in some way but he didn't. Instead, he gave us a smile and a look that said we were dismissed.

"Follow me," I said to Olivia before making my way to the stairs.

I didn't look back, knowing she'd follow. She had been taught to obey. I took a little pleasure in giving her that simple command.

Upstairs I showed her to Annabelle's room, flicking on the light. I wasn't surprised how clean and tidy it was. The room felt like a guest room with none of Annabelle's things anywhere. I had no doubt she spent zero time in here and would be surprised if her clothes were in the drawers.

Olivia looked around, her eyes wide, as she took it in. I closed the door behind us.

"This all looks so normal," she said. "There's even a bed."

I let out a laugh. "Luke doesn't buy into the whole women are property thing that a lot of the men believe here. He likes to keep things as normal as possible in his house, including letting us sleep in beds and sit on the furniture. But I'm afraid he may be the exception."

"What would it take to get Luke to acquire me?" Olivia asked.

I thought a moment. I knew Luke wasn't keen on having multiple women and honestly seemed like a one-woman kind of guy. I doubted he'd want to acquire anyone else but maybe there was a way to get him to acquire Olivia in order to save her from Mr. Martin.

"Maybe if I waited for him in his bedroom tonight," Olivia offered. "Show him what he could have?"

I wanted to laugh but I held it back. I knew that wouldn't work on Luke but I didn't want to hurt Olivia's feelings. Instead, I said, "Luke only has eyes for Annabelle so I wouldn't do that but I'm sure there has to be another way to convince him to bid on you. Maybe there's a chance Mr. Martin will like whatever women Master Owen hands over to him tonight so much that he will no longer be so keen on us. At least I hope so."

"Me, too," Olivia said. "I'm not sure I could handle Mr. Martin for long."

I pulled open a couple of Annabelle's drawers, surprised to find her dresses and gowns still tucked inside along with some of her work outfits. I pulled out one of Annabelle's sheer green dresses and held it up for Olivia to see.

"You can wear this tomorrow when we go out," I said, placing the garment in her hands. "The bathroom is across the hall so feel free to use it to shower or whatever whenever you want. There are all sorts of shampoos and such in there along with some makeup you're welcome to use. We'll head out first thing after breakfast. I'll show you around the women's side of town before getting whatever I need for dinner. Do you need anything else before I head back to my room? I need to just go to sleep."

Olivia looked at me with wide eyes, like she was a bit lost. My heart went out to her but my bed was calling. I hadn't realized how exhausted I was until the thought of a good night's sleep was finally in reach.

"Thank you," she finally said. "For everything. I'm not sure I could have gotten through all this without you."

My heart melted. I placed my hand on her shoulder. She tensed a little before looking down. A surge of something went through me. I lifted her chin so she had to look at me. Her green eyes looked uncertain. Something about her captivated me. I slowly leaned in and brushed my lips against hers. She gasped but didn't move, her eyes boring into mine, as I tasted her. She let out a sigh into my mouth that ran right through me.

My hand found its way to her hair as I pulled her toward me, my nipples brushing against hers, hard and wanting. I deepened the kiss, sinking into it. She opened up to me, allowing it, melting against me. She tasted sweet and savory, her lips soft and yielding. I closed my eyes and allowed myself to get lost in her for a moment. She didn't reach up to touch me and I didn't care. My whole focus was on her mouth and the vulnerability of her. She gave herself over to me so easily, kissing me back gently at first but then with more urgency.

My head spun as I continued to kiss her. I pulled on her hair, causing her to arch into me, her nipples grazing mine. I thought I was going to lose it. I pulled back and looked into her eyes, my hand still gripping her hair. Her eyes were wide and wild. Her breathing was shallow, a red blush across her chest. She looked haunted and beautiful. I had never been attracted to women before but there was something about her that pulled at me.

"You're beautiful," I said, my voice husky. "I want to taste you."

Her eyes widened even more.

"Can we do that?" she asked, her voice small.

"Who's going to know?" I asked. "Luke's house isn't monitored like Mr. Wood's or the training facility. Plus he'll be busy with Annabelle tonight. I guarantee it."

She looked at me for a minute. I could see the thoughts processing.

"Luke did say we could spend the evening any way we wanted," I said, feeling daring. I knew Luke wouldn't punish us even if he caught us together. He wasn't like that.

When she still didn't answer, I pushed her towards the bed, moving her until she fell back onto it. I spread her legs and kneeled in front of her, taking in her exposed pussy. Even though I was around naked women all the time, I rarely got to see them up close and personal.

I could smell Olivia's sweet arousal. I held her legs open as I took her in, captivated by the view. Her pussy looked like an ornate tropical flower, open and glistening. My mouth salivated at the sight.

I tentatively moved closer, reaching my tongue out until I lightly licked her delicate folds. She bucked her hips off the bed. I pushed her back down before burying my face in her sweet pussy. I slowly licked my way from the bottom to the top, stopping at her swollen clit, sucking it into my mouth. She tried to move under me but I managed to keep her still as my mouth worked over her, licking her again and again, not being able to get enough.

She gripped the comforter and let out a low moan as I sunk my tongue into her wet channel, my nose rubbing up against her clit. I had never done this before but was surprised by how much it turned me on. Feeling her squirm beneath me stirred something deep inside me, making me want to do more to please her. I wanted her to gush all around me, to let go for me. Suddenly I understood why men must find pleasing a woman so appealing.

I gripped her hips as I went down on her, pushing myself in as deep as I could, wanting to taste all of her. She squirmed beneath me, her breathing shallow, as I felt her getting close. I circled my tongue around her clit before sucking on it, causing her to moan and buck and finally let go. I sucked in her juices, a surge of pride and something else coursing through me. I felt satisfied and happy as I let go and sat back, looking at her exposed pussy all red and swollen in front of me.

I assumed my submissive pose naturally, hands on my thighs, as I watched her. Her body had gone slack, her legs still spread open, her pussy open and wanting. If I were a man, I could see the appeal of sinking into her, claiming her, making her gush all over again. She was beautiful how she was laid out before me, totally open, totally trusting.

I sat and waited, my heartbeat returning to normal. I didn't expect anything in return and, honestly, I didn't want it. This was all about her. I would have leaned forward and licked her some more if I didn't know from experience that she'd be tender and sensitive. I imagined her giggling if I tried, squirming away from me. The thought made me smile.

After a few minutes, she propped herself up on her elbows and looked at me down her body. Her green eyes were hooded and heavy, completely satisfied, as she took me in. I smiled at her, my heart full.

"What about you?" she asked.

I smiled. "This was all about you. I wanted to taste you. That's all. I got what I wanted."

I watched her as her body reacted. Her nipples hardened. Her eyes dilated.

"That was incredible," she said in a whisper. "Thank you. I needed that."

"Thank you," I said. "I never did that before but it was better than I had anticipated."

She let out a little laugh. "You seemed like an expert. How did you know what to do?"

"I just went with what I wanted to do," I said honestly. "My yearning to taste you surprised me but I'm so happy you let me do it."

"You can do that anytime. Now get up here so I can kiss you."

———

WE KISSED and fondled each other until we fell asleep in each other's arms. I never made it back to my room and I was OK with that. The morning came too soon, the sun waking me as it streamed in through the window. Olivia was still wrapped around me, sleeping heavily. I hated to wake her but I knew I needed to get us moving so I could get everything done in time for dinner.

I wiggled out from under her. She let out a little protest before curling up with a pillow. I liked watching her sleep, looking fully relaxed. I pulled the sheet up around her even though the room was hot enough. Something about her made me want to take care of her, protect her in some way. I knew there wasn't much I could do for her here but I wanted to do whatever I could.

I took a quick shower and slipped into a blue sheer dress, one of my favorites, before going down to the kitchen. Luke and Annabelle were gone already, probably to their jobs, which in a way was a relief. I grabbed an apple out of the fridge before sitting down at the counter to decide on the menu for tonight. I knew I wanted to make it special but also not too over the top. My cooking skills weren't that advanced but I wanted to impress Master Grant. I knew it didn't matter in the grand scheme of things—I'd more than likely be shipped off to Mr. Martin anyway—but it mattered to me to impress him at least a little, sort of a last hurrah.

I pulled out my cookbooks and got to work thinking through the menu complete with a starter course, a small salad, entree and dessert. I knew it'd be a lot but I had Olivia to help me. I knew she was good at following orders and nothing on the menu was too complex for her to handle.

I completed the list before going back upstairs to rouse Olivia. I leaned over and gently kissed her forehead before shaking her awake. She groaned in protest which made me smile. I knew they weren't this easy on her at the training facility and it was funny how quickly she reverted back to how she probably was in real life.

"Olivia, you need to get up," I said, keeping my voice soft. "We need to go shopping and I want to show you around town."

I kept shaking her until she stirred. Her eyes slowly opened, taking me in. I smiled at her as she started to wake up. I wouldn't have been surprised if she had forgotten where she was.

"Good morning," I said once she looked fully awake. "Take a quick shower and put on the dress I gave you yesterday. We can hit up one of the cafés on the women's side of town before we hit the shops. I think we both deserve a little treat. I'll meet you downstairs. Hurry up."

I left her without a glance back, trusting that she'd hurry. I was back in the kitchen when I heard the shower turn on. I smiled to myself. This was going to be a fun day.

NINETEEN

I handed Olivia an apple as we walked out the door. The sun greeted us. The day felt full and bright, and I couldn't keep the smile off my face. We walked arm in arm, quickly making it to the women's side of town without any fuss. I told Olivia how we'd be free to talk there as long as no men were around, which they rarely were. They liked the women to have some space where they could relax and talk freely. I reminded her that the men on the island wanted to keep the women happy since without us, there'd be no point to the island.

The women's side of the island was bustling as usual. It was refreshing to hear women talking freely as they walked down the streets and sat outside at various cafés. I took Olivia to one of my favorite cafés that had outdoor seating facing the bay. Everything was seat yourself so I snagged us seats outside at a table for two. The waitress brought our menus immediately, smiling at us as she asked us what we wanted to drink. We both ordered decaf coffees before turning our attention back to the menus.

"This is amazing," Olivia said, looking around. "I haven't been here before."

"It is nice that they have this for us," I said. "This should be one of the first places they take new women."

"I agree. All the women here look happy."

I looked around, seeing the place as she must see it. I never noticed it before but the women did look happy. Besides the way they were dressed or not dressed, I could have easily thought we were anywhere. Most of the women were smiling, talking to each other, looking like they were enjoying themselves. It was a nice reminder that the island wasn't all about being used by the men, that maybe there was something more here for the women, too.

The waitress returned to take our orders. I ordered one of the specialty omelets while Olivia ordered waffles with strawberries. The waitress smiled at us, refilled our coffees and left.

"I can hardly believe I'm here," Olivia said, her eyes wide. I thought for a minute she meant the women's side of the island but then it dawned on me that she was probably talking about being on the island itself.

"What brought you here?" I asked, taking a sip of coffee. Even though it was decaf, it hit the spot. There was something special about having coffee out.

Olivia smiled at me, gave out a little laugh then sort of looked away.

"It started as a dare," she said, unable to look at me. "One of my friends saw the ad online—she was in some alternative forum or something—and we all dared each other to apply. For some reason, they contacted me and my friends said that I had to do it. I thought meeting with them would be harmless. After all, I knew I could always say no. We didn't know the full extent of what this entailed until I went to that first meeting and then, God, I don't know, it all kind of fell into place."

She finally looked at me, her eyes wide, uncertain yet also solid. Like she knew exactly what she was getting herself into.

"I get it," I said, placing my hand over hers. "I felt the same way."

Her eyes widened. "Really?"

I laughed. "Yea. It was scary for me, too, but somehow, deep inside, I knew this was what I wanted and needed. I felt drawn to do it."

"That's how it was for me, too," she said with a bit of excitement in her voice. "Once I went to that initial meeting and learned more about the island, I knew I had to come. I knew I needed to experience this. It wasn't even about the money but about needing to do this. I know that sounds crazy and like what woman would want this but I knew I needed to come."

"Look around," I said. "Every woman chose to be here. No one's forced. That's the one thing that made me feel comfortable about coming here. I like that they want the women to be just as happy as the men. Everyone gets what they want. Ideally, it'd be a win/win."

"Until you get sold to someone you don't want," Olivia said, her voice suddenly small.

"Sometimes even then," I said, a glimmer of realization hitting me. "Sometimes surrendering to someone you don't want to surrender to is the ultimate form of surrender. At least here we can be assured that we'll always be safe and cared for regardless of who owns us. Sure, I think I'd like it better if I were owned by someone like Luke who let me do more of what I want but now that I'm thinking about it, maybe being owned by someone like Mr. Martin could be exactly what I need. It's part of the reason I came here—to relinquish full control over to someone else. Maybe it shouldn't be someone we want."

I watched as Olivia took this in. I could see her mind churning over the idea.

The waitress took this moment to return with our orders. My stomach growled at the sight of the food. Olivia looked just as pleased.

"The one good thing is if we do end up with Mr. Martin," I said, "we'll probably be there together. I know we can make the most of it."

Olivia took in a deep breath before letting it out slowly.

"I hope so," she said. "I want to be here. I want to stay."

AFTER BREAKFAST I showed Olivia around the women's side of town, taking her into a few of the boutiques and the bookstore. I explained how Luke had an account everywhere and how he was always telling me to buy whatever I wanted. I tried to convince Olivia to let me buy her something but she refused.

"I don't want to take advantage of Luke's generosity," she said. "I already feel privileged enough for him letting me stay the night. This has been a much needed break. I'm not looking forward to going back to the training facility."

"It doesn't sound like you'll be there very much longer anyway," I said, holding up a beautiful sheer green gown that would have looked stunning on her. I knew Luke would have liked seeing her in it but I didn't want to force her. "It sounds like your class will be auctioned soon with maybe me joining you."

"Oh right," Olivia said. "The auction. Why aren't they letting Mr. Martin buy us outright? You'd think that'd be simpler."

I thought a moment. "Perhaps but I don't think that's how it's done. I know Mr. Wood likes to do things by the book. Also, it might help him bring in a greater price for us if we're auctioned. Mr. Martin won't be the only man bidding."

"Right," Olivia said. "I didn't think of that but it makes sense. Every little bit counts."

We hit up the market last. I gave Olivia a tour of the place in case her new owner sent her there to retrieve stuff. The women on staff were super friendly and always helpful, even going as far as to help think through menu ideas and hand out recipes. They knew we were all trying to impress our men and did whatever they could to help make that possible. That was another thing I enjoyed about the island —the way the women came together to support one another. We were all in this together. Rarely did I witness outright jealousy or anything malicious among the women. We were often challenged enough without adding to it.

I wished I could have shown Olivia even more but I didn't want to overwhelm her. We carried the groceries back to Luke's, thankfully not bothered by anyone as we made our way back. Maybe the groceries deterred them. I was happy not to be bothered since I had a lot of cooking to do before Master Grant showed up.

I put Olivia to work in the kitchen, having her chop stuff while I worked to bring everything together. She admitted she wasn't much of a cook but wanted to learn. I told her how I had been hopeless before I came to the island and how much I learned since being here.

"What motivated you to learn to cook?" Olivia asked while she chopped mushrooms for the salad.

"I wanted to do something useful. I wanted to be able to offer something other than my body. And Luke encouraged me. I think he got it that I wanted something more. Learning to cook gave me an outlet, something to focus on outside of sex and submission. It helped ground me. Plus it made me happy to cook for Luke. He's not much for cooking so I knew he'd appreciate my learning. He never fails to compliment me. The more he appreciates it, the more I want to learn."

"It must be hard thinking about leaving Luke," Olivia said. "He seems like a great guy."

I put down the knife to give her my full attention. I mulled her words around in my mind. Sure, I would miss Luke and the life he provided me but I realized I wasn't agonized over leaving him. I was more distressed about moving towards Mr. Martin.

"Luke is a great guy but honestly I'm not as sorry to be leaving this household as I am worried about going to Mr. Martin. Ever since Annabelle joined Luke's household, I've felt like a third wheel. Luke and Annabelle have tried in their ways to include me but it's obvious that Luke and Annabelle are meant to be more one on one. I think Luke's only kept me around because men are encouraged to keep more than one woman in their household otherwise it might turn into a more traditional relationship."

"And that's bad?"

I laughed. "It's not why most of the men come here. At least that's not how Mr. Wood wants this community to be. He has a vision for the island that doesn't include love and romance. At first, I bought into that premise and it's one of the reasons I wanted to come. I liked the idea of sex without complications. But now that I've been here a while and have seen Luke and Annabelle's relationship up close, I'm not sure what I want."

"Have you thought about leaving?"

"I have," I admitted, the words heavy on my tongue. "My contract is up soon and it's a consideration. I could leave with my full compensation and start my life over at home. I have friends and family that I miss and who think I'm away doing some charity thing. They would love to have me back home."

"Do you want to go?" Olivia asked. Her eyes were wide with worry. It suddenly hit me that I may be her only friend here and what it would mean to her if I left. I knew I couldn't stay for her or anyone but it squeezed my heart.

"I honestly don't know. I have a little time left to figure it out."

"I hope you stay," Olivia said, a shyness to her voice.

I put my hand over hers. "I appreciate that but I know you'll be fine either way. The women here are amazing."

TWENTY

During the rest of the dinner prep, Olivia and I talked about other things, keeping the conversation light. I showed her some tricks in the kitchen while she shared more about her life back home. She had graduated college with an arts degree but had spent the past couple of years drifting, working at various galleries, feeling like she was getting nowhere. She had dated but no one seemed to stick. She had never had a long term relationship and wondered if she was even cut out for one.

"The men only ever seemed to want one thing," Olivia said as we were finishing up, "so I figured why not come here and give into that. I wanted to experience what it would be like to give myself fully to men like this. I wasn't having any luck back home so I figured why not. Plus I've always had a high libido."

"Have you ever been with a woman before?" I couldn't help asking. The question had been on my mind for a while. I knew it was none of my business but I wanted to know more about her.

Olivia blushed. "God, no. I never felt so inclined. But with you, I don't know, it was different. Maybe it's about being in this place where everything is about sex and out in the open. I wanted to see what it would be like."

"And?" I asked, the curiosity killing me.

Olivia laughed. "And it's been amazing. Maybe I'm a lesbian."

"Or maybe you're bi. It doesn't need to be all or nothing. Lots of people fall somewhere in the middle. I never felt attracted to a woman before you but I've always felt open to it."

"I'm happy about that," Olivia said, her shyness back. "I like being with you."

"I like being with you, too," I assured her. "Hopefully whoever obtains us will let us play together."

"I hope so. I'd like that."

We finished dinner just before Luke returned with Annabelle. I assumed they had been in the office together. They were laughing when they came through the door. Annabelle wore her work outfit, a white button-down blouse with most of the buttons undone and a black pencil skirt. She looked happy and a bit flushed and I wondered if they had a quickie before coming home. Surprisingly, I no longer felt jealous but simply happy for them.

"Something smells delicious," Luke said as he came into the kitchen. "Do you need help with anything?"

"No," I said. "We're good. Just head out into the dining room and we'll bring everything in."

"Don't forget we have a guest coming tonight," Luke said, a twinkle in his eye.

"Got it," I said as if I could forget. "We'll be right in with everything."

Luke left with Annabelle as I pulled the roast out of the oven. I directed Olivia to bring in the little appetizers we had created while I finished assembling the salads. I wanted tonight to be perfect, to showcase my talents, and to be a wonderful evening for everyone. I had tried not to think about our guest all day, continuously pushing him out of my mind, but it was a challenge. I knew he was in every preparation I made for this evening despite my trying to not make it about him. Something inside me wanted to please him more than anything.

I jumped when I heard the knock at the door just as I was about to bring the salads into the dining room. Unsure whether I should scurry to answer the door, I froze, salads in my hands. Thankfully I heard Luke at the door greeting our guest. Male voices flooded the front hall, causing a creep of anxiety to worm its way through me.

I swallowed it down and proceeded to bring the salads to the dining room. It'd take two trips and I wanted to get it completed as quickly as possible. I kept my eyes lowered even though that wasn't required in Luke's house, not wanting to meet the gaze of our guest.

I was headed back to the dining table when I came face to face with Master Grant. I inadvertently looked at him, his dark blue eyes penetrating as he took me in. I froze, my mind going blank, as my whole body reacted to him. Every part of me yearned for him. I quickly diverted my eyes but not before I saw the glimmer of amusement in them and something else, something deeper.

"Hello, Riley," he said, his voice deep and low. "How are you this fine evening?"

I kept my eyes lowered as I answered, "Hello, Master Grant. I'm well. How are you?"

"Fine now that I'm here. It's been a long day."

I wanted to ask him about his day like a normal couple would but I knew better than to ask. Instead, I kept my eyes lowered and made my way into the dining room with the rest of the salads. I felt him follow me. My face flushed at the thought of him watching my ass through the sheer dress. Even though he had seen me a thousand times before, tonight it felt more intimate, like friends gathering instead of women being summoned by men.

I set the salads down and took my usual seat. Annabelle was already seated with Luke tucked in beside her. It was only after I sat down that I realized that Master Grant would be sitting next to me with Olivia on his other side.

Master Grant slid into his seat, his hand finding its way to my thigh, before directing Olivia to sit next to him. I wondered if his other hand found its way to Olivia's leg and tried not to let jealousy bubble up inside me. It would make sense that he wanted to comfort her as much as he wanted to comfort me. I reminded myself that I was nothing special to him but only someone left under his care for a few days.

"Everything looks amazing," Luke said. "You've outdone yourself again, Riley."

"Olivia helped," I said, my voice small. I appreciated the compliment but I didn't feel like I could take all the credit.

"I think the words you're looking for are thank you," Master Grant said, squeezing my thigh until it almost hurt. "Try again."

Feeling chastised, I swallowed and took in a deep breath before saying, "Thank you, Luke. It was my pleasure."

I felt Luke's confusion but I kept my eyes lowered, not wanting to witness any of it. Master Grant's grip loosened before he trailed his hand lazily up my thigh until it graced my waxed mound. I tried not to react. I knew Master Grant wanted some sort of reaction but I refused to give it to him. Instead, I put my focus on the salad in front of me and started eating after Luke started.

Master Grant's fingers lightly stroked my clit, stirring an ache deep inside me. I wanted to squirm. I wanted to push into it. I knew I should have felt thrilled that he was touching me, paying attention to me, while he used his other hand to eat, leaving Olivia alone. A part of me sparkled under his attention while another part felt confused. Sure, I wore a black collar which meant any man could do anything to me at any time. However on the island men usually asked the woman's owner permission before touching her when he was present. As far as I knew, Master Grant hadn't asked. With his fingers slipping through my obvious wetness, I felt a rush of shame wash over me. I didn't want him to stop but I didn't want to upset Luke and have him sell me to Mr. Martin sooner.

I tried to ignore Master Grant's fingers as I finished my salad. Luke was talking with Annabelle about her day, discussing some of the changes Mr. Wood was making with his office. I tried focusing on their words but found it impossible when Master Grant slipped two fingers inside me. I bit my tongue to keep from gasping. I could almost see the smirk on his face.

He pushed his fingers in deeper, almost as if claiming me somehow. I opened my legs for him, making it easier, while wondering what the hell I was doing.

Annabelle popped up and started serving the roast. I knew I should be the one doing it but I wasn't sure how to extricate myself from Master Grant without making it obvious. For a moment I wondered if Annabelle knew my predicament and was helping me. She was kind that way.

I watched as she served Luke then came over and placed a plate in front of Master Grant. Even though the table cloth covered a lot, it was still obvious that his hand was somewhere on me. I blushed as I kept my eyes lowered. Annabelle served me then Olivia before serving herself, commenting on how it all smelled and looked wonderful.

"You've come a long way with your cooking, Riley," Annabelle said once she sat down. "I'm still struggling with it but I had some fun while you were gone. I think Luke found it edible."

"More than edible," Luke was quick to say. "You're coming along as well, Annabelle."

I heard the pride in his voice. It warmed my heart. It was nice to see them happy. I knew they'd miss me in their way but I knew they'd be fine without me.

Master Grant eased his fingers out of me before wiping them on the napkin on his lap. I felt vacant without him there. Empty. I closed my legs to try to contain the warmth he'd left. I knew I needed to accept my fate here or else I'd be miserable. I had been fortunate up until now and maybe I'd be fortunate again.

"Are you all set for the auction?" Luke asked Master Grant.

"Just about. The women are ready and excited. They've come a long way since day one and will be valuable additions to our community. Having them start at the training facility was a brilliant idea. Now they're better prepared for life here and hopefully will be happier for it."

"Are you expecting a big crowd of bidders this time around?" Luke asked.

"More than usual, I think. This will be our biggest auction to date with the most women being auctioned and the most men registered to attend. The men needed to register for it but they don't usually all show up. "

My stomach lurched. I put down my fork, no longer hungry. Somehow I had managed to block the fact that I'd be auctioned again. My first auction went smoothly with only me and another woman being auctioned. It was quick and not a lot of men were in attendance. Of course, Luke bought me and he made the transition to his house easy. I knew I wouldn't be so lucky this time.

"Are you OK, Riley?" Luke asked.

I looked up at him. I knew the blood had drained from my face. Suddenly I was facing my new reality and I didn't like it.

"I'm fine, Luke," I said. "Just not hungry."

Master Grant's hand was back on my thigh in a firm hold.

"Riley," Master Grant said my name in a growl. "Truth."

I swallowed.

"I'm a little scared," I admitted, my voice small. "I haven't lived with anyone other than Luke since I arrived. I don't think I'll like living with Mr. Martin."

Master Grant's grip on my thigh hardened.

"I need you to trust me," Master Grant said. "Trust Luke. We're doing what we can to ensure that doesn't happen. We have Mr. Martin being entertained right now by two of the more wild women from Olivia's class. They're more the type of women Mr. Martin wants and we're showing that to him."

"But he seemed set on us," I said. "I thought it was a done deal."

"It's not a done deal until the auction is over," Master Grant said. "And even then, things can be done."

He didn't elaborate and I knew I couldn't question him but I wasn't convinced. My mind felt overloaded from all of it. I didn't know what to think anymore. I knew if I wanted to stay that I needed to accept whatever happened even if I didn't like it. I felt a small sense of relief in knowing I could always leave. I always had that option even if it was one I didn't want to have to take.

I MANAGED TO SERVE DESSERT, pudding in little cups topped with rolled chocolate-filled wafers, despite my stomach being in knots. Everyone cooed over them, telling me how amazing they were. I only picked at mine, uninterested, wanting the whole evening to end. It was torture having Master Grant sitting next to me knowing that nothing could come of us. He didn't touch me again and my whole being felt the vacancy.

I cleared plates as soon as everyone was done, wanting to distance myself from the idle chatter happening at the table. Luke had always encouraged us to speak freely in his house, something I appreciated, so Annabelle helped carry the conversation, talking mostly with Luke and Master Grant. They didn't talk about the auction again which I was grateful for. I didn't want to think about it. The whole thing felt like a nightmare that was slowly creeping up on me.

Olivia joined me in the kitchen, plates in her hands.

"Where do you want these?" she asked.

"Just set them on the counter," I said, my back to her as I stacked the dishwasher. "I'll take care of them."

Olivia came around the kitchen island until she was standing next to me. She set the plates down as instructed but didn't move. I felt the tears threatening to tumble down my face and the last thing I wanted to do was cry in front of her.

"Are you ok?" she asked. "I know the auction is scary but is there something else?"

I knew I couldn't tell her about my crazy crush on Master Grant. I knew I needed to let that go. I had to assume that a lot of women crushed on him and Master Owen. They were both handsome men who knew how to bring out the best in a submissive woman. I would be crazy not to fall for one of them. But that didn't change the fact that nothing could happen between us. He was a trainer and, as far as I knew, had no intention of setting up a household.

"No, I'm fine," I said as I took the plates she brought in and stacked them in the dishwasher. "It's just nerves."

Olivia placed her hand on my arm.

"You can talk to me, you know," she said. "I might not be as knowledgeable about this place as you or anyone else but I do care about you. I want you to be able to talk with me about the scary stuff, too. You've been here for me so much. I'm not sure I could have made it through all the stuff I've been through if it hadn't been for you. You're my only real friend here and I want to be there for you, too."

I turned and looked at her then. Really looked at her. Concern clouded her pale green eyes but I also found comfort and friendship there. She really cared. Without thinking, I wrapped my arms around her. Her willowy body molded against mine as she returned the hug. I felt like I was hanging onto a life raft after being adrift at sea for ages. I hadn't realized how desperately I needed her until that moment.

She nuzzled into my neck, her breath warm against my skin. I ran my hand along her back and I pulled her even closer. I felt her body sigh and relax into me. A part of me felt like I was coming home.

I pulled back slightly so I could look at her. Her beautiful pale face was covered in a sprinkling of light freckles, covering almost every inch of her. Her large green eyes were wide and questioning as she looked at me. She wore no makeup and I loved how her natural beauty shined through. She didn't need makeup and I was happy she didn't feel the need to wear it. Most of the women here seemed to wear makeup almost as some kind of mask, as if wearing it would keep anyone from seeing the real them.

She blinked at me and I couldn't help my eyes moving down to her lush full lips that were slightly open, as if she wanted to say something but couldn't find the words. For a moment I felt frozen against her, thoughts and emotions rushing through my mind, confusing and overwhelming me. There was something about this woman that drew me in. I had never felt this way about a woman before.

Before I could talk myself out of it, my lips came down on hers. She seemed startled but kissed me back, her body melting into mine as she pulled me in tighter. Her tongue quickly found its way into my mouth, drinking me in, as she deepened the kiss. My head spun and my knees felt like they were about to buckle. Her kiss took the air right out of me.

She kissed me with a fierceness that made me lightheaded. Her hands were on my back, gliding up and down the length of me, as her mouth captured mine. I kept my eyes closed, afraid if I opened them that she'd disappear. The whole thing felt unreal and I wasn't ready to let it go.

I let myself get lost in her, in the moment, until I heard a male voice clear his throat from the kitchen entryway. I jumped back, breaking the kiss so quickly I nearly fell over. Olivia quickly lowered her eyes, cutting herself off from me, her face paling. Without thinking, I looked up to see Master Grant, his dark blue eyes unreadable looking straight at me.

"I see I'm interrupting something," he said, his tone low. "How long has this been going on?"

My body stiffened. I felt caught and I couldn't break eye contact with him even though I knew I shouldn't be looking at him, that I was breaking every rule I was ever given. He held my gaze, his expression unreadable, his eyes piercing through me. I felt like he had slammed me up against a wall and threatened to take me. My breathing went ragged as my body became inflamed with the need for him.

"Answer me, Riley."

I swallowed, my eyes still on his.

"It started last night," I said, my voice small. "We shared the same bed and I couldn't help myself. It's my fault, not hers."

Olivia kept her eyes down. I felt her next to me but I could only look at Master Grant. He didn't move towards us as I thought he would. Instead, he stood at the doorway, his arms crossed in front of his broad chest. I couldn't hear Luke and Annabelle talking anymore and I wondered where they were. Maybe Luke had taken Annabelle upstairs like he was known to do after dinner, enjoying some private time as the couple they were.

"Is this true, Olivia?" Master Grant asked.

Olivia kept her eyes down, her voice small. "We did connect last night but it wasn't all Riley's fault. I wanted her, too. I've wanted her since we met."

This revelation shocked me but I didn't say anything. Master Grant kept his eyes on me as if he was trying to read me. I had no idea what my expression said to him but I no longer tried to hide anything. I was done hiding.

He moved towards us, one solid step after another. My heart felt like it stopped as I held my breath, unsure if I was scared or excited or both. Master Grant's eyes never left mine as he moved towards me, his body suddenly large and strong and strangely foreboding.

"Do you know what serious trouble you two could get into if you were caught by somebody like Mr. Martin?" Master Grant asked once he was right in front of me. He stared me down, his eyes fierce. I thought he might reach out and grab me, maybe shake some sense into me, but he didn't. I felt the rage coursing through him, coming off him in waves, but he was able to contain it. He didn't so much as touch me or Olivia. "Something like that could send you both to the pillories for days or worse. Is that what you want?"

I swallowed, the realization crashing over me. My God, how could we have been so foolish?

"Answer me, Riley," Master Grant said, his eyes never leaving mine. "Is that what you want?"

"No, Master Grant," I said. "I'm sorry. That will never happen again."

He studied me a minute. His eyes never left mine as he asked Olivia the same thing.

"No, Master Grant," Olivia said. "I'm sorry."

"I won't always be around to protect you," he said. A flash of sadness crossed his eyes before they returned to being unreadable. "You need to abide by the rules of this island if you hope to stay here. Men like Mr. Martin will have no hesitation in punishing you and quite possibly severely for something like this. Women aren't allowed to have intimate relationships with one another without a man allowing it. Is that understood?"

"Yes, Master Grant," Olivia and I said in unison.

I had never felt so defeated in my life. I knew what we were doing wasn't allowed but Master Grant's disapproval crushed me. I never wanted to displease him. I knew now more than ever that there could never be anything between Master Grant and me. There was no way he'd want me after this. I held his gaze because I couldn't look away but I could see the disappointment and sadness there. I had blown it.

"Olivia, you're coming back to the training facility with me right now," Master Grant said. "Riley, you will be staying here. The auction is only a few days away so I need you both to stay out of trouble. I will let Luke know that he needs to tighten up his leniency with you so you'll be fully prepared once you transition to a new household."

His words put me back in my place. I was nothing to him. I was only a woman to be trained and taught how to be on this island. I made a promise to myself that I would follow all the rules and to give myself over fully to this process. I would somehow shut down my mind and allow myself to fully surrender.

Sadness crept through me when Master Grant finally broke his gaze with me, clipped a leash to Olivia's collar and took her out the door. I stood there feeling stunned and numb for I don't know how long, letting the whole evening sink in. Just when I thought I had found a little shred of something, it got snatched away. I knew what I was doing with Olivia wasn't right, at least not here, but there was a large part of me that still wanted it, even craved it. I wasn't sure how I was going to be able to shut that down.

TWENTY-ONE

I tossed and turned all night, my mind flooded with Master Grant's disapproval and what my life would be like from now on. I knew Mr. Martin would acquire me even though Master Grant had told me of his efforts to ensure that didn't happen. Mr. Martin didn't seem like the kind of man to be swayed once his mind was made up and his mind had seemed very made up.

I made breakfast almost in a trance, going through the motions. I made enough for Luke and Annabelle even though I doubted they'd eat it. I was up early enough to have it finished before they rushed off to the office. Annabelle came into the kitchen looking fresh and happy. I was happy for her, I really was, but my heart hurt looking at all she had and all that I'd never have.

"Good morning, Riley," Annabelle said as she took a seat at the counter. "Something smells amazing."

"I made breakfast," I said, stating the obvious. I put a plate of eggs with sausage and fruit in front of her along with a tall glass of water.

"Great. I'm starving."

Annabelle started eating a moment before she put her fork down and asked, "Aren't you eating?"

I realized I had been just standing there staring off into space.

Luke walked in, all smiles. When his eyes landed on me, he immediately asked, "What's wrong, Riley? Are you ok?"

My eyes went to his. I saw the concern there.

When I didn't answer, Luke came to me and wrapped me in his arms. All I could do was lean into him and cry. I didn't even know the tears had started until I felt them slide down my face and slip onto Luke's suit jacket. My whole body shook inside his arms but he didn't let go. Instead, he cradled my head, holding it firmly on his shoulder, while I let every frustration, sadness and doubt go.

"You're OK," Luke whispered into my ear. "We'll figure this out."

I knew in my heart there was nothing Luke could do to keep me from going to Mr. Martin but I didn't say anything. There was nothing I could say. Instead, I let myself be wrapped up by him and allowed myself a few moments of peace inside his arms.

"I would keep you if I could," Luke whispered, his words breaking my heart. "I hope you know that."

I didn't respond but let the tears fall. I knew there was nothing he could do and I didn't blame him for it. The only thing I could do was leave the island, an option that was becoming more appealing. But deep down I didn't want to leave. I didn't want to give into men like Mr. Martin and let him make me flee. I knew I was stronger than that but I hadn't yet figured out how to tap into it.

Luke slowly unfolded from me until he was looking me directly in the eyes. His dark green eyes showed concern along with something else I couldn't figure out. I blinked up at him through my tears.

"I value you," he said, his voice warm and sure. "You've been nothing but an asset to me. I wouldn't even think about giving you up unless it was something you wanted but right now my hands are tied. I've already consented to release you and I can't back out now. You have no idea how much this is killing me."

I believed him. He had no reason to lie. I had always trusted Luke but it didn't change anything.

"The auction is the day after tomorrow," Luke said, his arms around me, holding me steady. "I want you to do nothing more than relax and take it easy until then. Annabelle can cook and do all the shopping. I only want you to do whatever it is you want to do. If you want to go out to the woman's side of town, be my guest. Buy whatever you want. I'm not sure you'll be able to take your clothes and things with you but I'll see what I can do to make that happen. You deserve to take a break until then. Do you understand?"

"Yes, Luke," I said in a small voice. Resting sounded nice but it didn't keep my heart from breaking.

"Good," he said. "I need to go into the office today and tomorrow. Annabelle will be joining me but I'll try to get her home early both days in case you'd like to spend some time with her. It will all work out, Riley. One way or another."

I gave Luke a weak smile. I knew he was trying. I knew he was doing all he could. It just wasn't enough. It wasn't what I needed.

He kissed me on the forehead, gave me another hug then released me. Annabelle had finished breakfast and was busy stacking her plate in the dishwasher. I knew Luke would never let this happen to her and I had to bite back the jealousy that threatened to overtake me. I knew it wouldn't help if I started lashing out at Annabelle or Luke.

"I'll see you this evening," Luke said. "Don't forget to relax. I'll be mad if I come home and the house is spotless."

He gave me a half smile that almost made me smile back. His heart was in the right place.

I cleaned up the kitchen once they left, throwing the rest of the breakfast in the trash. I wasn't hungry and doubted I'd be anytime soon. Not having anything to do was almost worse than being ordered to do things. With Luke and Annabelle gone, the house felt empty.

I wandered to my room, thinking I'd find a little solace there. I had always appreciated having my own space in Luke's house to retreat to when needed. I knew other women weren't so lucky and I doubted I'd be so lucky at Mr. Martin's house.

I browsed through the postcards I had stuck to the walls. I slowly took them down one by one, reading each one, before sliding them into one of the novels I had bought in town. I knew I wanted to keep something from my time here and hoped Mr. Martin would allow it. Maybe Luke or Master Grant could convince him that allowing me to keep some of my things would help make the transition easier.

When I had arrived on the island I had been told that I'd be considered property and that property didn't own anything. It hadn't mattered at the time since I didn't come to the island with anything but the clothes on my back. I had been told during my interview before coming here that I wouldn't need to bring anything, that everything would be provided for me. But now that I had acquired a few things, I felt differently about it. I wanted to keep my few things, including the postcards and a few books. I felt they helped ground me and would help me through this next period of my time here.

With nothing left to do, I left my room and wandered to the front room. Part of me was tempted to go into Luke's bedroom and curl up on his bed, inhale his scent, surround myself with him in some way. I had a feeling he wouldn't be using me again before the auction, having already let me go. I wasn't craving sex but I missed the sweetness. I missed having someone who cared and wanted the best for me. I knew I wouldn't find that with Mr. Martin. To him, we were playthings to be used and probably discarded. I knew Mr. Martin wouldn't care about my interests or even my pleasure. The whole thing made me sad.

I wandered around the house, touching surfaces as if trying to memorize everything. I knew I wouldn't be back. There'd be no reason to be. I didn't imagine Mr. Martin giving me the freedom to roam around town like Luke had. I chastised myself for not taking more advantage of it.

I contemplated heading out, at least to the women's side of town. Luke told me to buy whatever I wanted but not knowing if I could take anything with me, and doubting I could, it seemed like it'd hurt more than help. I didn't have any friends outside of Olivia and Annabelle and even if I did, I'd have no way of connecting with them to meet up.

I kneeled on the soft rug, positioning myself in the waiting pose, wondering what it would be like to be owned by Mr. Martin. I hadn't allowed myself to think about it since thinking about it overwhelmed me. But now I felt like I needed to face it head-on since it was quickly becoming a reality.

I took in a few deep breaths, quieting my mind as I straightened my back. Through all the training I had learned how to be a proper submissive, to be patient and obedient, and to shut my mind down when needed. I knew I'd be called on to use these skills in the coming weeks if not months. I knew I could get through it and possibly emerge out the other side a more refined version of myself. I had come to the island to experience what it was like to surrender and I felt like I was about to find out what that meant.

I sat in that pose a long time, allowing myself to meditate and for my mind to wander. I was able to reach a place of peace and tried to cement it in my mind for future reference. I had a feeling I'd need it.

My mind kept wandering to Master Grant. His intense deep blue eyes kept finding their way to me along with his stern expression and the way his kiss took my breath away. He was able to capture a part of me that was so deep inside me that I hadn't even realized it was there. My heart ached at not being able to experience those times with him again. I knew Mr. Martin wouldn't allow it. Even though Mr. Martin would probably have no problem sharing me, I knew it wouldn't include sharing me with Master Grant.

Sometime during the day, I drifted off. I hadn't fallen asleep exactly but my mind quieted enough that I was no longer fully there. It wasn't until I felt a soft caress on my cheek that I startled and opened my eyes to find Annabelle kneeling in front of me.

"Sorry," she said, her voice soft, "I didn't want to scare you. I thought you heard me come in."

I hadn't but that didn't matter.

"It's fine," I said. "I was just resting."

"I see that," she said. Her eyes were warm and showed concern. "How are you doing?"

"Fine," I said automatically.

She gave me a half smile. "Really?"

No, not really, but what difference did it make? I knew she couldn't do anything to change things.

"I know it's hard," Annabelle said. "I'm sad to see you go. You've become a good friend to me."

My heart blossomed at her words. She caressed my cheek again, pushing my hair behind my ear. I felt cherished and cared for. Wanted.

"Luke would keep if you if he could," she said, her eyes on mine.

"I know," I said. And I did. This wasn't Luke's fault.

"Let's do something fun this evening. Luke will be gone for the evening at some work thing so we have the whole evening to ourselves. Would you like to go out to dinner on the women's side of town—or maybe the men's?"

She smiled at me in a knowing kind of way. I almost laughed. Going to the men's side of town was the last thing I wanted. But maybe a night out would help me get my mind off things.

"OK," I said. "That sounds fun. But let's stick to the women's side of town. At least for now."

ANNABELLE and I dressed up in our least revealing dresses which wasn't saying much. They were both sheer but I liked the idea of dressing up. I had gotten used to being nude around everyone so that was no longer a big deal. We put on full makeup, sharing the mirror and chatting away about nothing as we got ready. I missed having girl-friend time. Even though I had spent a lot of time with Olivia, it hadn't felt like this. There had always been an underlying sexual charge to it.

Annabelle didn't bring up the auction or anything to do with my precarious future the whole evening and for that, I was most grateful. We chatted more about our past and a little about her relationship with Luke. It sounded like things were going outstanding and they both wanted it to be long term. I couldn't have felt happier for her. I was happy they had found each other on this crazy island and were learning to navigate their needs in this place.

"What's going on with you and Master Grant?" Annabelle asked over dinner. We had stuck to the women's side of town so we could talk and not worry about being used. "I noticed a little something there."

I blushed as I shoveled in a forkful of my dinner.

"Nothing," I said. "He's just a trainer. You know that."

Annabelle smiled. "Yes, I know that but I also know there's something more going on between you two. It was obvious last night. He's so protective of you and willing to do whatever it takes to ensure Mr. Martin doesn't acquire you. That's not just nothing. There's something there."

I shrugged, not wanting to let the words seep in and give me even a shred of hope. I knew nothing could happen between Master Grant and me even if there was something there.

"He's just a caring guy," I said. "He'd do that for anyone."

Annabelle looked at me as if she didn't believe me. I didn't know what else to say to convince her and wasn't sure I could. Her mind seemed made up.

"He may be a caring guy, and I think he is, but you should have seen the way he went after you once you left the table after dessert. He told Luke that he needed to have a word with you and basically dismissed us to our rooms. He was very determined. What did he say to you?"

I blushed, remembering Master Grant finding me kissing Olivia. I knew I couldn't tell Annabelle about that. I didn't want that getting back to Luke. I didn't want to disrespect Luke in any way or upset him. He deserved better from me.

"He just told me that he was taking Olivia back to the training facility and to stay out of trouble until the auction."

Annabelle looked like she didn't believe me. I'm sure she didn't but I wasn't saying any more about it. I scooped up some fish instead, savoring the delicate flavors on my tongue. I had a feeling my life would be back to tasteless gruel in a matter of days.

We spent some time wandering around the shops, looking at jewelry and other adornments. Annabelle encouraged me to buy some of the things I liked but I shook my head and told her there was no point. I doubted I'd be able to take anything with me. She gave me a face but then quickly switched focus, pulling me out the door and back onto the street where the sun was just setting.

We stopped for ice cream and ate it outside while watching the waves crash onto the shore. The beach was mostly deserted this time of evening except for a few women laying out in the nude. I knew I would miss this place if I decided to leave. I had come to the island thinking I knew who I was but now I felt more lost than ever. Part of me didn't feel like I belonged here while another part of me knew I didn't belong back home either. I felt like a woman who had no idea how she fit into the world but I knew it wasn't being with Mr. Martin.

Back at Luke's house, we curled up on the sofa and talked about silly things. I asked Annabelle about how things were going at the office since she worked directly for Mr. Wood.

"Things have been a little tense lately with Mr. Wood trying to secure the casino deal with Mr. Martin. It's like he knows how much they want to close the deal so he's milking it for everything he can. He's not a nice man."

"That much I know," I said, not wanting to think about it.

"Oh, right. Of course. Sorry."

"It's ok. It is what it is. I'll adapt. Maybe it'll even be good for me."

Annabelle gave me a little smile. "Perhaps. I could see how it could push you to truly let go and embrace being fully submissive. It's always the most challenging when you're doing it for someone you don't like or something you don't want to do. I've had my share of that and I feel like it helped me to discover exactly who I want to be with Luke. I think it'll all come together for you."

I smiled at her, my first genuine smile in a while.

"I truly hope so."

TWENTY-TWO

The next day was more of the same. I tried not to do anything while Luke and Annabelle went into the office. I spent a lot of time in bed, luxuriating and reading, knowing that it could be a long time until I felt the comfort of a bed again. I had no idea how Mr. Martin intended to keep his women but I doubted we'd have our own rooms with comfy beds. I heard stories where some women slept on hardwood floors or in cages. None of these options appealed to me.

Annabelle made dinner for us. I tried to help but she wouldn't let me. Instead, I sat on the stool and watched while she made a recipe from one of my cookbooks, pushing back her auburn hair with the back of her hand every now and then.

Luke joined us for dinner, arriving right on time. He seemed in a happy mood but there was something right under the surface that I couldn't decipher. He kept the talk over dinner light and about nothing in particular, telling Annabelle over and over again how wonderful everything was. She smiled and accepted his praise graciously. I couldn't help feeling jealous, wanting what they had. I wanted someone to connect with, someone who got it, who could be in charge but also was yielding and caring. It was nice to see that it was possible even if I didn't think it was possible for me.

No one mentioned the auction happening tomorrow afternoon. It weighed heavily on my mind but I tried not to think about it. There was no point dwelling on it. It would only make me feel worse.

Annabelle made strawberry shortcake for dessert. I savored each bite while the two of them talked about inconsequential things happening around the office. It sounded like they were working in the same building again if not the same office. That was new. Usually Luke worked in a different building or, more recently, at the training facility. I wanted to ask him more about this change but I knew it didn't make a difference to me. I would still be auctioned off tomorrow and Mr. Martin would still be the one acquiring me.

Luke made a point to escort me into the living room while Annabelle cleared plates and cleaned up in the kitchen. He took my hand as if he was escorting me into a ballroom. He didn't say anything until we were in the living room and away from the kitchen. He quietly folded me in his arms, holding me to him. I heard his heart beating solid and strong underneath my head. His arms held me to him as if he was afraid if he let go I'd flee.

Emotions tumbled through me as he held me. I'd miss this man. He had been my rock throughout my time here, my safe place, even if I got jealous of his relationship with Annabelle at times. I knew he didn't want to let me go and I knew he didn't have a choice.

He nuzzled into my hair, his breath warm. I tried to soak it all in, memorizing as much as I could, knowing it would help me get through the next however many weeks with Mr. Martin. I trusted that Mr. Martin would get bored of me as new women arrived on the island and his attention was diverted elsewhere. Maybe by some miracle, Luke could acquire me back once Mr. Martin had moved on.

"I'll miss you," Luke whispered into my hair. "So much. Please know that I'm not letting you go easily or without a fight. I've done everything I could to keep you but it wasn't enough. My brother needs this deal to go through to ensure the vitality of the island and, unfortunately, you've become part of that deal."

I snuggled into him, appreciating his warmth and comfort. My heart ached for the simpler time when I first arrived on the island and

Luke bought me. I hadn't thought much of it, had taken it for granted, and knew I would never do that again.

Luke lifted my chin so I was looking into his dark green eyes. I saw his concern and compassion for me there. It made my heart ache.

He lowered his mouth to mine, kissing me gently at first but then deepening the kiss. I knew in my heart this was his way of saying goodbye and I let myself yield into it, allowing his strength and caring to wash over me as his mouth explored mine. He held me tightly as he deepened the kiss even more. I felt like I was clinging to him, as if he was somehow saving me even though I knew he'd soon have to let go. But at that moment, I let myself surrender to all of it, to let myself be kissed, to be appreciated, to be even loved in his own way.

Luke pulled back after a few minutes, his eyes finding mine. I blinked up at him, not sure how to feel, not sure of anything.

"Riley, what do you need right now?" Luke asked. "It's your last night here and I want to give you whatever you need."

I blinked at him, my mind spinning. I had no idea what I needed except a sense of security and knowing I wouldn't be auctioned off the next day but I knew that wasn't going to happen.

"Anything," Luke said, his voice low. "Tell me what you need."

I looked up at him, taking in his kindness and warmth. I gave him a small smile.

"I think I just need to be held," I said, letting the words roll off my tongue without analyzing them. "Just you and me if that's OK."

Luke smiled. "You got it."

He uncurled himself from me, took my hand and led me to his bedroom. I had no idea where Annabelle had gone and I told myself not to worry about her. She would have Luke for the rest of her life maybe while I would only have this one night.

Luke closed the door behind us once we entered his room. I wasn't sure what to do so I just stood there. I wasn't used to being in his room any more and wasn't sure what type of protocols, if any, we were following at the moment.

Luke must have sensed my hesitation because he came to me and wrapped his arms around me, pulling me into his warmth. I inhaled his fresh woodsy scent, grateful for him, grateful for this moment.

"I want you to dictate this night," Luke said as he held me. "I am yours."

My heart swelled and I felt like I might start to cry. I didn't know how I was going to be able to leave this and live with a man who would never hold me like this.

"Just hold me," I said after a minute.

Luke chuckled. "You got it."

At some point, we made it to the bed. I pulled off my sheer dress and slipped out of my heels while Luke undressed until he was standing naked in front of me. I hadn't seen his cock in a while and the sight of it warmed me. I wasn't sure if I wanted to have any kind of sex tonight but I liked the idea of it being an option. I was sure I would be more than used once I was in Mr. Martin's household and thought my body probably needed the rest.

Luke pulled me into bed and wrapped his strong arms around me. I laid my head on his chest, feeling the beat of his heart against my cheek, and allowed myself to drift into a deep sleep.

I WOKE up feeling refreshed with Luke's arms wrapped tight around me. He woke when I stirred, pulling me closer to him and planting a kiss on my forehead. I smiled at him, his eyes finding mine.

"Good morning," he said. "Sleep well?"

"So well," I said with a smile, almost forgetting what laid ahead of me.

"Good," he said, smiling back. "I want you to rest and relax until you have to leave. Be sure to shower but that's all you need to do. I'll leave it up to you whether you want to bother with makeup or whatever. I think you look gorgeous without it."

My smile faded.

"Thanks, Luke. I doubt it matters what I look like today but I'll make you proud."

He kissed the top of my forehead before pushing himself up.

"I know you will," he said. "You always do."

I laid in bed while Luke showered and moved downstairs. The smell of bacon and toast wafted up the stairs. My stomach growled, reminding me how hungry I was all of a sudden. I hopped in the shower before joining them in the kitchen. They were sitting at the kitchen counter eating.

"Hi, Riley," Annabelle said. "Please join us. There's more than enough."

"Thanks," I said, moving around the counter so I could grab a plate. Annabelle had outdone herself making scrambled eggs, bacon and toast along with cut-up grapefruits and strawberries. I had no idea when I would be able to eat this well again so I piled up my plate and sat down with them.

"Riley, I'm leaving Annabelle here until you need to leave," Luke said. "Someone from the training facility will collect you when it's time to go. I wish I could stay and be the one to bring you over but I'm needed in the office before then."

My heart dropped. I thought Luke would be with me until I needed to leave. I suddenly felt abandoned.

I ate the rest of my breakfast in silence, no longer tasting it as I shoveled it in. Just as I was finishing, Luke came around to stand next to me. He wrapped his arms around me, resting his head on top of my head.

"You're an amazing and wonderful woman," Luke said. "Know that you always have the option to leave this place if anything ever becomes too much for you. Your contract is up in a few weeks so if you can hold out until then, you'll receive your full compensation. I know you can do this. Mr. Martin isn't all that bad and they've been teaching him a thing or two at the training facility to ensure that he treats whatever women he ends up with well. I will always do whatever I can to protect you even if you're no longer in my care."

Tears sprung up as Luke gave me one last squeeze before releasing me.

"You'll do great," Luke said. "I believe in you."

He kissed me on the forehead then went lower and captured my lips with his in a gentle loving kiss. I let the tears fall, no longer caring. Luke gave me one last hug, whispered, "Take care of yourself," and left. I was too stunned to move. The reality of everything started to crash in. It was too much. I felt like I might hyperventilate.

Annabelle must have sensed my distress because she came around, placed a hand on my back and said, "Breathe, Riley. Just breathe."

I took in a deep breath and held it, slowly releasing it before taking in another. I did this several times while Annabelle continued to support me, her hand on my back, her other on my shoulder. She breathed along with me, deep cleansing breaths, until I felt my heartbeat come back down to normal. I had never hyperventilated before and I didn't want to start now.

"That's it," Annabelle said. "Nice and easy."

I took in another deep breath before letting it out in a long sigh. I felt better. More centered. I turned to her and thanked her.

"No worries, Riley. It's the least I can do. I know all of this isn't easy for you. If there's anything I can do to make it easier, I'll do it. I hope you know that."

I saw the kindness in her eyes and gave her a small smile.

"I know," I said. "Thank you."

She gave me a big hug as I continued to focus on my breathing, happy I was feeling more settled. I knew I couldn't think about it too much or I'd freak out. I needed to let go and allow whatever wanted to happen to happen. I knew I wasn't in control. The only thing I could do was leave the island early and after everything, that wasn't something I wanted to do. I could survive for a few more weeks. Then maybe I'd leave.

"Let me clean up then we can cuddle on the couch and talk if you want before you need to leave," Annabelle said as she started to let go of me. "Or whatever you want. You tell me."

I appreciated the offer but I didn't know what I wanted or needed. I smiled at her. "That'd be nice."

I wandered up to my room one last time, taking it in and ensuring I didn't miss packing anything. Luke had insisted that I pack a small bag of my belongings in case my new owner was cool with me having them. He knew it wasn't typical but he thought it was worth being prepared.

"I'll include in your write up how essential it is for you to have these things," Luke had said. "Especially the postcards from your friends and family. You should have those."

I was grateful for the effort but doubted I'd be able to keep anything. Mr. Martin didn't seem like the kind of man who considered other people's feelings.

I pushed down the dread that threatened to settle in my stomach as I surveyed my room one last time. The bed was made. The few dresses I had still hung in the closet. I had packed my favorite and left the rest. Annabelle could have them or any new woman Luke acquired although I doubted he'd acquire anyone else unless his brother pushed. I wished Luke had stood up to his brother more and refused to give me up but I knew it was pointless wishing for something that wasn't going to happen. I wanted to be with a man who was willing to fight for me, who would do everything it took to ensure my happiness.

I smiled at the thought. It hadn't occurred to me until that moment that I had this want. I had assumed I had no idea what I wanted in a relationship or if I even wanted a relationship but there it was. I wanted someone who would fight for me and make me feel safe and secure. I did want that in my life. Maybe I'd be able to find it once I was back home in a few weeks.

I returned downstairs feeling more buoyant. I had a plan. I knew what I wanted and I knew I was going to go after it. I had decided to leave the island and trust that I could find what I wanted outside of this place. I knew people lived all sorts of kinks and I would be able to find a man who could give me exactly what I needed and wanted. And hopefully, I'd be able to give him exactly what he needed and wanted, too. Wasn't that how it was supposed to work? I could manage a few more weeks even if it meant being Mr. Martin's sex slave. I knew I could do it and then I'd be out of here.

Annabelle smiled when I returned. She was curled on the sofa. I joined her on the other end, our legs and feet between us. We spent the next hour talking about everything and nothing. It was wonderful to let go of the impending auction for a while. I felt myself start to relax. I knew I could handle whatever came my way.

TWENTY-THREE

The knock on the door startled us. I knew what it was but I couldn't move. Annabelle hopped up and answered the door. I heard a deep male voice from the front door yet I still couldn't move.

"She's right in there," Annabelle said before a tall man with lots of muscles I had never seen before rounded the corner. He had dark eyes and dark skin and looked all sorts of intimidating. My heart raced as he approached me, a leash in his hand.

"You must be Riley," he said, his voice deep and smooth. "I'm Master Jax. I'm here to escort you to the auction."

He approached me with a clear collar and leash in his hand. I still hadn't moved. I wasn't sure I was capable. But when he motioned for me to stand, I somehow found my legs and stood before him. He was tall and handsome. He didn't smile but his eyes were kind. I quickly checked myself and lowered my eyes, fear washing over me at my blunder. I had gotten too comfortable with Luke to remember how to be around a man on the island.

"I'll let it slide," Master Jax said, his voice firm. "But do understand other men won't."

"Yes, Master Jax," I said. "I apologize."

Master Jax unclicked Luke's collar before fastening the clear collar around my neck and clicking the leash to it. It felt cool against my skin. Foreign. I swallowed a few times, quickly crushing the fear that threatened to overtake me.

"Good," Master Jax said. "Let's go."

I didn't say goodbye to Annabelle as we left out the front door, remembering myself and that women weren't allowed to talk when a man was present without permission. Walking out the front door felt like walking into a different world, one I wasn't sure I wanted to be a part of anymore.

The walk to the training facility was uneventful. Men looked but no one touched. I had a feeling it had to do with Master Jax who looked like the kind of man who didn't share. I wasn't sure what a clear collar told the men. I felt relieved not to have to deal with anyone and let out a sigh of relief once we entered the training facility.

As soon as we entered, Master Jax stopped and turned to me. Without a word he fastened a black blindfold over my eyes, plunging me into darkness. I only knew to start walking again when I felt the tug of the leash. I followed him blindly through the building, my ears trying to pick up clues to where exactly we were but I heard nothing but the sound of his boots against the concrete.

Doors opened and closed. We moved forward through the space. He had me walk up some steps until I was on what I assumed was some sort of platform. I heard other people around but no one was talking. I felt the weight of their breathing and the shuffling of their feet. My heart hammered, feeling overwhelmed and scared, not sure what to expect, not liking any of this.

Master Jax fastened my leash to something, pulling it taut. I knew enough not to lean into it. I knew it must be that way for a reason.

He didn't say anything before he left, his heavy boots pounding against the floor. A door opened and closed and I assumed he was gone. I took in deep breaths to steady myself. I knew I could get through this. I only had a few more weeks to go then I could go back home with a pile of money and start my life over. I had no idea what that'd look like but I knew I'd figure it out.

I stood there, focusing on breathing, my ears perked for any movement around me. I could hear other people breathing, feet shuffling and the occasional murmur. I assumed we were all waiting to be auctioned and I hoped it wouldn't be much longer before things got started. I wondered if Olivia was among the women waiting and if we would end up at Mr. Martin's together. Having her along with me would make things easier even though I knew we wouldn't have the leniency we had at Luke's place.

My heart quickened as I heard the door open and male voices enter the space. The mingled voices made it impossible for me to make sense out of any of it but I was comforted to know that we'd be starting soon. What I didn't expect were the hands that quickly found their way to me.

All of a sudden hands were squeezing my ass, groping my breasts and pinching my nipples. I kept my eyes lowered even though I was blindfolded and gave myself over to the sensations. The men continued to talk, their conversations more clear now they were closer, making comments about our bodies, who looked more fuckable than others, what they wanted to do with each of us.

Someone pinched and pulled on my nipples until I was almost thrown off balance. It took everything I had not to lean forward, to take off some of the pressure, and I was amazed as the pain shot straight through to my pussy. I knew I was wet before fingers found their way there and pushed inside me. Someone flicked on my clit, making me squirm, while hands continued to pinch and pull on my nipples.

"Look at this one, Bill," a man in front of me said. "She's fucking wet. I'm sure she'll go for a high price."

More hands were on me. More fingers sliding in and out of my pussy.

"I wish we could fuck them right now," another man said. "Take them for a test drive."

Someone laughed. "That'd be great but I doubt we'd ever get to the auction and I can't wait to take one of these bitches home."

The hands and fingers came and went as the men moved from one woman to the next. I tried to figure out how many of us there were but couldn't. I assumed these were all the women from Olivia's class, at least the ones who hadn't left. They were trained for this but it was something else to be manhandled by so many men at once without being able to see them.

I tried to escape inside myself as the groping and fondling continued. My body responded, wanting more, wanting one of the men to stay with me long enough to push an orgasm or two out of me. Instead, I was left dripping and wanting, my body revved up with no hope for release.

More men made crude comments about me, sharing how they wanted to fuck me and what they would do with me. I knew I should have felt some relief knowing I'd be going to Mr. Martin but I had no idea who I'd end up with. More men were coming to the island all the time. There was a possibility that another man would have deeper pockets than Mr. Martin or that Mr. Martin had decided on someone else.

I pushed back the prickling of fear that threatened to overtake me. I reminded myself that I could do this, that I came to the island for this, and that I could handle whatever these men put me through for the next few weeks until I could leave.

As quickly as the groping started, it ended. A predominant male voice announced that the auction would be starting and for the men to find their seats. I imagined who knew how many men sitting audience style facing us. I wore nothing more than heels, feeling barer than ever as I felt eyes taking me in. This felt worse than when the men were up close and personal. At least that I could relate to. Being on display in front of a crowd wasn't something I had ever experienced.

I took in deep breaths as I willed myself to remain calm. I told myself that this would be over before I knew it and then I would know what I had to deal with for the next few weeks.

The announcer started the auction, listing stats that were not mine. I listened while he talked about the woman's attributes, including her measurements and how much she could deep-throat without gagging. It sounded like he was demonstrating as he went, showing the audience what they could expect from her, driving the price higher. I had overheard during training with Olivia's group that the men auctioned using tablets so there was no shouting out numbers but there were feedback and hollers from the crowd.

This went on, woman after woman, until it came to me. The auctioneer announced my name along with my measurements and how I had been on the island for almost six months and through the advanced training at the facility. He pinched and pulled on my nipples until they hardened into little peaks.

"As you can see, this one is super responsive," he said before sliding his hand between my legs and plunging two fingers inside me. He pulled out almost immediately as I imagined him showing the audience. "She's wet and ready for all that you have to give her. She's super obedient and willing to please. She comes with high recommendations from her owner as well as from Master Grant at the training facility."

My heart quickened at the mention of Master Grant. I wondered if he was watching me and what was going through his head. I knew I was just another one of the women to come through the training facility but a small part of me hoped I meant a little bit more.

The auctioneer went on, pinching and pulling my nipples, smacking my ass, showing me off while the crowd grew louder around me. I tried my best to block it out, to imagine myself somewhere else, but it was a challenge. My body responded to the manhandling, wanting more while at the same time wanting none of it.

My breathing got shallow as the auction continued. The auctioneer shoved his fingers inside me, circling my clit with his thumb, sending my body into overdrive while he continued to sell me to the crowd. He quickened the pace, his thumb driving me mad, until I gave in and let myself come all around him.

He chuckled and pulled out, selling the virtues of my orgasm and how delightful it would be to deny them.

I let my body hang loose as the groping continued, my mind finally somewhere else. I had given in, fully surrendered, and no longer cared where I ended up. It didn't matter. Maybe I was only a body to be used, like all these men seemed to think about women. I'd go through the motions, allow myself to surrender to it, counting down the days until I could leave.

The auctioneer gave my ass one more slap before announcing me sold. I felt momentarily stunned even though I knew it was coming. The finality of it sunk in while someone escorted me off the platform, down some steps and out of the main room. We walked a little way until a door opened and closed and my blindfold was taken off.

Master Jax smiled at me. We were in a small room with a desk and a chair and no windows.

"You went for a high price," he told me as he unfastened the leash then took off the collar. "The highest so far. You should feel proud."

Proud was the last thing I felt. I kept my eyes lowered as I tried not to let the enormity of what just happened to overwhelm me. I needed to keep it together. It was only a few more weeks.

"There's a bathroom through that door," Master Jax said, indicating a door behind me that I hadn't noticed. "Take a shower, freshen up, and we'll be back to collect you when you're new owner is ready to pick you up. It shouldn't be too long. He seemed very excited about acquiring you."

My heart sank.

"Yes, Sir," I said, my voice small.

"Very good," Master Jax said then left.

I took my time showering, washing off as much of the day as I could. I wasn't concerned about being fresh for my new owner but I liked the idea of feeling clean. I had no idea how often I'd be afforded this luxury with my new owner so I knew enough to appreciate it.

I toweled off slowly, wishing there was some way I could avoid being picked up by my new owner. At least I had some hope that Olivia would be joining me at my new household. That was something to hang onto. It would be easier not to be alone in this.

I had nothing to change into so I slipped my heels back on and waited on my knees in the little room. The walls were painted a dull grey, making the room feel depressing, the floor a raw concrete. My knees ached as I waited but I allowed the pain to give me a focal point, something to concentrate on to keep my mind from wandering.

I didn't wait long before the door opened and Master Jax stood in front of me.

"Up," he said.

I uncurled myself until I was standing in front of him, my eyes lowered.

He placed a blindfold over my eyes, plunging me back into darkness.

"Your new owner requested that you be blindfolded until you arrive home," Master Jax explained. "Since you no longer have a collar —your new owner will see to that—I cannot attach a leash to you to help guide you. Instead, place your hand on my arm and follow my every command."

"Yes, Sir," I said as Master Jax moved my hand to his arm. I gripped on tight, afraid to lose him. He chuckled before walking out of the room with me trailing along.

We didn't walk far before he told me to duck and placed me into some sort of vehicle. There weren't cars on the island, only golf carts, so I assumed that's where I was. I felt the warm breeze swirl around me as someone buckled me in and we started out. With the blindfold on, I had no idea where we were headed so sat back and tried to relax.

The trip didn't take long. I tried to control my breathing as the cart stopped and I was guided out of it. My heart hammered as I was led, told to step up a few times, and brought into my new owner's house. I wondered if Olivia had been bought by Mr. Martin, too, and if so, when she'd be arriving. It would have been more comforting if we had been brought in together. But what if she wasn't bought by Mr. Martin? My head swam with the possibility. I could be in this alone.

I tried not to think about it as I was moved further into the house. I wondered if Mr. Martin had purchased a house or if he was still staying with Mr. Wood. Either way, it didn't matter. My mind was trying desperately to latch on to anything it could focus on, something concrete it could be sure of.

"Kneel and wait for your new owner," Master Jax instructed.

I kneeled on what felt like soft carpet which surprised me. I got into waiting pose with my hands palms up on my lap, the blindfold still in place.

"Good, Riley," Master Jax said. "Try to breathe. Everything will work out."

I almost laughed. I had been holding my breath without even knowing it. I took in a deep breath and then another until my mind started to calm. I heard Master Jax leave, his footsteps quiet on the soft carpet. Then I was alone.

TWENTY-FOUR

I didn't have to wait long before I heard a door open and close. Soft footsteps descended on me. I held my breath as I waited, my heart hammering, my body tense. This would be my life for the next few weeks and I wasn't sure how I was going to get through it.

A hand reached out and caressed my cheek. I was startled by the tenderness. I half expected it to be followed by a slap but it never came. Instead, the hand caressed the other cheek before cupping my chin and lifting my head as if he was looking at me. I willed myself to stay calm but it was almost too much.

He released my chin before walking around me, his fingers trailing lightly over my shoulder. He didn't say a word but I could hear his steady breathing. My nipples hardened in anticipation. He traced his fingers over my back lightly as he circled back around to stand in front of me. A finger grazed over one of my nipples, sending a shiver through me. My body responded to his touch in a way that surprised me. I had never been turned on by Mr. Martin before.

His fingers grazed the other nipple before pinching it lightly. I wanted to arch into it, my body aroused by his simple touch. My mind started to calm. This I could do. Maybe it wouldn't be so bad.

I heard a deep chuckle as he released me, obviously pleased by my response. The voice sounded familiar but I couldn't place it. My mind felt overloaded like it was taking in too much at once.

The hand was back at my cheek, caressing it softly.

"Stand, Riley."

I quickly uncurled myself until I was standing. I took in a deep breath, trying to anticipate his next move. Part of me felt thrilled and I had no idea why. I had just been sold to some unknown man. I should have been mortified but something told me this wasn't Mr. Martin. This was someone else. Someone who knew how to work my body, who possibly knew how to work me.

I felt his lips softly press against mine as his hand went into my hair, pulling me closer. I automatically opened my mouth to him, accepting his kiss, as his mouth captured mine.

My mind exploded from the intensity of the kiss, making me breathless, as the kiss intensified. I gave myself over completely to it, to him, no longer worried who this mystery man was. I knew somewhere deep in my soul that this was the man for me, that this was how it was supposed to be. Everything else had just been leading to this moment.

I lost track of time as his mouth devoured mine, drinking me in. One hand stayed in my hair, pulling me in closer, while his other cupped my ass, pulling me into his obvious erection.

He kissed me like that for a long time as if he couldn't get enough. Flames licked through me as my desire rose. He hadn't touched my nipples again or my pussy but I knew there wasn't anything I wouldn't do for this man. He had me with this one kiss.

He pulled back, his breathing hard.

"God, you're beautiful," he said, his voice deep and husky. "You're everything I always wanted and here you are, all mine."

I took in a deep breath, my heart hammering but for a whole different reason.

He ran his hand softly over my cheek again before he pulled off the blindfold.

I blinked a few times before my eyes settled on deep blue eyes and a devilish grin. My heart stopped. I couldn't believe who I was seeing.

"Did I say you can look at me?" Master Grant teased, his eyes not leaving mine.

Before I could respond, his mouth crashed down on mine. Gone was the gentle kiss from before, replaced by fierceness and urgency. My mind was still whirling, trying to make sense of why Master Grant was here. Had Mr. Martin sent him to greet his new acquisitions? I couldn't wrap my mind around it. Would Master Grant be able to steal moments like this with me?

I gave up trying to figure it out as I gave myself over to his kiss. He devoured me like he couldn't get enough. This time his hands made their way to my breasts, cupping one, while the other held onto my ass, pulling me in tighter until I was molded against his muscled body. My body yielded to him, wanting him in the worst way, wanting all of him.

He lifted me as if I were nothing. My legs wrapped around his waist as he carried me deeper into the house into one of the bedrooms. He practically threw me on the king-size bed before climbing on top of me. He still wore his dark jeans and a long sleeve white t-shirt that he quickly pulled over his head and threw on the floor.

My hands found their way to his shoulders, pulling him in, as his mouth found mine. I no longer worried about rules or whether or not I would get in trouble. None of that mattered. All that mattered was this moment with Master Grant, especially since I had no idea how long I'd have him.

Master Grant opened his pants, his mouth still on mine, releasing his impressive cock. I felt the head of it against my opening. I spread my legs, welcoming him in, burning for him. I was so aroused that I nearly came as he sank himself into me with one swift movement.

I arched up to meet him as he pulled back and thrust in again. I clamped down on him as if trying to keep him there as he hammered into me. My hands were on his back, loving the feel of the muscles beneath my hands. His mouth was on my neck. I heard his heavy breathing as I threw my head back and came. I felt like I was bursting open, releasing everything I had been holding over the past several weeks. It all came bursting out. I even think I screamed his name, calling him Grant instead of Master Grant.

He pushed into me a few more times, his breathing getting more ragged.

"God, Riley," he said before pushing all the way in and spilling himself inside me.

He rolled over next to me, his breathing still ragged. I had never felt so satiated. He pulled me into him. I curled myself against his bare chest, inhaling him, a warmth spreading over me. I felt content and protected in his arms. I wished I could stay there forever.

"God, Riley, that was amazing," he said into my hair. "I knew it would be great once I had you but I never thought it'd be like this."

My heart flipped. Did that mean what I hoped it meant?

I nuzzled into him more, not wanting to break my illusion.

He kissed the top of my head.

"How was it for you?" he asked. "I want you to be satisfied, too. I want you to know that."

I looked up at him. His deep blue eyes locked on mine, causing my heart to skip. I smiled at him.

"It was beyond amazing," I said. "Every time with you is like that. I just wish we could have more of this. I wish we didn't need to sneak around."

His smile widened.

"We don't need to sneak around. Not anymore. I bought you. You're mine."

My heart stopped. My eyes widened.

He laughed at my reaction, kissing my nose.

"But how?" I asked. "What happened with Mr. Martin? He was so set on us."

"I helped shift Mr. Martin in another direction, one that would be more suited for the lifestyle he wants to create here. It took some convincing but he finally caved. I also reminded him that your contract was up in a few weeks which meant you could leave the island and he'd be left with nothing. I think that's what did it. He wanted to secure women who'd be here a while."

I stared at him, letting the words sink in. I was his. I was Master Grant's. My heart felt like it was going to burst. This couldn't be happening. This couldn't be real. I couldn't possibly be getting everything I ever wanted.

"What about Olivia?" I asked, my mind shifting to her. "Did Mr. Martin get her?"

My heart sunk a little as I started to worry about her there alone with Mr. Martin, feeling crushed that I wasn't there to help make things easier. She had to have friends from her class so maybe she wouldn't feel completely alone but my heart still went out to her.

"I acquired Olivia, too," Master Grant said with a smile. "Mr. Wood encouraged me to have more than one woman if I was going to start building a household here and I always thought you two came as a set."

"Oh my God, really?" I asked. I couldn't believe it.

Master Grant smiled at me. "Yes, really. I set her up in her room before coming to spend time with you. I hope that's OK with you. I wasn't sure how you'd feel about sharing me."

I laughed. I couldn't believe this was happening.

"I never knew what I wanted but now it all sounds perfect, especially since it's Olivia. Somehow she fits with me."

Master Grant smiled. "That's what I thought but I'm happy to hear it."

I FELL ASLEEP A VERY happy woman tucked inside Master Grant's arms. I didn't ask any more about Olivia. I was simply happy to hear that she'd be part of our household. I hoped she wasn't jealous that I got the first night alone with Master Grant but I had a feeling she'd just be relieved to be here with us instead of with Mr. Martin.

I woke up with Master Grant nuzzling in my neck. I smiled and wrapped my arms around him. I couldn't believe I was here, in his bed, finally.

He kissed my neck, trailing kisses down my chest before he found a nipple and sucked it in. My body didn't hesitate to respond to him. Heat pulsed through me. He shifted so he was over me, both of his hands on either side of me. I marveled at the movement of the muscles in his arms as he held himself up. His eyes met mine and he smiled. He looked happy and the thought thrilled me.

"Things are going to be different in my house," Master Grant said, his eyes sparkling, before he captured my mouth with his.

I caved into him completely. I felt swept away by him and it was the most wonderful feeling. He deepened the kiss, his tongue exploring mine, making me ache for more. I didn't think I could get enough of this man and that was a wonderful new feeling. There was something about him that just clicked.

He positioned himself over me and slid in easily, never breaking the kiss. I opened to him, happy to be filled by him. He moved slowly at first as if savoring each moment, driving me mad, before picking up the pace and plowing me with swift determination.

I came in no time, unable to contain myself. He broke the kiss before he came deep inside me, pushing in deep as if wanting me to capture all of him, before collapsing beside me.

"I'm going to want to do that every day," Master Grant said next to me, his breathing labored. "I hope you're OK with that."

"More than OK with that," I said, smiling.

I turned and snuggled into him. He put his arm around me and pulled me in so my head was resting on his chest. I could hear his heartbeat and inhaled in his clean male scent. I still wasn't convinced I wasn't living a dream or some cruel practical joke. Like what if Mr. Martin had Master Grant take me back to his place but I'd be taken over to Mr. Martin's by the end of the day.

I pushed that thought away. I needed to enjoy this moment no matter what happened next. It was everything I had ever wanted and more.

"We should go get Olivia," Master Grant said. "I don't want her to be on her own for too long. I told her to make a quick breakfast this morning when she got up so hopefully, she's already in the kitchen."

I couldn't smell breakfast but that didn't mean anything. Master Grant's door was closed.

"Let's take a quick shower then we'll go down," he said.

I watched as he pushed himself off the bed before he extended a hand to me. He lifted me in his arms which surprised me and carried me to the bathroom attached to his room. Everything was in whites and greys, simple yet sophisticated. The shower was big enough for two or more and was lined with simple white subway tiles. He turned the water on, jets spraying from every direction, before he pulled me in.

He took his time washing me, including my hair with a conditioner rinse, before he turned his attention to himself. I wanted to run my hands all over him but since I didn't know what the rules were yet with him, I didn't want to push it. I was already busted for making direct eye contact and touching him while we were in bed without permission.

He smiled at me and kissed me one more time before he turned the water off. He handed me a big white fluffy towel before grabbing one himself.

"Let's get dried off so we can go see Olivia," Master Grant said. "I don't want her waiting for too long."

I toweled myself off. Master Grant hung both our towels on a towel bar near the shower before grabbing my hand and leading me back into his bedroom. I finally got a moment to look around his room. It was simple yet sophisticated, same as the bathroom, with a king-size bed dominating the room and a white dresser against one wall with a mirror above it. I didn't notice any pictures or anything personal in the space which made me think he either didn't bring any of that stuff to the island or he had just moved in.

He handed me a white chiffon sundress that was more opaque than sheer. I slipped it on over my head, liking how it lightly hugged my curves while mostly covering me. He handed me a pair of silver heels that weren't as high as I was used to. I slipped them on, happy with how they fit.

I looked at him as if to ask how he knew my size but he simply smiled at me, grabbed my hand and dragged me out the door. His place was all on one level. We passed a simple living space with big picture windows overlooking a garden before making our way to the kitchen.

Olivia smiled at us as we entered, her eyes bright and happy. She wore a dress similar to mine, more opaque than sheer, in a deep green that brought out her eyes. My heart ached at the sight of her and I wanted to rush into her arms and squeeze her tight. We had somehow made it out of Mr. Martin's grasp and here we were with Master Grant. I couldn't have been happier.

Olivia looked like she felt the same but she stayed put, quickly lowering her eyes. I hadn't thought to do the same and could only imagine the punishment Master Grant would roll out for that. I wasn't even here a day and I was already in trouble.

Master Grant walked us over to Olivia until we stood right in front of her. I lowered my eyes in case he looked at me. I wanted to show him I could be respectful, too.

He looked between us and chuckled before wrapping his arms around both of us, pulling us in for a hug. I wrapped my arms around the both of them, breathing them in, my heart feeling like it might burst.

"My girls," he said over our heads. "At last. I can't tell you how happy I am to have you here."

He released us so he could look at us. I lowered my eyes, a smile on my face. I couldn't be happier.

He lifted both of our chins until we were looking directly at him. His deep blue eyes sparkled. He looked overjoyed.

"Rule number one," he said. "You have permission to look directly at me whenever we're alone. I prefer it. I want to connect with you and always see what your eyes have to say. I will be more upset with you if you don't look directly at me. I understand while we're in public, you will need to keep your eyes lowered. That's fine. But here, in my house, you will always look at me. Do you understand?"

"Yes, Master Grant," we said in unison. I already felt in sync with her.

"Rule number two, call me Grant when we're not in public. You may continue to use Master Grant when we're around others. I also expect you to address other men by their proper designations, including Luke. You will now address him as Mr. Wood. Do you understand?"

"Yes, Grant," we said. It felt odd dropping the master but I knew I'd get used to it. I liked how his name rolled off my tongue.

"Very good," he said, a smile on his face. I loved being able to look at him. He shifted his gaze from me to Olivia, his eyes happy. "Now for rule number three. After careful consideration, I have decided to give you each yellow collars. This allows you to be groped in public but nothing more. Now that I have you, I plan to be a little possessive. I hope you're OK with that."

I beamed at him.

"Yes, Grant," I said. Olivia answered the same right behind me. I was done being used by random men for a while.

"Wonderful," he said. He pulled out two yellow leather collars from the kitchen drawer and slipped them around Olivia's neck then mine. I reached up to feel the smooth buttery leather. It was missing the O hook in the front that my black collar had. I wondered if that meant he had no intention of leashing us. The thought warmed me.

"You both look amazing," he said. "My girls. All mine at last."

I couldn't stop smiling at him. I had no idea what life would be like with Grant but I knew it'd be wonderful.

CONNECT WITH EROTICWRITERGIRL

THANK YOU SO MUCH FOR READING MY BOOK. I HOPE YOU LOVED IT!

Please take a moment to leave a brief review on Amazon. I'd truly appreciate it.

Don't miss out! Sign up for my email newsletter to stay in the know.

Email me at connect@eroticwritergirl.com. I'd love to hear from you.

ACKNOWLEDGMENTS

Thank you to my amazing readers. You make writing worth every minute. I appreciate you more than you know. I have always felt that writing isn't complete until it has an audience. Thank you for showing up to help support my dreams.

Thank you to my amazing husband who continues to support me even when I'm not being my best self. He keeps me going even when I'm ready to give up, reminding me to have fun and to enjoy the process. Because of him, my life is richer.

Thank you to my wonderful beta readers, especially Anne who has seen this series through since the beginning. She has helped talk me through storylines and always manages to find the depth to my stories and characters.

ABOUT THE AUTHOR

eroticwritergirl is the pen name of a super introverted and creative writer who loves to explore women's submissive nature in super sensual, romantic and surprising ways. She wrote her first full-length romance novel at age 13 and has been writing ever since. She writes contemporary romance along with erotic romance and loves to push boundaries and explore human nature through her writing.

When not writing, eroticwritergirl reads everything from YA to the steamiest erotic romance, spends time at the beach (she's a total water girl), dances around to her latest playlist, plays her electric guitar and paints using her intuition.

She grew up outside of Detroit, has lived in Chicago and currently resides back in Michigan off the shores of Lake Michigan with her husband and two spoiled cats.

Please leave a review on Amazon and Goodreads. It'd be greatly appreciated.

instagram.com/kinkyinkpress
facebook.com/kinkyinkpress
youtube.com/@eroticwritergirl

www.ingramcontent.com/pod-product-compliance
Lightning Source LLC
Chambersburg PA
CBHW051507260626
47162CB00008B/2859